"I'm worried about you."

"I appreciate that, Marcus, more than you know." Nicole reached tentatively for his hand, willing him to understand what she couldn't seem to come right out and say. "Soon things will be different. My brother and I will move away from my father and be free to go where we want...*see* who we want."

Marcus opened his mouth as if to argue, then he blinked. The next thing she knew, he was jumping out of the car.

"Say hello to Beau for me," Marcus prattled cheerfully, striding away.

Nicole blew out a short breath. What was *that* about? Had the mere suggestion that she'd like to date him sent him running for the hills?

At first, Nicole was disheartened, then realized there was plenty of time to change his mind. She was sure Marcus cared, and maybe one day *he* would get used to the idea....

Books by Arlene James

Love Inspired

The Perfect Wedding #3
An Old-Fashioned Love #9
A Wife Worth Waiting For #14
With Baby in Mind #21
To Heal a Heart #285
Deck the Halls #321
A Family To Share #331
Butterfly Summer #356
A Love So Strong #363

*Everyday Miracles

ARLENE JAMES

says, "Camp meetings, mission work and the church where my parents and grandparents were prominent members permeate my Oklahoma childhood memories. It was a golden time, which sustains me yet. However, only as a young, widowed mother did I truly begin growing in my personal relationship with the Lord. Through adversity, He blessed me in countless ways, one of which is a second marriage so loving and romantic, it still feels like courtship!"

The author of over sixty novels, Arlene James now resides outside of Dallas, Texas, with her husband. Arlene says, "The rewards of motherhood have indeed been extraordinary for me. Yet I've looked forward to this new stage of my life." Her need to write is greater than ever, a fact that frankly amazes her, as she's been at it since the eighth grade!

ARLENE JAMES

A Love So Strong

Steeple
Hill®

Published by Steeple Hill Books™

STEEPLE HILL BOOKS

Steeple
Hill®

ISBN-13: 978-0-373-87391-3
ISBN-10:   373-87391-3

A LOVE SO STRONG

www.SteepleHill.com

Printed in U.S.A.

And this I pray,
that your love may abound still more and more
in real knowledge and all discernment.
—*Philippians* 1:9

For Lauren, because granddaughters
are one of God's greatest blessings,
and Granna loves you very, very much.

Chapter One

"Happy birthday! Happy birthday, Marcus!"

Marcus Wheeler lifted his hands and addressed the two dozen or so assembled guests.

"You shouldn't have gone to so much trouble. The church already gave me a nice monetary gift. A man blessed with that and a family such as this can't ask for more." He grinned, then added, "But I'm mighty appreciative, all the same."

"Good grief, man. We have six sisters between us," Vince, husband of Marcus's sister Jolie and scion of the boisterous Cutler clan, stated ruefully. "Did you really think your two sisters and my four would let your birthday slip by without a family celebration?"

Everyone laughed, and the rippling sound warmed Marcus to the very center of his soul. Not so long ago he'd been struggling to hold on to some semblance of his fractured family, and now, thanks to his two younger sisters—especially Jolie, the eldest of them—he had more family than he could keep track of.

"So far as I can tell," drawled Kendal Oakes, husband of

Marcus's youngest sister, Connie, "the Cutlers don't let any excuse to celebrate get past them."

This elicited more laughter and a general chorus of "Amen, brother!"

An only child himself, Kendal confessed to Marcus that he still didn't seem to know what to make of the loving horde who were the Cutlers, but after almost a year as a member of the clan, he was more at ease. Even his daughter, Larissa, who would be three in a couple months and was often over-whelmed by too much stimulation, had relaxed into the midst of what had proven to be a loving, sheltering family.

It was also a growing family, with Jolie and Vince expecting their first child in late June. Marcus knew that Jolie would be as wonderful a mother to her own child as she had been to her nephew, Russell, Connie's thirty-month-old son, in his first year when Connie couldn't take care of him.

"Can't have too much celebration," Connie murmured, smoothing Russell's bright red hair as he leaned against her leg, eagerly awaiting his piece of the birthday cake.

Marcus couldn't have agreed with her more. So much had changed in the past two years.

Connie had gotten out of prison and had since been exon-erated of having taken any knowing part in the armed robbery and subsequent murder perpetrated by Russell's biological father. The split that had occurred in the family when Connie had reclaimed Russell from Jolie's care had been mended, thanks to Vince Cutler, who had married Jolie last Valen-tine's Day, almost a year ago now. Most amazing of all, Connie and Kendal had found each other, and what had begun as a marriage of convenience had joined two broken homes into one strong, Christ-centered family.

Marcus thanked God daily for the masterful way in which

He had mended the bonds shattered by death and separation, and the spotty care of the foster child system in which he and his sisters had grown up. Truly, what else could a man of God possibly ask for?

Looking around the room at no fewer than seven happy couples, Marcus had to admit to himself that it was proving to be surprisingly difficult to be the only unmarried adult member of the family. Here he sat, a single minister in want of a wife, and suddenly thirty felt positively ancient. It seemed ungrateful, even selfish, to keep asking God where his mate was, but he couldn't help wondering. Marcus closed his eyes and sent a swift, silent prayer heavenward.

Lord, I thank You for all with which You've blessed me. I thank You for every person in this room. I even thank You for the room itself! You've given Jolie and Vince a lovely home. Connie and Kendal, too, for that matter. And I thank You for my church, Lord. Help me be satisfied with what I already have. That's my birthday prayer. Amen.

Jolie shoved another box onto his lap.

"Ya'll, this is just too much," he insisted, mentally cataloging the stack of dress shirts, ties, bookmarks and religious CDs already littering the floor around his chair.

"Hush up and rip in," Jolie counseled, dropping a kiss on his forehead as she moved back to her husband's side on the sofa that occupied one wall of the living room, to which the party had relocated after indulging the children's demand for cake. "That's the last one anyway."

Relieved to hear it, Marcus eagerly tore away the wrapping paper and pried apart the white pasteboard box beneath to reveal a large photo album tastefully bound in brown leather. A cross and the word "Wheeler" had been embossed on the front in gold.

Somewhat warily, Marcus cracked the cover. The front page contained grainy black-and-white photographs of their great-grandparents Edna and Bledsoe Wheeler.

"I remember these!" Marcus exclaimed happily. "But I thought they were lost."

"Jo had them," Connie apprised him, obviously pleased.

He turned another page and found a color eight-by-ten of his mother, Velma, as a high school senior. The youngest of two daughters born almost twenty years apart, Velma had been the late child of elderly parents and too quickly left alone in the world. After Marcus's father died she'd tried to fill the void with one man after another, eventually abandoning her own children in search of a love she'd never truly understood, only to die in an auto accident.

As difficult as it had been to be separated at ten from his younger sisters, Marcus thanked God that he'd landed with a family who had taught him to love the Lord and saved him from repeating his mother's fate. His sisters hadn't been blessed in that fashion. But now wasn't the time for bad memories. Today was his birthday, a time to celebrate. He and his sisters were back together again. That was all that mattered.

He turned the page and saw a small photo of their father, Carl, who had died of heart failure in his thirties, brought on by extensive alcohol and drug abuse. Marcus barely remembered him. Mostly he remembered the loud arguments that had preceded his departure from the household when Connie had still been a baby.

He'd been a nice-looking man, with Connie's bright, golden blond hair. What a pity that he'd allowed himself to be controlled by his addictions. Still, it was nice to have this reminder of him.

Pictures of Marcus and his sisters as children followed. Most included various members of the foster families with whom they'd resided. Next came a picture of Jolie's wedding. Marcus smiled at that and then at the photo of Connie and Kendal's *second* wedding, which followed. Now that was an interesting story.

Their first ceremony had been a somber affair performed in Kendal's home. They married because Russell needed a father, and Larissa needed a mother. Only some months later did the two realize that God had brought them together for more than the sake of their children and made their sham marriage a real one with a ceremony in church. It had been Marcus's distinct privilege to perform all *three* of his sisters' ceremonies.

He chuckled at photos of his nephew, Russell, and niece, Larissa. The two had taken to each other like bark on a tree. Soon the cross adoption of each child by the other's natural parent would be finalized.

The last picture was a puzzle. It looked like an ink blot at first, and then Marcus realized that it more closely resembled a printed negative of an X-ray. He turned the album sideways, trying to get a better look, prompting Vince to lean forward and announce, "That's your *other* nephew."

Jolie patted her slightly rounded belly with a self-satisfied smile. "We made you a print of the sonogram."

Ovida Cutler, Vince's mother, launched to her feet. All rounded curves and beaming smile, with fading red hair curling about her face, she was the quintessential grandmother.

"It's a boy!" she exclaimed, as if she didn't already have four grandsons.

"And this one will have the Cutler name," once of Vince's sisters pointed out.

"Actually," Jolie said, glowing at Marcus, "we're thinking that Aaron Lawrence Cutler is a fine name for a son, if you don't mind us appropriating your middle name, Marcus."

Marcus glanced at Larry Cutler, Ovida's husband, who was beaming ear to ear, obviously having no compunction about his given name coming in second to Marcus's middle one.

"I'd be honored, sis," he told her in a thick voice.

Fortunately the doorbell rang just then, preventing the whole room from erupting into happy tears.

While Vince hurried out to answer the door, Marcus quickly flipped through the remainder of the pages in the photo album to be certain that they were empty, then yielded to the clamor to pass it around. Within seconds the women were all "oohing" over the sonogram. Marcus himself hadn't seen anything that actually looked like a baby in the print, but that didn't lessen his delight in having it. Aaron Lawrence Cutler. Wow.

He wondered if he would ever have a son whom he might want to name after himself.

Vince returned with a girl in tow. Striking, with long hair the color of black coffee falling past her slender shoulders, she wore a somewhat outlandish costume of lime-green leggings, a long, straight denim skirt, a black turtleneck and muffler, a sky-blue fringed poncho and red leather flats. The shoes matched her gloves, which left only her wrists, ankles and heart-shaped face bare to the February chill.

A lime-green headband held back her sleek, dark hair, revealing an intriguing widow's peak that emphasized her wide, prominent cheekbones and slightly pointed chin. It was an exotic face, with large, round, tip-tilted eyes that gave a feline grace to a small nose and a wide, full, strawberry mouth. What galvanized, Marcus, however, were the shiny tracks of tears that marked her pale cheeks.

Without even thinking about it, he was out of his chair a heartbeat after Jolie's mother-in-law, Ovida, and was striding across the room, certain that he was needed.

"Nicole Archer!" Ovida exclaimed, opening her arms. "Honey, what's wrong?"

The newcomer shook her head, eyes flicking self-consciously around the room. If her hair was black coffee, Marcus noted inanely, then those sparkling, soft brown eyes were café au lait. The cream in the coffee would be her skin.

Despite her lithe build, she was not a teenager, he saw upon closer inspection, but not far past it. He liked the fact that she wore no cosmetics, her skin appearing freshly scrubbed and utterly flawless.

A number of private conversations immediately began, their intent patently obvious. Marcus felt a spurt of gratitude for any effort to put this obviously troubled young lady at ease.

"I'm sorry to bother you," she said in a soft, warbling voice as Ovida's round arms encircled her slender shoulders.

"Nonsense. Suzanne's daughter could never be a bother to me." Ovida pulled back slightly and asked, "Now, what's he done?"

Those coffee-with-cream eyes again flickered with uncertainty. Sensing her discomfiture, Marcus stepped up and pointed an arm toward the door beyond the formal dining area as if he had every right to offer this young woman the use of the house.

"It's quiet in the kitchen," he suggested.

Ovida looked up at that, her worried gaze easing somewhat. She patted his cheek with one plump hand.

"I don't want to impose," Nicole protested softly, sniffing and ducking her head.

"No problem," Marcus assured her as Ovida turned the girl toward the door and gently but firmly urged her forward.

A couple of Ovida's daughters rose to follow, but Marcus lifted a proprietary hand. They would, of course, want to help, but ministry had some privileges, and he found himself compelled to exercise them for once. Both instantly subsided, and he nodded in gratitude before swiftly following Ovida and her guest.

He caught up with and passed them in time to push back the swinging door on its silent hinges. As she passed through into the kitchen, Nicole looked up and whispered her thanks.

"You're welcome," Marcus murmured, unashamedly following the pair into the brick-and-oak kitchen and letting the door swing closed behind him.

Ovida parked Nicole at the wrought-iron table in the breakfast nook. "Can I get you something to drink, honey?"

Nicole glanced at the half-empty coffeepot on the counter. Marcus had noticed that wherever Ovida and Larry Cutler were, the coffeepot was kept in service. It seemed fitting that this girl, for she was little more than that, surely, should show a preference for the dark beverage.

Without being asked, he turned to the cabinet and took down a stoneware coffee mug. Then he filled it with strong, black coffee and carried it to the table, placing it gently in front of this dark-haired beauty. She was beautiful, he realized with a jolt. But very young.

"There's cream and sugar, if you like."

Smiling wanly, she shook her head, tugged off her worn red leather gloves and wrapped a slender hand around the mug.

"Thank you. Again."

"You're welcome. Again."

As she sipped, he pulled out a chair for Ovida and nodded her down into it.

"Now tell me, honey," Ovida urged, "what's wrong?"

Nicole glanced quickly at Marcus before dropping both hands into her lap in a gesture that bespoke both helplessness and frustration. Marcus pulled out another chair and sat, bracing his forearms against the glass tabletop.

"Forgive me if I'm intruding where I'm not wanted, but if there's a problem, I'd like to help. My name is Marcus Wheeler, by the way."

"Nicole Archer."

He smiled to put her at ease. "It's nice to meet you, Nicole. I take it that you know my sister Jolie."

Nicole shook her head. "I know she's married to Vince, that this is their house."

"If you know the Cutlers, then you must realize that, through Jolie, I'm part of the family now. You probably don't know that I'm also a minister."

Her slender, dark brows rose into pronounced arches.

"Really? You seem too…young."

Marcus chuckled. "That's good to hear today of all days." He leaned closer and confessed in a conspiratorial tone. "Today's my birthday. My twenties are now officially behind me."

"Happy birthday." Wrinkling her button of a nose, she added, "I didn't mean to crash the party."

"No problem." He folded his hands. "I'd like to help, if you'll allow it."

She sighed, braced an elbow against the tabletop, turned up her palm and dropped her forehead into it.

"There's nothing you can do. There's nothing anyone can do." Straightening, she shook her head. "I don't even know why I bothered to come here. It's just that…" She looked at

Ovida, and fresh tears clouded her eyes. "You said this was where you'd be if I needed you."

Ovida reached across the table to squeeze her hand. "You did exactly right. Now, then, what's Dillard done this time?"

"Same old, same old," came the muttered answer.

"That man!" Ovida snapped. "Did he hurt you?"

Marcus stiffened as alarm and something he didn't normally feel, anger, flashed through him.

"Who is Dillard?"

"Nicole's father," Ovida divulged. "Dillard Archer's been mad at the world and living in a bottle ever since his wife died more than three years ago."

"He was never like this when Mom was alive," Nicole said, shaking her head. "He'd lose his temper once in a while, even put his fist through a wall a time or two, but now…" She bit her lip.

Marcus reached for the sheltering mantle of his professional detachment. For some reason that seemed more difficult than usual, but he managed, asking gently, "Is he abusive?"

Nicole bowed her head and whispered, "The worst part is the things he says sometimes, especially to my little brother."

"What's your brother's name?"

"Beau. He turned thirteen at the end of November."

An emotional age, as Marcus remembered all too well. The next question was, to him, all important.

"Has your father ever hit either one of you, Nicole?"

She sucked in a deep breath, her stillness indicating that she was deciding what to tell him.

"Not really. He's shoved us around a little, Beau mostly. I'm afraid my little brother hasn't learned when it's best to keep quiet."

Ovida shared a grim look with Marcus, saying, "Your poor mother's heart would break if she wasn't beyond such emotion, thank the good Lord."

"I just don't know what to do with him anymore," Nicole admitted tearfully. "I know he misses Mom, but we all do."

"Of course we do," Ovida crooned. "For her I'm happy, though. No more illness or pain. Just the peace and joy of heaven."

Nicole nodded, sniffing. "I believe that, but Dad doesn't."

Marcus sighed inwardly, unsurprised to hear that Dillard Archer was not a believer.

"Have you considered calling the authorities?"

Nicole shook her head, blurting, "I don't want him to go to jail!"

"It might be the only way to get him the help he needs."

"But what would happen to my little brother?"

Marcus knew the probable answer to that, but he needed more information to make an informed guess.

"How old are you?"

"Twenty."

So young, Marcus thought, *to be shouldering such responsibility.*

"Do you work?"

"Part-time. School doesn't leave a lot of time for work."

"You're in college then?"

"UTA."

He'd attended the University of Texas at Arlington himself, before seminary.

"Studying what, may I ask?"

"Early childhood education."

He smiled at that and heard himself saying, "We have a day care center at our church."

"Oh? I'd like to work in day care again, but waiting tables pays better, especially for part-time." She looked down at her hands, mumbling, "Dad's on disability because of his back, and that really doesn't go very far. If we hadn't used Mom's life insurance to pay off the house, I don't know how we'd make it."

"His drinking can't help any," Marcus pointed out gently, "and he isn't likely to quit on his own."

"Look," Nicole said firmly, "I promised my mom." Her beautiful brown eyes implored Marcus to understand. "I promised that I'd take care of them, Beau and Dad. Mom wouldn't want me to turn him in to the police."

"Nicole, your mother never imagined that your dad would fall apart like this," Ovida pointed out. "She wouldn't want you to risk yours or your brother's safety."

"It's not that bad," Nicole insisted. "It's just that I never know what's going to set him off, and he can say some really ugly things. I shouldn't let them bother me. I know it's the alcohol talking, but…" She sighed intensely.

"Don't make excuses for him, honey," Ovida advised, "and don't let him get to you."

She lifted big, wounded eyes to Ovida, whispering, "He said that Mom would be disappointed in me."

Ovida scoffed at that. "No way! Your mother thought the sun rose and set in you and Beau. Your father's the one she'd be disappointed in, not you. Never you, sugar. And no one knew Suzanne better than I did. I knew your mom from the time she was eleven years old. I was her Sunday School teacher. Trust me on this."

Nicole smiled wanly. "Mom always said you were the big sister she never had."

"Oh, and I loved her like a sister."

"He loved her, too, you know," Nicole said wistfully.

"I know," Ovida conceded. "I know. But that doesn't give him the right to behave this way."

"Would you like me to speak to him?" Marcus asked. "I think he needs to hear that God still loves him."

Nicole looked at him, wide-eyed, and shook her head. "I—I don't think he'd sit still for that. Maybe later, once he's calmed down."

"He'd have to be more open than the last time I tried to talk to him," Ovida warned sadly. "He threw me out of his house—me, who he's known for decades. He said God and church didn't do Suzanne any good and he didn't want to hear any more mealymouthed Bible-thumpers telling him it was for the best."

"Ah." Marcus nodded, understanding the problem exactly. He'd seen it before, a weak faith trying to believe that a desired outcome was the only right one, then shattering completely when God's will didn't follow the proscribed path. Jolie had succumbed to that kind of disappointment and doubt after Connie had reclaimed her son, Russell, but with prayer and patience and a willingness on Vince's part to be used by God, she'd come to see the truth. Marcus made a mental pact with himself to pray regularly for the Archers, starting now.

At his request, Nicole bowed her head and sat quietly while he spoke to God about protection for her and her brother and emotional and spiritual healing for Dillard Archer. Afterward, he spoke to Nicole about AlAnon, the support organization for the family and dependents of alcoholics, and she seemed interested in possibly attending a meeting, if her schedule permitted. Marcus promised to locate the nearest meeting for her, although it sounded as if she already had a pretty full timetable with classes and work and her family.

"Where do you live exactly?"

"Dalworthington Gardens."

"We're practically neighbors then. I'm at First Church in Pantego."

"I know that church," Nicole said, surprising and pleasing him. "I pass it on my way to school. I like the way it looks, sort of homey and old-fashioned, almost like its own little town."

Marcus felt his grin stretch to ridiculous proportions. Something odd shimmered through him, something he couldn't quite identify that snatched at his breath. He cleared his throat and said, "That's exactly the impression we were going for, a community of believers with the church at its center."

"But don't be fooled by the exterior," Ovida advised Nicole. "It's a powerful little church, a real asset to the city, and pretty cutting-edge when it comes to technology and worship."

"We do try," Marcus conceded. "It's been an exciting pastorate so far."

"You ought to visit, Nicole," Ovida urged. "You and Beau might like it there."

Nicole looked at Marcus, her warm brown eyes measuring him. "We might," she said, and then she dropped her gaze pointedly.

Marcus felt a jolt. That hadn't been *personal* interest he'd seen in her eyes, surely? No, of course not. To her, he must seem like the next thing to an old man, which, comparably speaking, he was. That seemed a particularly dismal thought.

As talk became more chatter than confession and hand-wringing, Marcus made himself sit silently, a mere observer now that the emotional crisis had passed. It was what he did, part of his calling. He was good at stepping up to the plate when called upon to bat and equally good at retiring once he'd taken his swing. He couldn't help wondering why this time it was proving so difficult.

Perhaps he should rejoin the party in the other room. He, after all, was the guest of honor. Yes, he should definitely excuse himself. Yet, he sat right there, listening as Ovida and Nicole talked of events in which he'd had no part and people whom he didn't know.

For some reason he couldn't tear himself away. Yet, this time, observation felt strangely like being on the outside looking in.

Was he suddenly so old, Marcus wondered, that he'd lost touch already with such fresh-faced youth as this? If so, then surely it was past time for God to bring him a wife.

That wasn't too much for a man to ask on his thirtieth birthday, was it? Then again, hadn't he just told God that he'd be happy with those blessings already granted him?

He stared at Nicole's pretty profile, observing the animation with which she spoke, and knew that if his interest could be elicited by this mere *girl,* then he was in big trouble. Not only was she too young for him, she was entirely unsuitable.

A minister's wife did not dress in such eccentric fashion. She didn't bounce around in her seat and gesture broadly as if physically incapable of sitting still. And she sure wouldn't slide alarmingly coy looks across a table at a man she'd just met.

It struck him then how laughingly desperate he had become.

Nicole was little more than a child, whose life was, nevertheless, chock-full of stress and responsibility. At her age she probably batted her eyelashes at every male in the immediate vicinity without even knowing that she was doing it.

And he was a thirty-year-old fool who obviously needed to remember that his priority in life was his ministry. That ministry included helping emotionally beleaguered young ladies find the faith to make difficult decisions. If the opportunity arose, that was precisely what he would do for Miss Nicole Archer.

He had the unsettling feeling that such an opportunity would, indeed, arise and no understanding at all why that should alarm him.

Chapter Two

Nicole allowed both Marcus Wheeler and Ovida Cutler to escort her to the door, even though she knew it was an imposition for him. This was his birthday, after all, and the party had been going on without him for some time already. Still, she couldn't resist. He was so...calm. Serene, even. And gorgeous—in a very buttoned-down and conservative way, which, oddly enough, she didn't mind at all.

Once in the spacious entry hall, Nicole took some time to look around her, stalling the moment when she must actually leave. Western chic wasn't her thing, but the sheer proportions of the place were impressive, and she liked the colors and the rustic light fixture overhead.

She'd barely noticed her surroundings when she'd arrived. Her pain and desperation had blinded her to everything except the need to find a little reassurance, some measure of comfort. At times like that she missed her mother so much that she literally hurt. That was when she reached out to Ovida.

Lately, her father's drinking had escalated and she'd been reaching out more and more. Surely things would calm down soon, though. Her father seemed to cycle in and out of these ongoing rages.

He'd be surly and withdrawn for a while, then gradually would grow more belligerent until he began exploding over the smallest things. Finally he'd rage for hours, saying cruel, hurtful things to her and her brother. Eventually he'd drink himself into oblivion. Misery and apologies would follow the hangover. Then the cycle would begin again.

She hoped they were at the end of that ugly cycle now, but even if they weren't she still couldn't bring herself to follow the pastor's advice to call the police or even Family Services. She couldn't bear the thought of her father in detox or jail or her brother in foster care. Such a thing would have been inconceivable while her mother lived. Every time Nicole thought of calling the police, she'd picture her mother's face, see the sadness, disappointment and anguish in her eyes, and she couldn't do it.

No, she just couldn't see herself following the good minister's advice. That didn't mean, however, that Nicole wasn't glad to have met Marcus Wheeler. Far from it. Looking up now into his warm, moss-green eyes she felt safe, reassured, and not a little thrilled.

Who knew that ministers were this good-looking? Not to mention young.

Okay, he was a little older than the college crowd, but thirty wasn't exactly over the hill. Besides, she didn't fit in with that group all that well herself. She didn't fit in anywhere, truth be told. In some ways she felt aeons older than her friends. In others she felt like a complete innocent. They were into partying and carefree escapades. She was into her family and fulfilling her responsibilities.

For Nicole, it was all about making a future for herself and her little brother. She didn't have time for parties and dates. She'd be tempted to make an exception for someone like Marcus, though. All antique gold and polished bronze, Marcus was not only handsome, he radiated strength, gentle confidence and genuine concern. Surely such a man would be a good influence on her little brother.

At first, mortified to have broken in on a family gathering, Nicole was now glad that she had come here today. She'd found what she needed: the strength to go home again and put up with whatever awaited her there a little longer. On the way, she'd swing by the library and pick up Beau. Meanwhile, she owed this man, if only for his kindness.

"I'm sorry about interrupting your birthday party."

He shook his head, smiling as laughter spilled out of the living room. "Doesn't sound to me like you put a crimp in anything."

"Still, it was good of you to take time away from your guests to talk to me."

"It was my pleasure. I'll be praying for you."

"Thank you."

"We'll both be praying for you, honey," Ovida broke in, hugging her. "Think about what the pastor said, will you?"

Nicole nodded. She'd think about it, but she knew that she wouldn't call the authorities.

"I'd better go," she said reluctantly. "The library closes at nine."

"Hug that brother of yours for me," Ovida instructed.

"I will."

"And don't hesitate to reach out again if you need me."

"But if you should need another ally," Marcus interjected smoothly, reaching into his shirt pocket and producing a small card, "I can usually be reached at one of these numbers."

Ridiculously pleased, Nicole took the card and slipped it into her glove. She would definitely be calling on the young minister, just as soon as she could come up with a valid reason. With one last squeeze of Ovida's hand and a warm smile for Marcus Wheeler, Nicole slipped through the door that he opened for her.

He stepped outside onto the low front stoop and watched from beneath the tall brick arch until she was safely inside her old car. In his shirtsleeves against the frosty February temperatures, he continued to stand there while she cranked and cranked the starter on her rattletrap vehicle. Then, once the engine finally turned over, he lifted a hand in farewell before rejoining the party inside. It seemed a very gentlemanly thing to do.

Nicole smiled to herself as she drove off into the night, feeling the edges of his card against the back of her hand, where it nestled inside her glove.

Their paths would cross again.

Connie stirred honey into her herbal tea, tapped the spoon on the rim of the cup and laid it aside before slipping her forefinger into the dainty hole formed by the handle and lifting the hot, fragrant brew to her lips.

"So, find out any interesting tidbits about our unexpected guest at the birthday party the other night?" Jolie asked, lifting her straight, thick, biscuit-brown hair so she could lean back in her kitchen chair without trapping it.

Connie blew on her tea, then shook her bright gold hair. They'd both been curious about Nicole Archer. Something about that girl made a person sit up and take notice, something besides the wardrobe, which was even odder than those of the young women one saw on the streets these days.

"You know Marcus and his ministerial ethics," Connie

said. "All I could get out of him is that her mother and your mother-in-law were friends."

"*Were* is the operative word," Jolie divulged, absently rubbing her swollen belly. "Mrs. Archer died over three years ago. Cancer. Ovida was her Sunday School teacher at one time, and the two stayed close over the years. Now Ovida's become sort of a surrogate mother for Nicole. Supposedly, Nicole's father drinks a lot."

Connie sipped from her cup and set it down again.

"I guess mothers-in-law don't have the same ethical concerns as ministers."

Jolie chuckled. Conversation turned to their plans for the upcoming weekend. Vince and Jolie planned to shop for the baby's room. Connie and Kendal were taking their children to a popular pizza arcade for the birthday celebration of one of their young friends.

"We may not stay long," Connie said. "It depends on how well Larissa does in that environment."

Little Larissa still suffered the occasional meltdown when overstimulated, but her conduct had improved by leaps and bounds in the ten months since Connie and sweet, placid Russell had come into her life. Still, Connie and Kendal were careful to monitor her environment and coach her behavior. They made a good team and, Jolie had to admit, were excellent parents.

Jolie no longer grieved or resented the removal of her nephew from her care. The way she looked at it, everything was as it should be. As God had wanted it to be. She could be Russell's aunt now without wishing she was still his de facto mom, and she again enjoyed the company and companionship of her sister and brother. Best of all, she and Vince were going to have their own child, who was even then turning somersaults inside her womb.

"Goodness, this boy's going to be an athlete of some sort. He's always in motion lately."

It was no secret that the Cutlers were football fanatics, and Jolie knew that Vince was dreaming of sitting on the sidelines to watch his son play. Connie opened her mouth to comment, but just then the doorbell rang.

"I'll go," she said, slipping out of her chair and waving Jolie back down into hers.

"Can't imagine who it is," Jolie murmured, arching her back to relieve an ache in her spine.

It was probably someone wanting to clean her carpet or sell her a magazine subscription. While she waited for Connie to return, she decided that she'd have another cup of herbal tea and rose to move to the kettle cheerfully steaming on the stovetop.

The tea bag was steeping when Connie appeared on the other side of the bar that separated the den from the kitchen. She was not alone.

"Do you happen to know where Ovida is now?" Connie asked, glancing meaningfully at the young woman at her side. "Nicole is looking for her."

Jolie shook her head. "I think she was going over to Sharon's, but that was hours ago." Sharon was the oldest of Vince's four sisters.

Nicole frowned. "I went by there," she said, "but no one was at home."

Jolie considered. "Obviously they went somewhere. That woman really ought to get a cell phone." She snapped her fingers. "Sharon's got one. Why don't I give her a call?"

Nicole brightened visibly.

"Would you mind? I don't usually work on Friday afternoons, but I've been called in to cover for another server, and I really need someone to pick up my little brother from school."

Jolie went to the telephone and dialed Sharon's number, but the cell went straight to voice mail. She left a brief message and hung up before turning back to Nicole.

"Sorry," she said, leaning against the counter. "Sharon isn't answering. She probably forgot to turn the phone on."

Nicole sighed and shifted her weight, one hip sliding out. Jolie glanced at Connie, who lifted her eyebrows, then studied the girl.

Girl wasn't exactly the right word. She was young, yes, and a little quirky with her dark hair twisted up on top of her head and sticking out in all directions. Fat, sleek tendrils of it hung down beside her face, which was really very pretty, no thanks to artifice.

Jolie didn't much like to wear makeup herself and considered that it would have been a crime to cover up Nicole's flawless ivory complexion. Nicole was really very striking, Jolie decided, despite the slender, fraying cropped jeans that she wore with clashing stripes.

Her oversize, rainbow-hued sweater was striped vertically in wide bands of vivid color, but the black-and-white stripes of the turtleneck that she wore beneath it ran horizontally, while her socks sported a diagonal pattern of yellow-and-orange bands.

It was enough to make an innocent observer dizzy.

Jolie cleared her throat and concentrated on Nicole's pretty eyes. They were almost leonine in their shape and size, and the slight tilt at the outer edges gave her an exotic air. It was the frankness in those warm brown eyes that most appealed to Jolie, however. They seemed to speak volumes, and one thing came through loud and clear.

This girl was worried about her brother.

"I could do it," Jolie said impulsively.

"Oh, Jo," Connie put in quickly, "you don't need to go out."

She turned to Nicole. "I'll do it. Just tell me where his school is, and I'll drive by on my way home, pick him up and drop him off at your house."

Nicole made a face. "Actually, I don't want him dropped off. I—I was hoping Ovida would take him home with her until I get off work. I mean, he's thirteen, he hardly needs babysitting, but...well, he spends a lot of time alone."

Jolie looked at Connie and saw the same conclusion in her gaze. Nicole didn't want her brother to go home because their father was drinking.

"Do you think," Nicole began hesitantly, "that your brother, Marcus, might...?"

"That's brilliant!" Jolie exclaimed. "Why don't we give him a call?"

Nicole lifted a shoulder, already backing away. "Maybe I'll just drop by the church on my way to work."

"Oh." Again Jolie traded glances with her sister, her instincts perking up. "That'll work. And if for some reason he can't help you, just ask him to give one of us a call."

"Thank you. I appreciate that," Nicole said, practically out of the room.

Jolie followed, trying to see her unexpected guest out. She barely got to the entry hall before Nicole opened the front door. "Thanks again. Everyone in your family is so nice."

"Think nothing..." The door closed before she could get the rest of it out. Jolie folded her arms consideringly before turning back toward the kitchen.

"She was certainly in a hurry," she told Connie as she re-entered the room.

"Guess she had to get to work."

"Somehow I think it's more than that," Jolie said, sending her sister a droll look.

Connie set down her cup and folded her arms against the table. "I thought she seemed a little taken with him the other day. Not that he would notice."

"True." Sighing, Jolie lowered herself into her chair. "That's a big part of the problem, you know. He's just oblivious."

Connie shrugged. "Well, maybe a minister has to be."

"Maybe. On the other hand, how does he ever expect to find anyone if he doesn't at least open himself up to the possibility?"

Connie smiled. "Oh, the same way we did, maybe."

Jolie burst out laughing. "In other words, God will have to drop her on his head."

"Something like that." Connie grinned.

What neither of them said aloud was that Nicole Archer couldn't possibly be the one. Indeed, it went without saying. Just as well then, that Marcus would probably never even realize that quirky little Nicole was developing a crush on him.

"I don't get home until almost ten. The restaurant closes at nine on Fridays, but we have to clear out the electronic till and help clean up before we go."

"No problem," Marcus told her.

They'd met on the sidewalk in the midst of the church compound. He'd pulled in just ahead of her, having returned from the office supply store. His heart had leaped when her little jalopy had nosed into the space beside his dependable, late-model sedan and again when she'd clambered out to smile at him, costumed in the most outrageous stripes he'd ever seen. He could hardly look at her—and couldn't look away.

Nicole gusted a huge sigh of relief and turned those big, tilted eyes up at him. "Thank you so much. It's a huge weight off my shoulders. We need the extra money, you know, but right now Beau can't be home with…out me," she finished weakly.

It was cold out, but Marcus set the bag of office supplies on the hood of his sedan and leaned a hip against the fender, crossing his arms. "Have you given any more thought to what I said about calling the authorities?"

She shook her head. "It's just not an option."

"Nicole, it's not going to get better until he's faced with reality."

"Look," she said, skipping closer. "I'm less than two semesters away from graduation. Then Beau and I can afford to take off on our own."

"Just like that?"

"No, not…I mean, we're making real plans."

Marcus didn't have the heart to point out that their father might have a good deal more to say about that than either of them realized.

"Well, we can talk about this later. You just go on to work and leave Beau to me," Marcus told her. "Which school is it?"

Nicole told him the name of the middle school where Beau was an eighth grader and launched into directions. "You go out here and turn right." She pointed toward the street. "Then it's the third light—"

"I know it well," Marcus interrupted. "Several of our youngsters attend there, and some of our adult members are on the staff."

She clapped her gloved hands together. "Great! I'll call from work and let them know you'll be picking him up."

"Just have him wait in the office."

"You're sure you don't mind entertaining him for the evening?"

"Not at all."

She dug a toe into a crack in the pavement. "I thought maybe you had other plans or something."

"None. I'm looking forward to the company." He leaned toward her, aware that it wasn't a gesture he normally employed and a little puzzled by the urge to do so now. "Gives me a good excuse to play video games." She laughed, and the sound made him smile.

"As if any guy needs an excuse to play video games."

"Hey, you reach a certain age," he said with a helpless shrug.

"Puh-leeze." Reaching out, she gave his shoulder a little shove. "You're not exactly a grandfather."

His first impulse was to playfully shove back, but he kept his arms tightly folded, surprised by the discipline required to do so. "I'm not exactly a kid, either."

"Not exactly."

She didn't sound as if that was a bad thing. He didn't want to think about why. Instead, he reminded himself what his purpose was.

"I do have a favor to ask in return, though," he said.

She spread her hands. "Anything I can do. Anything at all."

"I'd like for you and your brother to attend church."

"Ah." She dropped her gaze and rocked back on her heels.

"You said you might," he cajoled.

She shined a blindingly bright smile on him. "I'd already planned on it."

"Excellent." He pushed away from the car and reached for the shopping bag. "This is what I call a real win-win situation."

"Yeah, well, don't be surprised tonight if Beau's not quite so…enthusiastic." She wrinkled her nose. "He is thirteen."

Marcus chuckled. "He doesn't like to be babysat."

"Exactly."

"Fine. I won't babysit him. I'll just pick him up, feed him and allow him to keep me company until I drop him off at your house."

"Oh, you don't have to do that. I'll pick him up."

Marcus shook his head. "No way. Not at that time of night."

"But I'm out at that hour all the time."

"Not if I can help it."

She rolled her eyes. "I'm not the thirteen-year-old."

"I'm aware of that. Nevertheless, I'd feel better if you'd go straight home after work."

Nicole flattened her mouth. It was a very pretty mouth, too pretty to appear stern. He smiled, and she threw up her hands.

"Oh, all right. But don't think I'm going to let you get away with treating me like a child, Marcus Wheeler, because I'm not."

"You are, however, young and female and too pretty for your own good." He snapped his mouth shut, wondering where on earth that had come from.

She had beamed before. Now her smile could have warned ships at sea.

He gulped and said, "I—I wouldn't let my mother wander around on her own late at night. In fact, if I could have stopped that, she might still be alive."

Nicole's smile softened. "It's terrible to lose your mom, isn't it?"

He nodded, suddenly swamped with emotion. "She died in an auto accident."

"I'm sorry to hear that."

"No sorrier than I was to hear about your loss. I was only seven when she disappeared. We didn't know she'd died for years." Now why had he told her that?

Long, slender fingers wrapped around his hand. Even through the leather of her gloves, he felt the heat of her hand.

"That's so sad," she said, "At least I had my mom until I was grown."

He almost snorted at that. She was barely grown now.

Barely, but grown.

Abruptly he stepped back. As if sensing that she'd made him uncomfortable, she swiftly turned away, saying, "I'd better run. Thanks again."

"Don't worry about it," he called after her.

She flashed him a smile and dropped behind the wheel of her car. That thing looked as if it was held together with baling wire and prayer. Another reason she ought not to be running around on her own late at night. He stood where he was until she managed to crank the engine to sputtering life and bully the transmission into reverse. Only as she drove away did he turn toward the office.

He hoped that restaurant where she worked made their servers wear uniforms. Otherwise, customers were bound to lose their appetites. He laughed at the memory of all those stripes as he pushed through the heavy glass door into the outer office.

Glancing at the clock on the wall behind his secretary's desk, he made note of the time. Ten minutes after three. He had plenty of time, but it wouldn't hurt to be in the principal's office waiting for Beau when the bell rang at four o'clock. Even as he deposited the bag on Carlita's desk and shrugged out of his overcoat, he told himself that he had known he would cross paths with the Archer family again.

He tossed the three-quarter-length tan coat over a chair, explaining, "I'm going out again in a few minutes. I just want to grab a few video games from David's office."

David Calloway was their part-time minister of youth. Marcus hoped to introduce him to Beau very soon.

"You shouldn't be here at all," Carlita reminded him in her tart, Spanish-tinged English. "It *is* Friday."

The single mom of four children and several years his senior, Carlita was prone to mother him a bit. He didn't mind. Having someone care about you was not an onerous burden.

He knew that Carlita and his sisters thought he worked too much, but he liked his work. Besides, some weeks emergency calls and visitation kept him out of the office, so Friday might be the only day he had to catch up on things, like picking up supplies he'd failed to have delivered with the regular monthly order.

Even as he rifled through the stack of video game discs on a shelf in David's tiny office, Marcus mused that he had no reason *not* to work. What use was a day off if it was spent alone? It was good to have the prospect of company, any prospect of company. Even if Beau Archer proved less engaging than his sister, Marcus would be grateful for the companionship.

It had been almost a year since Connie and Russell had moved out, but he still missed them. Not that he would have changed anything. They were happy as could be with Kendal and Larissa. It was just that he'd never been much good at living alone. The parsonage was small, but it could still feel lonely for one person.

In the early years after their mother had disappeared, he'd missed his sisters terribly, but at least he hadn't been alone. His foster parents had looked after a houseful of boys. Then when he'd first gone off to college he'd lived in a dorm, and after that he'd shared apartments or houses with various buddies.

He'd spent a few months on his own after the church had

called him, but that had been a very busy time. Then Connie had gotten out of prison and she and Russell had come to live with him.

Those had been good months, especially after God had brought Vince into Jolie's life and spurred her to forgive him and Connie for removing Russell from her custody. Now the family was not only together again, it was expanding.

His sisters' happy marriages had seen to that. If it felt as though something was missing from his own life, well, he expected God to put that right one of these days, too. He was trying not to be impatient about it.

Unbidden, an image of Nicole Archer standing in his sister's foyer came to him, and he resolutely pushed it away. Nicole was an opportunity to minister, not a prospective spouse. The very idea was ludicrous for a number of reasons. Besides, she needed his help, not his desperate, misplaced attentions. She probably had a boyfriend, anyway.

The thought made him wince, and he resolved to put it firmly out of mind, unwilling to picture Nicole flirting and smiling with some boy and managing to do so just the same. He was forced to admit that he couldn't see her with a *boy*. Some guy like David was much more her speed. Thankfully, er, fortunately, the young minister of youth was engaged, a matter of no little irony to Marcus's mind.

Not even out of seminary yet and already engaged to be married. It was enough to make a mature, older man just a tad envious.

Marcus strolled past Carlita's desk, tossed on his coat, pocketed the game discs and moved toward the door again, saying, "I'm gone now. Have a good weekend."

"You, too, Pastor," she called as he pushed through the door.

The winter air was bracing, and the weather forecast predicted sleet in the wee hours of the coming morning. Marcus stood for a moment and inhaled deeply, clearing his head of unwanted thoughts. He hoped the prognosticators were correct about the timing of the coming sleet storm.

February always brought at least one ice storm to north central Texas, and it invariably shut down the entire Dallas-Fort Worth Metroplex area for a day or more. For the sake of road safety, it was better that it happen on a weekend than a workday, even if it meant that church attendance would be down this Sunday.

Marcus let himself into his sedan and started up the engine, warm inside his coat. Lots of the kids around here routinely walked to and from school, regardless of the weather; Marcus was glad that Beau wouldn't be one of them, at least for today.

He was curious about Nicole's brother. Actually, he was curious about everything having to do with Nicole Archer. After only one meeting, he'd known that she was a very unusual young lady. Something about her had stuck with him since their initial meeting two days ago. In fact, he hadn't been able to get her out of his mind. That, no doubt, was because God was calling him to perform this service for her and her family, this and others to come.

Marcus was glad to do so. That's what his life, his calling, was about. God would take care of everything else in His own good time.

Chapter Three

When Marcus walked into the school, he was instantly recognized by the attendance officer and the vice principal, Joyce Ballard, who was a member of his church. He greeted both by their given names and stated his purpose for being there.

"I didn't realize you knew Beau," the vice principal observed nonchalantly.

A tall, thin woman, she looked older than her forty-something years and could be very stern, but Marcus knew that she genuinely cared about her young charges.

"Actually, we haven't met yet. I know his sister."

"Some of our parents could take a lesson from that girl," Joyce said.

"She does seem devoted to her brother."

"No doubt about it," the woman said, going back to the paperwork she'd been doing when he'd entered.

Marcus removed his coat and sat down to wait for the bell to ring. As she worked, the vice principal gave him the rundown on some of their church kids. One had done very well in a University Interscholastic League competition that week. Another had been out ill with a cold, and a third had recently won the lead role in a school drama. Marcus made the appropriate mental notes and was about to ask about another youngster when the bell rang.

Instantly, kids spilled out into the hallways. Noise swelled, happy voices punctuated the sounds of heavy footsteps and the slamming of locker doors. Rising, Marcus reached for his overcoat just as a group of youngsters swarmed into the office, talking loudly. Among them was a solemn boy with medium brown hair and dark brown eyes. The vice principal singled him out at once.

"Beau, this is Pastor Wheeler. Your sister sent him to pick you up."

Marcus stuck out his hand, saying, "Hello, Beau. I'm Marcus."

The boy hesitated, sizing up this newcomer. Marcus openly returned his regard, patiently keeping his hand out.

Beau's blocky build and squarish face had nothing in common with his sister's. Though of only average height at present, he was destined to make a big man. Only his coloring was similar to Nicole's, if reversed. Where her hair was dark and her eyes lighter, the opposite was true for Beau.

Unlike his sister's, his choice of wardrobe was mundane: athletic shoes, a maroon T-shirt that was a bit too small and faded, baggy jeans. What struck Marcus most, however, was the wariness in Beau's dark eyes. Marcus had seen that wounded, haunted, uncertain look before. He'd seen it far too many times, in fact, most often in the mirror.

Finally Beau shifted his bright blue backpack to the other shoulder and shook Marcus's hand. Marcus let his smile broaden.

After a farewell wave to the adults in the office, Marcus

followed the boy out into the busy hallway. The boy didn't appear to have a coat, but Marcus said nothing, all too aware of the prickly pride of a thirteen-year-old boy whose parents didn't live up to their responsibilities. Instead, he folded his own coat over his arm and headed for the wall of doors at the end of the hall. If Beau was going to suffer the cold, Marcus would, as well, not that Beau seemed to notice.

The boy seemed uninterested in conversing. He sat hunched in the passenger seat of Marcus's sedan, his attitude clearly wary and defensive. The only reply Beau made to Marcus's explanation for why Nicole hadn't picked him up and to the series of polite questions about what he'd like to do that evening was, "I'm hungry."

So Marcus took him to the closest fast-food joint, where he ordered a hamburger and a cola. Marcus said nothing about the possibility of him ruining his dinner. He knew from experience that boys the age of Beau could eat their own weight three times a day and still be hungry.

When Beau pulled a couple of bucks out of his pants pocket, Marcus politely ignored him, ordered a milk shake and fries for himself, neither of which he really wanted, and paid for everything. The food came quickly, and they carried it to a corner booth where they sat in silence for several minutes.

Marcus picked a fry from a tiny paper bag and munched it, turning sideways on the bench to stretch out his legs. Having allowed the boy to eat undisturbed for some time, Marcus adopted a nonchalant tone and prepared to gently prod.

"So tell me about yourself, Beau."

"Like what?" came the doubtful reply.

Marcus said the first thing that came into his head. "Do you have a favorite subject in school?"

The boy bit off a huge chunk of hamburger and studiously chewed it. Marcus figured it was an excuse not to speak, but then the boy surprised him.

Marcus discovered that Beau was an indifferent student with a passion for music. He was not, however, in band classes, either because he couldn't afford it or he didn't like the band director. Or both.

"It's whack," Beau grumbled. "Mr. Placid doesn't like guitar. Says there's no future in it. Like there's a huge future in tuba and xylophone. Truth is, he just doesn't know squat about it."

Marcus was familiar with that term *whack*. In the parlance of the modern youth it meant the opposite of cool, but he had no intention of trying to demonstrate his grasp of current teen lingo. Kids were quick to spot a patronizing adult. Instead, he played it straight down the line.

"So you play the guitar, then. I'm envious. It's all I can do to follow along in the hymnal."

"My grandpa taught me when I was a baby," Beau said softly, and Marcus instantly picked up on the significance of that.

"Yeah? Does your grandpa live around here?"

Beau shook his head before explaining that his grandfather had died the same year as his mom.

"Tell me something good you remember about him," Marcus urged.

A light shone in Beau's eyes. The sullen, wary teenager had gone, and in his place sat a simple boy who had lost too much.

"He had this cabin up in Oklahoma. We used to go up there in the summertime. It's right on the river. You ever been on the Illinois River?"

Marcus shook his head and swung his legs around to sit facing the boy again. "No, I'm sorry to say that I haven't."

Beau began a monologue on an old canoe that they'd kept at the campground at the bottom of the bluff below the cabin and all the times he and his grandfather had taken it out.

"There's these pools, where the water's still, and that's where you get the most fish," he said wistfully. "I wish I could go back there for good."

"What about your grandmother?" Marcus asked. "Doesn't she still live there?"

Beau shook his head. "She lives up in Seattle with my great-aunt. Her mind got bad even before my mom got sick, and she pretty much forgot everything. When Grandpa died, Nicole wanted to take care of her, but Aunt Margaret said she'd do it so Nic could go to college."

"That was good of your great-aunt."

"Yeah. She's pretty old herself."

Marcus wanted the boy to know that he was blessed despite all of his losses and problems, so he made a confession. "I don't have any great-aunts or anybody like that, and I don't have anything good to remember about any of my family except my sisters."

Beau furrowed his brow at that, asking, "How come?"

"My grandparents died before I was born. They didn't have any family except my mom. I never knew my dad's family or anything about them. My dad wasn't around much, and he split when I was about four. Then my mom took off a few years later and was killed in an auto accident."

"That stinks."

"It sure did. My foster parents tried to make things fun for the boys who lived with them, but there wasn't much money and my foster mom was crippled up pretty bad with arthritis. Besides, it was kind of hard to have fun without my little sisters there. All that's changed now, though." He sat back, aware that he had Beau's full attention. "Everybody's good now. My sisters are both married to really great guys. They both have nice homes, and I have a nephew and a niece with one more on the way. Plus, there are the Cutlers."

"You know the Cutlers?"

"My sister Jolie is married to Vince."

"No kidding?"

"That's how I met *your* sister."

"Nicole says the Cutlers are like a tribe. There are so many of them, and they've got all these rituals and stuff, like football, and everybody's always hanging out together. Man, that's gotta be bananas."

Marcus laughed. "Close." He pushed the milk shake over, saying offhandedly, "Want that? I'm not as hungry as I thought I was."

Beau drained his cola in one long swig and reached for the milk shake, asking, "So how come you're not married?"

Marcus was a bit taken aback. "Been wondering that same thing myself. Just haven't found the right woman yet."

Talk turned to other things. Beau never once mentioned his father, but he obviously depended on his sister for everything. Marcus hoped Beau knew how blessed he was in that sister of his, but he wasn't sure that a thirteen-year-old was capable of understanding how unique Nicole was.

Most young ladies her age were all about guys and friends and accumulating things, not providing stable homes for their younger siblings. Marcus understood her motivation better than most, but Beau likely took her somewhat for granted, which probably was as it should be. Someday, though, Beau would look back and understand what his sister had done for him. At least Marcus wanted to think he would, for Beau's sake as much as Nicole's.

Beau finished his "snack," including what was left of Marcus's French fries, and allowed Marcus to lead him outside. As predicted, clouds had swept in on a new pressure system, obscuring the sun and dropping the temperature into the twenties.

Marcus hustled the boy into the car and resumed his place behind the steering wheel. He started the engine and cranked up the heater, hoping that it wouldn't take long to warm up.

Beau's lack of a coat was troubling, and Marcus tried to think how to address the situation, finally coming up with a rather obvious approach. "Would you like to drop by your house to pick up your coat?"

Obviously alarmed, Beau exclaimed, "No!"

Knowing what he did about Dillard Archer, Marcus considered that response ominous, but he didn't want to judge the man unfairly. "Mind if I ask why?" When the boy pressed his lips together sullenly, Marcus explained, "It's too cold for you to be running around without a coat."

"Mine's dirty," Beau mumbled.

"A dirty coat is better than no coat, Beau," Marcus pointed out.

The boy suddenly erupted. "My dad threw up on it, okay? He was sloppy hungover and he barfed all over my coat this morning!" He turned his face away, ashamed.

Marcus surreptitiously fortified himself with a deep breath, his heart going out to the boy, and carefully chose his next words. "Your father's alcoholism is a real problem for you. I'm sorry about that. With my dad it was drugs."

Beau slid a curious look over Marcus. "Yeah?"

"He overdosed not long before my mom left with her boyfriend. She used it as an excuse, actually. She kept saying that she had to provide my sisters and me with a father, as if my dad had ever really been a part of our lives. I couldn't figure out how taking off without us was supposed to provide us with parents, anyway."

"My mom would never do something like that," Beau vowed.

"I understand she was a fine Christian woman," Marcus said softly. "You must be very proud of that."

Beau nodded, whispering, "Before she died, everything was real good."

"It will be good again, Beau," Marcus promised. "I'm living proof of that. Now about that coat…"

"He'll be drinking again by now," Beau said miserably, shaking his head and staring out the windshield.

"Actually," Marcus said, "I was thinking about an old coat I have that you can use. Want to go take a look at it?"

Beau hunched a shoulder in a seemingly unconcerned shrug. Marcus took that for assent and headed for the parsonage.

When they turned into the church grounds, Beau seemed surprised. Looking around him quickly, he exclaimed, "It's almost like a town."

"A very small town perhaps," Marcus said, guiding the car past the church offices and day care center.

He explained that the membership had needed to expand the church but they hadn't wanted to abandon their beloved old sanctuary. The solution had been to purchase, one by one, the houses which had faced the original church on every side.

The buildings were then renovated according to their assigned purpose and linked via covered walkways. In some cases, two buildings had been joined by an addition to form a larger space. Marcus pointed out the education building, the fellowship hall, the youth department and the music center. A house still undergoing renovation would soon serve as a furlough home for missionaries and their families returning to the U.S. on leave or for some other reason.

As Marcus eased the sedan into the narrow garage of the tiny parsonage, Beau pointed out that the "missionary house" was much larger than the home occupied by Marcus.

"Well, maybe someday I'll get married and need the larger house," Marcus said, unconcerned. "Then this house will be the furlough house, although we might have to add a bedroom or two."

Marcus tossed his own coat over the counter that separated the small kitchen from the combined dining and living area, flipping on the overhead light as he did so. He'd forgotten that the place was so cluttered. A necktie, which went with the shirt draped over the back of a dining chair, lay in a snaky heap next to this morning's unwashed breakfast bowl and an empty milk carton. Books were stacked on the dining table. Today's newspaper had drifted off the old-fashioned, green vinyl sofa onto the floor, and Marcus wondered suddenly when he'd last vacuumed the sand-colored carpet.

Beau chuckled and commented, "Man, Nicole would send you to your room if she got a load of this."

Marcus sent him a bemused glance, bringing his hands to his hips before once again surveying the place. "She'd be justified, too."

He started gathering up his errant clothing. Beau leaned an elbow on the counter and parked his chin on the palm of his hand.

"What's for dinner?"

Marcus nearly dropped everything he'd gathered. They had just eaten, hadn't they? Growing boys. "Pizza?"

"I'll call it in!" Beau exclaimed eagerly. Marcus chuckled and pointed out the phone.

By the time he'd dumped his load and reached into his closet for the coat he had in mind for Beau, the pizza was on its way.

Made of quilted gray nylon with snaps up the front and ribbed cuffs, the coat was a couple sizes too large for Marcus, having once belonged to his foster father, which meant that it would swallow the boy. Marcus counted on the inexplicable teenage fixation with oversize clothing to make the coat acceptable to Beau, and it did exactly that.

"Über!" Beau exclaimed, pushing up the sleeves to expose his hands.

Marcus recognized the German word for *super.* "You can keep it if you want," he offered. "I never wear it."

Beau looked pleased, then doubtful. "Nicole may not like it. She says we have to do for ourselves."

"I don't think she'll object."

Still unconvinced, Beau peeled off the coat and laid it across the chrome-banded, wood coffee table.

"Well, you can return it later, if you want," Marcus said lightly. "How about a video game?"

It was glaringly obvious long before the pizza came that Marcus was no competition for the boy at all, but that didn't seem to matter. As the pizza swiftly disappeared into the boy's mouth, Marcus silently marveled, remembering well when he, too, had eaten like a human garbage disposal. It seemed long ago now.

When they finally turned off the game, Marcus was surprised to find that the evening news was just signing off.

"We've got to get you home!"

Beau didn't argue, just popped up and tossed on his borrowed coat. Marcus grabbed his own coat, and the two hurried out.

The winter night was brittle with cold, but the clouds had

unexpectedly cleared away, leaving the city lights to sparkle and glow against the pitch-black backdrop of the starry sky. Their breath puffed out in little fogs until the car warmed up, which wasn't long before they reached the Archer house.

A long, low, red brick ranch-style built on a generous lot at the top of a cul-de-sac, the home of Beau and Nicole Archer and their father had a welcoming air, despite overgrown shrubs, broken tree limbs and the wildly canted mailbox at the curb. Though an older home, it appeared to be a good place to raise a family and boasted a large, double-car garage that Marcus could easily covet.

He parked his late-model sedan behind an aging pickup truck.

"Thanks for everything," Beau said, yanking open the passenger door and reaching toward the floorboard for his backpack.

"I don't see Nicole's car," Marcus pointed out.

"She parks in the garage when it's cold. Otherwise her old heap won't start in the morning."

That wasn't surprising. "I'll just walk you to the door," Marcus said, "I'd like to speak to her." In truth, he wanted to be sure she was all right.

The interior light of the car clearly illuminated Beau's worried gaze. "I could have her call you."

Marcus signaled his understanding with a smile. "I won't antagonize your father, I promise, Beau, but I'm going to walk you to the door and be sure your sister arrived home safely. Okay?"

Beau muttered something under his breath and climbed out of the car. Marcus followed suit, and together they walked to the front of the house. A motion-sensitive light flicked on as they drew near the multi-paneled door, and almost at once it opened. Nicole stood there, framed in the open doorway.

Marcus couldn't help smiling at her outlandish clothing. Something about her propensity to costume herself like this was rather endearing. The stripes going in every direction did make him want to cross his eyes, but at the same time for some reason his heart seemed to climb up into his throat and lodge there. He knew he should say something, but she smiled at him, and his mind went completely blank. The words that seemed to roll so easily off his tongue from the pulpit were simply nowhere to be found. It was perhaps the scariest moment of his life.

Nicole smiled at Marcus and reached out a hand to her brother, who attempted to slip past her into the house. Only then did her mind register what her eyes were telling her.

"Hey, where'd you get this coat?"

Marcus coughed, cleared his throat and rasped, "It's an old one that I had in my closet."

She looked at Beau. "Where's your other coat?"

"In the hamper," Beau mumbled, turning to Marcus. "Thanks for everything."

"My pleasure."

Beau escaped into the house, his backpack bumping Nicole and rocking her sideways. She looked to Marcus with her brows arched in question.

He cleared his throat and croaked, "Uh, if he doesn't want it—the coat, that is—maybe you can give it to someone else. I never wear it."

"All right. Are you feeling okay? You sound like you're coming down with something."

He seemed flushed to her, but he shook his head. "No, no. I'm fine. Just—" he swallowed "—something in my throat."

"How'd it go with Beau?"

"Just fine." He looked down, and she felt a spurt of unease, but then he looked up again, a smile crooking up one corner of his mouth. "I have one question, though. Do you have to work a second job to feed him?"

She laughed. "Sometimes. I hope he didn't clean you out of groceries."

"Impossible. I didn't have anything in the house. We had pizza. And burgers." He grinned. "Fries. Milk shakes. Cookies…"

She rolled her eyes. "What do I owe—"

"Don't even say it," Marcus warned, holding up a hand. "I was really glad of the company."

A loud, slurred voice shouted from inside, "Shut that blasted door! You're letting out all the heat!"

Nicole immediately stepped outside, pulling the door closed behind her. She folded her arms against the cold and said, "Thank you. And thank you for the coat. He likes it. I can tell."

"Very fashionable for him," Marcus quipped.

"Obviously. I—I just don't want you to think that I routinely let him go to school without a proper coat. I have an early class on Fridays, so he rides with a friend. I can't imagine why he didn't take his coat. You know how kids are."

"Too well. Speaking of coats. It's too cold for you out here without one."

"I'm okay. D-Did he say anything about, you know, Dad?"

"Yeah, but listen, we can't talk standing out in the cold like this." Marcus glanced around, then took her by the arm. "Come on. Let's sit in the car."

Nicole let him tug her toward his roomy sedan. "Good idea."

He walked her swiftly around to the passenger side and handed her into the car's interior. It was still warm from the drive over but rapidly cooling. Thankfully, after taking his seat behind the wheel, he started the engine and switched on the heater.

"There. That's better." For good measure, though, he lifted his scarf over his head and draped it around her shoulders, spreading it out like a shawl, a narrow one but surprisingly effective, warmed as it was from his body.

He started to shrug out of his coat, but she put a stop to that. "I'm quite comfortable now, thank you."

"You sure?"

"Absolutely. So what did Beau say about Dad?"

"He said he was 'sloppy hungover this morning,'" Marcus answered. "That's why his other coat's in the hamper."

She grimaced, not even wanting to know what that meant. She'd find out soon enough anyway. Tossing one end of Marcus's scarf across her throat, she inhaled. It smelled just as she'd imagined it would, just as she'd imagined he would.

"I thought he was just saying that so you wouldn't know that he left it home on purpose. His old coat's too small, and the other kids make fun of him because of it. You know how it is."

"Yeah, well, the way things are these days, too small could actually mean that it fits, not that these kids would see it that way."

She laughed. "True. I hate that we can't afford new things for him, but the way he's growing it's all I can do to keep him covered."

"There are worse things than not keeping up with fashion trends," Marcus said.

"That's the way I see it," she agreed sincerely, but then he got this big grin on his face.

"What?"

"Oh, nothing. I'm just glad to see that you have your priorities straight."

"Oh. Well, I'm glad you think so. Beau doesn't always agree."

"He's thirteen. I think agreement is a biological impossibility at this point."

She chuckled. "You're telling me! He's not a bad kid, though."

"I can see that. I meant it when I said I enjoyed his company."

"I'm sure he enjoyed your company, too, a lot more than he would have the Cutlers. They're wonderful people, but to Beau anyone over thirty is the enemy right now." Marcus winced, and she quickly reached out a hand. "I'm sorry. I didn't mean that literally. I just meant—"

"I know what you meant. Don't worry about it. Guess I'm just feeling my age these days."

"Well, it's not like you're arthritic or anything." Now she winced. "Are you?"

He laughed. "Not that I've noticed."

"Some young people are, you know. I mean, there's a girl in one of my classes with juvenile arthritis. She's stiff all the time, and you can, like, hear her joints popping when she moves."

"No arthritic joints here," he said merrily. "Not yet, anyway. Thank God."

"I'd better go in before I wind up with the other foot in my mouth," she muttered. And before her father took enough note of her absence to ask some awkward questions that she didn't want to answer.

"Beau's probably wondering what happened to you," Marcus agreed softly.

Reluctantly she removed the scarf from around her neck and offered it to him, but he shook his head.

"No, you keep it for now. You can return it on Sunday. Right?"

Nicole draped the scarf around her shoulders and tossed one end across her throat, smiling. "Right. I won't forget."

"Okay. See you then."

"See you then," she confirmed, opening the door and quickly hopping out. "Thank you, Marcus," she said just before she closed the door. "Bye."

He waved and put the car into reverse, but he just sat there with his foot on the brake until she reached the house.

"See you Sunday," Nicole whispered as she slipped inside.

It wouldn't be wise to let her father find out what she was planning. He'd had a thing about church ever since her mom had fallen ill. But she knew that going was the right thing to do, if only because she'd promised Marcus. It wasn't only that, though. Her mother would want them to go, her and Beau.

For too long Nicole had catered to her father's anger on this subject. Somehow she'd allowed herself to fall into the trap of trying to appease him when she knew only too well that nothing could.

She hoped that Beau wouldn't put up a fuss. He probably wouldn't. She thought he'd go because he liked Marcus, but he was going even if she had to bully him. One way or another, Sunday morning was going to find them both sitting on a church pew again.

Her fingers slid over the soft wool draped about her shoulders. It took a moment for her to realize that the feeling growing inside her chest was hope.

It had always lived there. She couldn't have kept on keeping on otherwise. Suddenly it seemed to be branching out, though, and in some surprising directions.

Smiling to herself, she fairly danced down the hall to her brother's room.

Chapter Four

Nicole sat on the foot of her brother's bed and waited for him to get off the computer. He ended the game he was playing and swiveled around on the seat of his chair, one arm on the desk, the other draped over the chair's hardwood back.

"Where's Dad?"

"Asleep in front of the TV, probably."

"You mean he passed out in front of the TV," Beau corrected.

She didn't deny it, but she wasn't here to discuss their father or his drinking problems. She had another matter entirely on her mind. "So what do you think of the pastor?"

Beau shrugged and said nonchalantly, "I like him."

"Really? You're not just saying that because you think I want you to?"

"Chillax. I said I like him."

"So you wouldn't mind spending time with him again?" Nicole probed carefully.

"I'll kick it with the pastor whenever you want," Beau said, turning his chair around to straddle it and fold his arms across the top of the back. "He's easy to talk to, like one of the guys almost, not like he tries to *be* one of the guys, though."

"I know what you mean," Nicole said. "It's like he's really interested in you and what you have to say."

Beau nodded. Then he asked, "Doesn't it seem funny that he's not married?"

Nicole's heart gave a pronounced thump, but she kept her expression cool. She hadn't even considered that he might be married. Why hadn't she looked at his ring finger? Why hadn't she asked Ovida Cutler?

"How do you know he's not married?"

"He told me so."

"Oh? What did he say?"

"Just that he hadn't found the right woman yet."

"So he's looking, then?"

Beau screwed up his face, complaining, "I don't know. What're you asking me for?"

"No reason," she answered nonchalantly. "It's just that I promised him we'd try out his church this Sunday, and I wanted to know what you thought about him. That's all."

Dropping his chin, Beau sent her a pointed look. Clearly she wasn't fooling him. He knew she was interested in Marcus. She rolled her eyes as if to say she wasn't, and for some reason Beau chose to let it go. She wondered if that signaled approval or if it meant that he figured she had no chance of attracting Marcus's interest for herself.

She cleared her throat. "Well? Do you want to go to church on Sunday or not?"

He thought about it before asking, "What about Dad?"

"The way I figure it," Nicole said, "is that if he goes out on Saturday night, then he'll be sleeping in on Sunday morning."

"And he always goes out on Saturday night," Beau said matter-of-factly.

They stared at each other for several long moments, neither saying aloud what they both knew. It would be better if their father didn't realize they were attending church, at least initially. Maybe once he saw that it wouldn't interfere with his lifestyle, he would be amenable. That had proven the case with the issue of Nicole attending college.

For some time before she'd graduated from high school, Dillard had grumbled that Nicole should put any plans to further her education on hold until Beau was old enough to take care of himself. Wisely, Nicole had said nothing, and when the time had come to enroll she had not sought Dillard's permission. Instead she'd simply taken herself down to the university, signed up for classes and applied for every grant, scholarship and tuition aid she could find. She was halfway through the first semester before her father had realized that she was attending college and his life had not truly been impacted at all. Hopefully, it would be the same way when he found out that they were attending church.

On the other hand, it might turn out to be a one-time deal. Marcus Wheeler's church might not be to their liking. They might not go back. That's what she told herself anyway. In her heart, Nicole knew that regular attendance was definitely in her future. She missed going to church, but she hadn't seen any point in risking her father's wrath until now.

"You'd better try on your dress slacks," she told Beau, rising to her feet. "You'll probably have to wear one of Dad's shirts."

Beau nodded, shrugged and turned back to the computer, muttering, "Guess you'll be going through your boxes."

"Oh, yeah," she admitted. This occasion definitely called for something special.

She headed for the garage and the half-dozen boxes that contained everything that was left over from her mother's and grandmother's closets. Nicole loved digging through them and wearing the clothes. Not only did it play to her personal tastes, it also saved her a lot of money on her wardrobe. Plus, it made her feel closer to those whom she missed most.

Luckily, retro was "in" right now, not that Nicole cared a fig for being in style. Some of the old stuff in those boxes was worth a good deal in resale shops, though. Once in a while, when money was especially tight, she'd pick out a piece to sell. Usually it was one of her grandmother's old handbags. Grandma Jean had claimed to have a handbag fetish. She'd accumulated dozens by the time she'd forgotten what the word *fetish* meant, along with so much else, including the family.

Dillard claimed that Jean was lucky because she couldn't remember the pain of losing her daughter and husband. Nicole didn't buy that philosophy, though. She was glad to remember. Every memory was a treasure to her, and she hung on to the memories much as she hung on to those boxes of old clothes.

It was too cold to go through her boxes in the garage, so Nicole towed them into her bedroom, one by one. A couple of them were actually made for garments, with poles for hangers. The rest were neatly stacked with smaller items. She knew exactly what each box held, but at times like this she would pull out every article and spread them around her colorful room, arranged by category. Once the contents of the boxes were properly displayed, Nicole would spend hours choosing what she would wear before lovingly packing it all away again.

On this occasion, she pulled everything out, then went to

bed beneath an extra blanket of garments, leaving the decision-making process for the morrow. She wanted to relish this turn that her life seemed to be taking. Even if the ultimate destination was not what she hoped, she intended to enjoy the journey.

Marcus couldn't contain his pleasure when he looked out across his congregation on Sunday morning at the smiling faces of Nicole and Beau Archer. There were other visitors, as well, of course. The place was packed, in fact, as it often was of late. Even the tiny balcony section, reached via a narrow, winding staircase hidden in the back hall, was stuffed with bodies.

Marcus recognized several families whose children attended day care at the church and was glad that preparations were underway for adding a second morning service in the spring, even though it would mean more work for him. Meanwhile, all those involved in the actual production and execution of worship were busily planning what that second service would involve. At times, like this morning, the excitement was palpable as the church poised itself for that next big step forward.

As he moved into the pulpit, Marcus felt lifted up, his words imbued with a special power. Though he considered himself more of a thoughtful teacher than a spellbinding preacher, he seemed linked to his audience in an unusual manner that morning. It was as if he shared a special connection with every person present, and when all was said and done, the church had added three new families, numbering ten souls in all, to the membership roll. Through every moment, he was aware of the Archers.

Even as he stood at the vestibule door, shaking hands and sharing smiles and comments with the exiting throng, Marcus was keenly aware of Beau and Nicole Archer near the back of the line. Beau seemed somewhat hesitant when Marcus paused to speak with him, but Marcus assumed that it had to do with his painfully awkward appearance.

Beau looked like a poster boy for the underprivileged, dressed as he was in a faded black tie and a white shirt which was considerably too large for him. The cuffs of his shirt sleeves had been rolled back several times to keep them from hanging over the boy's hands, and the collar was in no danger of choking him, despite the tightly knotted tie. To make matters worse, his charcoal-gray dress slacks were a little too short, showing a bit of white sock above worn black shoes. In addition, his shaggy brown hair slid haphazardly in several directions at once, despite having obviously been parted and wet-combed earlier. He held the coat Marcus had given him, clutched in both arms, like a security blanket.

Marcus knew he had to do something. He called over a couple of youngsters around Beau's age and introduced them. As the trio stepped aside to talk stiltedly among themselves, Marcus at last turned his attention to Nicole.

While Beau's attire branded him as a poor kid barely surviving in a harsh world, Nicole managed to look amazingly pretty in her odd getup. Considering the last two times he'd seen her, this outfit was fairly subdued, which was not to say conventional.

Her dark hair fell sleekly past her shoulders from beneath a yellow crocheted cap pulled almost to her delicately arched brows. The crochet was repeated in the ankle-length, purple vest that she wore over a slender, black, short-sleeved sheath, yellow stockings and knee-high, white vinyl boots. She clutched her red gloves in one hand and carried a familiar striped scarf folded over one arm with what appeared to be a royal-blue cape, though it could have been a voluminous coat arranged so that the sleeves were hidden.

Marcus couldn't help laughing. Not because she looked ridiculous—she didn't, oddly enough—but because something about her just inspired that reaction. It was as if the sun came out from behind drab clouds when Nicole appeared, as if color suddenly washed a black-and-white world with sparkling, breathtaking hues. Yet, no one could deny that she was a quirky character. Marcus saw the way that others looked at her, the smiles hidden behind coughs and throat clearings, the surreptitious glances and whispered comments. She seemed happily oblivious.

"That was great!" she gushed, rocking up onto her tiptoes as she held his hand. "Inspiring. Honestly!"

"Glad you enjoyed it. I'm delighted to see you and Beau here this morning."

"We'll be back," she announced, beaming.

"Wonderful. If you have a few minutes now, though, I'd like a word with you when I'm done here." A shadow passed across her eyes, dimming them momentarily. "Won't take long, I promise," he added quickly, then glanced pointedly over his shoulder at Beau.

"Oh, um, okay. Sure."

He directed her to a bench against one wall of the vestibule and made quick work of the few remaining farewells before joining her.

"As I said, I'm really glad to see you and Beau here this morning, Nicole," he told her. "I'm even happier that you plan to return, and I'd like to help Beau fit in, if I can."

"I'm sure once he gets to know people…" she began.

"Oh, absolutely," Marcus agreed. "If I could make one suggestion, though?"

Her slender brows drew together, and her voice carried a wary note despite her polite reply. "Of course."

"Let him lose the tie, or at least wear it loose and drooping." He touched his own neat Windsor knot and chuckled. "That's how our minister of youth wears his. Very cool, I'm told."

She made a face and relaxed. "I guess we were both thinking about the last time we attended church." Dropping her head she admitted, "It's been a long time, you know. Beau was just ten, and what was considered appropriate for a boy that age back then and what's considered okay now…" She waved a hand.

Marcus chuckled. "Yeah, I know. Some of the older folks complain when they see these kids with baggy pants and the shirttails out and hanging down to their knees, but I figure that this is their church, too, and they should be comfortable. That they're here is much more important to me than how they're dressed."

"I see what you mean."

"We do have standards," he went on. "We draw the line at T-shirts with slogans other than Christian ones and head coverings indoors for the boys. We don't even allow the girls to wear those backward caps that are so popular. Those so-called 'belly shirts' are absolutely forbidden, too, and we quietly monitor the length of skirts and, in the summertime, shorts. Otherwise, we pretty much try to go with the flow."

"Okay. I'll remember that," Nicole said. "I mean, it's bad enough that everything he owns is practically worn out. No reason he should stick out like a sore thumb, too."

Marcus bowed his head, fingering his chin, and said uncertainly, "Nicole, I could…that is, I'd be glad to—how should I put this?—front you some money on Beau's behalf."

She was on her feet and shaking her head before he got the words out. "Uh-uh. No way. Treating him to dinner is one thing, but buying clothes is something else."

"Think of it as a loan," he urged, but she was even more adamant in her refusal of that.

"Absolutely not. I couldn't pay it back, not for a long, long time, anyway." She folded her arms. "We've held out this long. We can hold out until I've paid next semester's tuition. After that we can start taking care of some of this other stuff."

He wanted to argue. It tore at Marcus's heart to see Beau going around so bedraggled because Marcus so vividly remembered being that boy. But he remembered, too, the pride that had gotten him through the worst of it, and well-deserved pride was better than new clothes. He wasn't thinking of the sort of pride that Scripture warned caused downfall but rather the pride that came from doing the difficult thing for the right reasons. Funny that Nicole should be the one to remind him of that.

"You're right," he said, rising to his feet. "Forget I mentioned it."

"That's okay." She smiled. "It just shows you care."

"Yes," he agreed unthinkingly. "Exactly. I do care."

"Thank you for that," she said, and then to his shock, she flung her arms around him in a hug.

For a moment Marcus froze, his arms trapped between them. Heat flashed through him, exploding into red blossoms on his cheeks. To his horror he realized that several of the kids were standing in the open doorway looking in at them, Beau in their midst, with none other than David Calloway in the background.

A couple of the teenagers giggled speculatively. Others seemed shocked. The minister of youth looked as embarrassed for him as Marcus felt. His throat burned and his face pulsed red by the time Nicole released him from what was surely nothing more than an impulsive display of gratitude, but he couldn't remember ever being quite so shaken before. He did his best to appear unconcerned, even casual. He said something about it being lunchtime and having to lock up before quickly turning away and immediately getting so busy that he didn't even see her leave.

Indeed, he didn't see much of anything after that. A red haze seemed to fog his vision. He felt disoriented, tongue-tied, glaringly conspicuous. It must have been obvious, for when David finally joined him, he asked peremptorily, "You okay?"

"Sure," he answered, wincing inwardly because it seemed too loud. "Just trying to get out of here. As usual, my sisters are expecting me for lunch."

"Ah." David grinned. Fair and blue-eyed, he was an engaging young man, a bit on the small side, but good-looking in a trendy, polished way with his artfully spiked hair and designer attire. More importantly, he was very, very good at youth ministry. It wasn't his fault that he sometimes made Marcus feel as if he were teetering on the brink of old age. Like now. "I don't think I've ever seen her before," David went on thoughtfully.

"Who?" That was painting it entirely too brown, and Marcus knew it, but he was stuck now.

"Long, dark hair," David said, a twinkle in his eye that made Marcus want to drop through a hole in the floor.

"Oh, you mean Nicole Archer. The new kid's her brother."

"Hmm. I didn't get much out of him."

"It's a long story," Marcus said. "I'll tell you about it in the office tomorrow."

David nodded. "Must be interesting."

"Interesting but sad," Marcus said gravely. "The Archers are in a very difficult situation."

That doused the speculative gleam in David's blue eyes. "Is there anything we can do?"

"I don't know. Maybe. For now, just pray, I suppose. His name's Beau, by the way. Beau Archer."

"I'll add his name to my list," David said.

"Great. Now would you check that back door for me? I'm starving."

"Go ahead and take off," David said, hurrying away.

Marcus did, for once, as quickly as possible, but he couldn't seem to recover his aplomb. While he drove toward his sister's house, he kept thinking about that hug, and for the life of him, he couldn't figure out why it had flustered him so.

As a single man in ministry, he was acutely aware that his conduct must be above reproach. For that reason he had always been very circumspect in his dealings with females of all ages, especially the young ones, and that included Nicole.

Why, a full decade stood between them. And it showed. Anybody could see it.

That didn't really explain why that hug had sent him into a panic, though. It wasn't the first time such a thing had happened. Usually he just disengaged and kept a polite distance, and that was the end of it. He couldn't understand why this felt different.

Walking up the gently winding pavement toward Jolie's front door, a picture of Nicole climbing into her battered little car suddenly assailed him. He stopped in his tracks, remembering that he'd felt an odd kinship with her even then. It was as if he knew her somehow, although they'd never met before.

He hadn't even been aware of her existence before! Surely that kinship was nothing more than his ability to identify on an innate level with what she was going through. Wasn't it?

Yes, of course. It had to be. What other explanation was there?

"The explanation, my man," he told himself aloud, the thought coming to him in a flash of insight, "is that the devil always hits you hardest when you're at your weakest point, and you have got to stop feeling sorry for yourself."

That was it. This feeling of being alone in a world of happy pairs was clouding his judgment and muddling his emotions. He had no reason to be embarrassed by a public hug from a funny girl who simply needed a friend, and he had no reason for this maudlin lonesomeness, either. When the time was right, God would bring someone into his life. Until then he was just borrowing trouble by letting it prey on his mind.

He bowed his head right where he was and confessed his weakness to God, adding a petition for the Archer family before ending his silent prayer. Feeling better, he went inside to dinner and the warmth of his sister's home.

Nicole handed the paper bag and bucket of chicken to her brother before fastening her safety belt. The drive-through lane had been ten cars deep when she'd pulled up to the fast-food restaurant, and she hadn't wanted to burn expensive gasoline or waste precious time idling in line, so she'd parked and gone inside to place their order. Now the car was cold again. She started the engine and began wrestling the gearshift into reverse.

"Sorry, I didn't have enough money for all the sides you wanted, but I got the gravy, and we can make instant potatoes."

Beau shrugged and pulled a steaming biscuit from the paper bag. A yeasty odor immediately permeated the bare interior of the small car. The crystal rainbow that hung from the rearview mirror on a string reeled crazily as the transmission finally caught and the little jalopy lurched backward in an arc.

"'At's o-hay," he said around a mouthful of hot biscuit.

He gulped and shoved the second half of the biscuit into his mouth. Apparently it had cooled enough to allow him to actually chew, for he mauled it once or twice before swallowing this time.

As he reached for a second helping, Nicole mentally said goodbye to her share of the hot bread. The kid ate as if constantly starving. She imagined that he'd be shooting up another couple of inches soon, which meant that his feet were going to get bigger, too.

That part of the equation worried her. He could wear his pants too short; with warmer weather coming on, she could always cut them off. As for shirts, he'd have to make do with Dillard's castoffs and cheap tees. But shoes were something else.

Beau detested secondhand shoes like those on his feet at that moment, and the cheap new ones, the ones she could afford, came apart within an appallingly short period of time. It was as if he wore them out from the *inside,* as if he steeped his feet in acid before he put on the things.

Anything durable enough to last longer than a few weeks was going to cost upward of sixty bucks. She could buy two or three pairs of the cheap ones for that, but in the end it would wind up costing her the same as the better ones. The only advantage was that she could parcel the money out in smaller portions. But Beau would be unhappy about it the whole time.

Sighing inwardly, she thought of the offer Marcus had made earlier, but she couldn't take his money, his or anyone else's. It was her job to care for her brother, hers and their father's, but she saw no point in dwelling on that. What

Dillard did, Dillard did. She couldn't answer for anyone but herself. The thing was, she'd promised at her mother's deathbed to take care of Beau, and that's what she had to do. She'd realized early on that if she didn't stand firm, she'd be swept aside by those who thought youth automatically trumped responsibility, which was exactly why she couldn't reach out to the authorities as Marcus had suggested.

She pictured Marcus as he'd appeared that morning. The fit of his dark brown suit had been perfect. She'd have jazzed things up with a pink shirt and neon-green tie and socks, but the pale yellow and gold had been nice, too, especially with Marcus's coloring. The shoes he'd worn were positively elegant, gleaming, butter-soft slip-ons with tiny leather pleats across the toe box.

She wished Beau could wear clothes like that. Then again, even if she could afford to outfit him in such style, he'd only grouse about it. He wanted to be like the rest of the kids in their expensive, baggy, oversize gear. Nicole supposed it was understandable, even though she had never wanted to look like anyone else. It was much more fun to be one of a kind.

"So what'd you think?" Beau asked, having had his fill of hot biscuits or, perhaps, realizing that he'd better leave the rest for their dad.

"About church?"

"No, about traffic. Duh. The music wasn't as whack as I figured it'd be, and those kids said they're going to start doing a service with guitars and drums and everything."

"Really? That sounds like fun."

"Could be."

"So you liked it, then?"

"Yeah, I liked it."

"Me, too. Especially the sermon."

Beau snorted. "Especially the preacher, you mean."

Nicole shot him a startled glance but kept her tone nonchalant as she said, "What of it? You like him, too."

"But *I* don't want him for a boyfriend," Beau teased.

"I never said—"

"You were hugging him, Nic."

She fought the impulse to tighten her hands on the steering wheel and trained her gaze straight ahead. "I was just thanking him. You're making mountains out of molehills. Now, back to the sermon."

Beau snorted again, but he let the matter go, asking, "What was that Phillips thing he read?"

"Philippians. It's in the New Testament."

"I didn't get that part about dying being gain."

"It's about knowing that you're going to heaven when you die. See, it's like…" She had to gather together the right words to explain it to him. "Okay. We think this life is good because it's all we know. And there's plenty to like about it. Living is a good thing. But heaven's even better, so death isn't about losing this life as much as it's about gaining a better one. That's what it means."

Beau nodded. "I can get with that. I've always believed that Mom and Gramps were in a better place. It's getting left behind that stinks."

"I know, but even that's not all bad. It's not even mostly bad once you get over the worst part."

"That's Dad's problem, isn't it?" Beau said matter-of-factly. "He can't get over the worst part of missing Mom."

Can't or won't, Nicole thought, preferring to stick with the sermon, which had moved her. "Anyway," she went on, "that Scripture passage wasn't really about dying. It was about living the way we ought to."

"'Only conduct yourselves in a manner worthy of the gospel of Christ,'" Beau quoted, proving that he'd been paying attention.

Nicole smiled to show her approval. "Exactly."

She hoped Beau was thinking about the things that Marcus had said were part of worthy living, things like reading the Bible and praying every day, being honest and kind and "wholesome." She knew she was going to be thinking about that a lot. The honest part niggled at her because she and Beau were not being honest with their father about attending church.

What else could they do, though? If they asked, he'd say no. At least this way they'd get to go for a while.

Which meant that she'd get to see Marcus.

That thought made her feel even worse, because church shouldn't be about getting to see a guy you liked. Church was about worship. She remembered her mom saying that over and over again. Back then for Nicole church had been more about seeing her friends than anything else. Once her mother had fallen ill, however, church had become all about God healing her. Suzanne had realized it and said that shouldn't be the case. Nicole had wondered how it could be about anything else, and she remembered sitting in that pew next to her mom, her friends forgotten, pleading with God to spare her mother's life.

…to live is Christ, and to die is gain.

It was as if Marcus had been saying to her with his sermon that now she could put behind her the deaths of her mother and grandfather and live the rest of her life in a manner that would prove the reality and wonder of heaven. And that was just what she intended to do. As soon as she figured out how.

She smiled to herself, knowing exactly who could help her with that.

Chapter Five

Nicole handed two cans of soup to her brother and reached for the handle of the refrigerator door.

"Open these while I make us some grilled cheese sandwiches."

Beau turned one can in his hand in order to read the label, making a face. "Oh, man, I hate this stuff!"

"The other is chicken noodle," Nicole pointed out, slapping a stick of margarine onto the counter. Ignoring his second grimace, she bent over the deli drawer in the refrigerator, looking for the sliced cheese.

"Why couldn't we nab a pizza or something?" he whined, having gotten used to picking up dinner after church these past four weeks.

It had become their cover. On the one occasion when their father had actually been awake when they'd come in, he'd seen the food sacks and assumed they'd gone out for that and no other reason. The trouble was, carrying in fast food was expensive.

"I told you," Nicole reminded her brother, "I'm broke."

"Man, there's got to be something else here to eat," Beau grumbled. Setting aside the soup cans, he shuffled over to the pantry and began poking around inside.

"Do not," said a raspy voice, freezing them in place, "try to tell me that you've been out getting lunch this time."

Her heart in her throat, Nicole made herself remove the sliced cheese from the drawer, close it and rise, giving the re-frigerator door a gentle shove as she turned. Beau put his back to the counter and folded his arms defiantly. She carefully did not look at him. Instead, she fixed her father with a level gaze.

"No, we didn't go out to get lunch," she admitted calmly. "We're scraping the pantry today, but I get paid tomorrow, so no sweat."

Carrying the cheese to the counter, she took the remains of a loaf of bread from her grandmother's old-fashioned bread box, then reached into a cabinet for a skillet.

"So where were you?" Dillard demanded, pulling out a rickety chair at the equally rickety kitchen table. "And don't give me any guff about being broke and payday coming."

Well, what had she expected? This day had to come sooner or later. She was surprised that they'd gotten away with it this long.

Nicole turned to face him just as he lowered himself into the chair. He stretched out his long, thick legs, crossing his stocking feet at the ankles. He was a mess. The heel was out of one sock, and the hems of his jeans were ragged. His faded T-shirt had holes in it and looked none too clean. He hadn't shaved in days—or bathed, by the greasy look of his lank, untrimmed hair.

A much larger, older version of Beau, Dillard Archer still retained some of the heavy musculature that had once made Nicole believe that her daddy was the strongest man alive. His middle had given way to a pronounced paunch. By the way he held one arm across it, he was probably nauseous, and the furrow of his brow said that his head likely ached, too, all of which meant that he was hungover. But perhaps a little less hungover than normal, unfortunately.

Beau walked across the room to stand beside her, belligerence in his every move. She rubbed his arm soothingly, then took a deep breath, relief warring with dread. "We've been going to church."

Dillard's face wrinkled and bunched. "Now why would you want to do a fool thing like that?"

Nicole used her greatest weapon without a single compunction. "Mama would have wanted us to."

Dillard clamped his jaw and looked away. After a moment he lifted a hand to massage his temples with thumb and forefinger. "You'd better not be putting my money in the collection plate," he groused, "then expecting me to eat soup!"

Beau made a rude sound. Nicole sent him a quelling glance and figuratively bit her tongue. They all knew that Dillard routinely drank up nearly every bit of his small disability check. If she hadn't made sure that the electricity bill was debited from it and a portion automatically set aside to pay their property taxes at the end of every year, he wouldn't contribute to supporting the household at all.

Her heart pounding, Nicole carried the skillet to the stove and turned on a burner. Beau started rummaging around in a drawer, looking for the can opener, which was sitting in the dish drainer next to the sink.

"You two little idiots have really been getting up, pawing through the ragbag and hauling yourselves to church?" Dillard demanded in the acid tone that always meant he was spoiling for a fight.

Nicole was determined not to give it to him. "What kind of soup do you want," she asked calmly, "chicken noodle or tomato?" When he didn't immediately answer, she glanced over one shoulder.

Scowling, Dillard brought his hands to his hips, but then his shoulders drooped, and he rumbled, "Tomato, but put some sherry in it, for pity's sake." Nicole tried to keep her expression bland, but he saw her disapproval and immediately snapped, "It's how your mother would have made it."

"I remember," she said lightly, reaching toward the dish drainer, "but we don't have any cooking sherry."

She handed the can opener to Beau with a very pointed look. He was glowering, but he kept his back to their father as he opened the can and dumped the contents into a bowl. She concentrated on preparing the grilled cheese sandwiches, while Beau heated the soup in their old microwave.

After a moment, Dillard got up and shambled out of the room.

A minute or two later, Beau tapped her on the shoulder. When she turned her head, he pumped one fist in a gesture of victory. Nicole smiled, but she wasn't so sure that they'd won anything yet. Still, their father hadn't forbidden them to continue attending church, and that in itself was more than she'd expected. Maybe, as Marcus's sermon had asserted that morning, God really was at work in their lives.

Marcus watched as the enthusiastic young minister of youth drove away in his shiny red pickup truck. David was great with the kids, who met weekly on Wednesday evenings for Bible study and fellowship. Marcus liked to put in an appearance at those weekly meetings himself, and David seemed to welcome his input. The two of them made a pretty

good team, and Marcus liked the young man immensely—
and envied him almost as much.

David was cool, popular and had his life together. His
parents came down from Oklahoma occasionally and stood
around beaming with undisguised and fully-merited pride. He
was engaged to a pretty, wholesome young woman from
another solid family, who couldn't have been more fitted to the
calling of a youth minister's wife, and they were happily
planning a wedding that was apt to set her parents back several
thousand dollars in another year or so. Marcus begrudged
them not a bit of any of it. He just wanted some of that for
himself, and he couldn't figure out where this unwarranted, un-
attractive and counterproductive discontent was coming from.

Crossing the square toward the parsonage, he cut through
the parking lot and a corner of the lawn surrounding the sanctuary. Sand-colored grass crunched beneath his feet. February
had gone, but the first day of March had brought only the
slightest promise of spring. He dug his hands deeper into his
coat pockets and hunched his shoulders against the frosty air
nipping at his ears.

He admitted to himself that he was disappointed because
Beau Archer hadn't attended the youth meeting this evening.
Marcus had invited the boy personally on Sunday, but he'd
mumbled something about Nicole having enrolled him in a
computer program at the local library. Marcus figured she'd
paid a fee and that Beau didn't want her to lose her hard-
earned money.

Marcus knew that for Nicole it was probably more about
keeping her brother away from their father than having him
taught about computers. If he asked her, she might well drop
the computer course so Beau could attend youth meetings
instead, but should he?

He saw her in his mind's eye as he had last Sunday. He hadn't meant to look her up and down like that, but the long orange silk shirt with the slender, red cotton skirt under it could not be ignored, especially with that chain-link belt slung low around her waist. By the time his gaze had finished its upward journey, she was looking very pleased with herself, and no wonder.

With the sides of her hair swept back and caught loosely at the nape of her neck and the collar of that vibrant orange blouse turned up to frame her face, she looked like a particularly tasty piece of fruit. He'd had the distinct impression she'd cultivated that particular look just for him, and it wasn't the first time he'd gotten that sense about her.

She hadn't hugged him again, thankfully, but she had a way of brushing her hand down his arm that literally stopped his lungs from working. Then there was that little look she gave him from time to time, her pert chin tucked low so that her eyes appeared as big as full, tip-tilted moons. And unless he missed his guess, she'd taken to wearing lip gloss. At least he had this picture of full, shiny lips in his head that he couldn't seem to turn off.

Given all that and the way she'd started hanging around until everyone else had left the building so she could engage him in private conversation, he was fairly certain that Nicole was flirting with him. Now maybe *that* was something he should be talking to her about—if only he could bring himself to do it.

Bringing the subject up with her could do more harm than good. Besides, it might just be a figment of his tortured, overwrought imagination. Surely it was a figment of his tortured, overwrought—warped, self-centered—imagination. It *had* to be a figment of his imagination.

Marcus climbed the few steps and let himself into the house. The place felt as empty as a tomb. Switching on lights, he divested himself of his outerwear and tossed his coat over the low shelving unit that separated the entryway from the living area. He walked across the dining space and around the bar counter into the kitchen.

Opening the refrigerator door, he tried to turn his mind to dinner, but the contents of his larder left him uninspired. Finally, he took out a carton of milk and snagged a box of crackers and a jar of peanut butter from the cabinet. After plucking a clean spoon from a drawer, he carried the lot back into the living room, where he collapsed into the armchair and kicked off his shoes.

With only the television for company, he made a cursory meal, washing down the crackers and peanut butter with milk directly from the carton. Suddenly exhausted, he shut off the TV, put everything away and moved into the bedroom.

He got ready for bed and slid beneath the covers. Leaning back against the headboard, he reached for the Bible on his bedside table. After reading for a while, he closed the book and put it away. Folding his hands, he closed his eyes and prepared his mind for prayer, mentally reviewing the list he'd been constructing in his mind all day.

"Gracious Lord God," he whispered, "Creator of all things, Author of salvation, Fount of wisdom, I praise Your holy name. Forgive me for my shortcomings, all those sins I so thoughtlessly commit during the course of a day, the envy, the unkind thoughts, the irritations…"

The words dwindled away, and with them every thought in his head.

Blinking, he stared at himself in the mirror on the dresser opposite the bed. Everything looked perfectly in order, the covers smoothed and folded across his chest, the lamp shining down on the Bible on the bedside table. It was exactly the same picture he saw every evening, except for one thing: the look of panic in his own eyes.

He got out of bed and onto his knees. "I don't know what's wrong with me, Lord."

Yes, you do.

"What am I supposed to do? Tell me, please. What am I supposed to do?"

Your job.

Of course. And cravenly keeping his distance from Nicole Archer—and her brother in the process—just because he was lonely and couldn't seem to stop thinking about her was *not* doing his job. Marcus sighed and gave in. After all, he had no real excuse. What God willed, the Holy Spirit empowered, as he well knew.

With the impediment to his communication with God removed, he finished his prayers, got back into bed and turned out the light, settling down to sleep. But just as consciousness slipped away, a picture formed in his mind: Nicole in flaming orange, smile gleaming, brown eyes shining, a white veil floating about her dark head as she walked toward him, flowers clutched in her hands. He carried that incongruous image into his dreams and woke with it the next morning.

Maybe, he told himself with a groan, he needed a vacation.

By Friday Marcus had sufficiently steeled himself enough to do what he knew he should and decided how to go about it. He'd thought about calling the house, but he couldn't be sure how her father would react, and the very last thing he wanted to do was stir that pot. He could've waited until Sunday, but after what had happened the last time he'd pulled her aside for conversation there, that didn't seem a particularly wise move.

On the other hand, he knew right where she'd be about a quarter of four this afternoon. Plus, the street in front of the school seemed a perfect spot for a talk, public enough to be impersonal, private enough for a quick chat. Yes, that would do nicely.

So resolved, Marcus put in only a brief appearance at the office on Friday morning, much to Carlita's delight. If he hadn't known better he'd have thought his secretary liked having him out of the office. He knew, though, that her pleasure stemmed from genuine concern for him, and she was right.

Friday was his day off; he needed to learn how to relax and enjoy it. To that end, he spent the remainder of the morning sprawled on the couch watching old Westerns, a diversion in which he hadn't indulged in years.

After lunch he took himself off to perform several small, personal errands, things he'd been meaning to do for weeks, like having his tires rotated and purchasing some new socks. He got a haircut, too, and walked around a baby goods store trying to figure out what to purchase as a welcome gift for his namesake nephew's eventual entry into the world. All the while, his miserable little mind hummed with the knowledge that he would soon see Nicole again.

Just doing his job, of course.

The Bahamas sounded really nice right about then.

Nicole's head jerked up at the rap of knuckles against her car window, and then she laughed at the sight of Marcus bent at the waist, head cocked at an awkward angle, one hand cranking in a bid for her to roll down the passenger side window. Instead, she leaned over and opened the door.

"It falls off the track if I roll it down. Get in. Beau won't be out for some time. The bell hasn't even rung yet."

He dropped onto the ragged seat. "I had a car with a window that would fall off the track once."

"Yeah, what'd you do?"

"Drove around with the window open for months. It was on the driver's side, so that made it convenient for drive-through windows, at least."

"What about rain?"

"That was a problem. I learned to close an old raincoat in the door." He shook his head, remembering. "I kept hoping somebody would steal that thing so I'd have a good excuse to get a new one."

"A new raincoat?"

"A new car."

Laughing, she twisted sideways in her seat. "If you could afford a new car, why not just buy one and be done with it?"

"I couldn't afford the new *raincoat*," he said, mossy-green eyes twinkling, "but I was spiritually immature enough to think that if my car was stolen, the Lord would magically provide me with another. And, of course, whoever did would naturally need a broken-down old rattletrap of a car much worse than I did, which meant I wouldn't even have to report it." He closed his eyes and smiled. "Sweet justification. Unfortunately, the delusion disappears around the age of nineteen. At least it did for me."

Nicole laughed. "I can't imagine you being delusional at any age."

"I'm delusional now," he said, suddenly serious, "just about different subjects."

She could be just as serious as he could. "I don't believe that."

He looked away, smiling almost sadly, then looked back again and said, "I understand that Beau attends a computer class at the library on Wednesday evenings."

"He used to," Nicole answered, somewhat confused, "when I had a class on Wednesday evening." She was apparently no less confused than Marcus, who scratched his head.

He'd cut his hair, and she wished he hadn't. He had beautiful hair, and it would grow out again.

"Beau told me that he was taking a computer class when I invited him to youth group on Wednesdays," Marcus revealed.

"Ah." Nicole nodded, understanding now. "He didn't want to tell you that there'd be trouble if Dad found out he was actually going to church *twice* a week."

Marcus's gaze turned inward suddenly. "I see." He sounded just the opposite, confused.

"I explained Dad's view of church."

"I—I guess I thought that was just for himself, that he was okay with you and Beau going to church now."

"I don't know if he's *okay* with it, exactly. I think it's more that he can't justify kicking up a fuss about it so long as it doesn't directly impact his life. See, Dad's always hungover on Sunday morning. He likes to stay out late with his drinking buddies on Saturday night."

"And he's home on Wednesdays," Marcus stated.

"Yep. That's one of his favorite TV nights."

Marcus sighed. "Maybe I could talk to him, get him to see reason."

Nicole straightened in her seat. "That's not a good idea. Let's just leave it as it is right now."

"You don't think Beau would benefit from Bible study tailor-made for his age group?"

"I don't think Beau would benefit from getting into it with our father. The two walk tightropes around each other as it is."

Marcus looked straight into her eyes, and it struck her suddenly that it had been a while since he'd done so. "Nicole," he said, "you have to think about calling—"

"Don't say it," she interrupted, yanking her gaze away. "There's no reason to call the authorities. Things are fine now."

"*Now*," he echoed pointedly. "But they won't stay that way. You know they won't, and I'm worried about you."

She bowed her head, delighted to hear that he gave her a single passing thought on any level. "I appreciate that, Marcus, more than you know, but I'll graduate at the end of the fall semester. Then…" She reached tentatively for his hand, willing him to understand from mere inference what she couldn't seem to come right out and say. "Then things will be different. Beau and I will move out and be free to go where we want…*see* who we want."

Marcus opened his mouth as if to argue that point, but then he blinked, and the next thing she knew he was climbing out of the car.

"Well, that's all I wanted to say."

"You don't have to go," she pointed out. "The bell hasn't even rung yet."

The bell rang, a loud, irritating, mechanical bleat that Nicole would have silenced without a second thought if she could have.

"Say hello to Beau for me," Marcus prattled cheerfully, and then he was striding away. She didn't even get a chance to suggest that he could do that himself in another minute or two.

Brow beetled, Nicole blew out a short breath. What was *that* about? Maybe he had an appointment he'd suddenly remembered.

And maybe the mere suggestion that she'd like to see him in a dating capacity at some point in the nebulous future had sent him running for the hills.

Disheartened, Nicole leaned her head against the window, frowning. Then the thought came that she had plenty of time in which to change his mind. It wasn't as if she was ready for any sort of relationship herself. With school and work and Beau, she barely had a social life, seeing her friends mostly in class. She could just imagine how her father would react if she started seeing someone—especially a minister! No, this wasn't the time for that, which meant, really, that nothing had changed. Yet.

But maybe one day. And in the meantime, Marcus could very well get used to the idea. He cared, that was what she had to remember.

By the time Beau threw his backpack over the seat and plopped down beside her, she was smiling again.

Marcus dropped his head into his hands and groaned aloud. It wasn't that speaking to Nicole today had been a mistake. No, he hadn't mistaken God's intent there. He'd done what he should've done, and he'd learned what he'd needed to know, which was what had brought him to his knees at a time when he would normally be thinking about dinner and what he was going to do with his Saturday.

He could just as easily have gone to God in his own living room or his office, anywhere, really. But what he'd seen earlier in Nicole's eyes, what he'd felt in the touch of her hand, had rocked him right down to his soul, and he needed to be in God's house for this.

"I'm so sorry, Lord," he said, kneeling by the front pew. "I should've seen it coming. I did see it coming, I just didn't want to face it. Nicole needs a friend, someone to show her how to tap into Your power. She doesn't need to develop some silly crush on a man who's not right for her."

A man she's not right for, you mean.

"Yes, that, too. It's not just that she's young, she's spiritually immature, troubled, flamboyant… Lord, You know I want, need, a wife, and I've let that mess up my mind, interfere with my judgment. I understand that I'm called to help Nicole and her brother, and I'm committed to that. You'll take care of the other when the time is right. I believe that with all my heart. And I'll do my very best for them, just as I should. But please, Lord, in the meantime, is it too much to ask that Nicole not think of me in a romantic way?"

And that you not think of her in the same vein?

"Okay, I know that's the real problem here, so I'm asking you now to just take these feelings away. She and I could never be a couple, and I can't allow her to think that we ever could. So please don't let her look at me in a romantic way. I'm walking a fine line here, already, and I need Your help in this. I need You to guide my feet, to keep me from slipping and falling."

Falling in love?

"Falling out of Your will."

The words of Hebrews flowed through his mind. *Let us hold fast the confession of our hope without wavering, for He who promised is faithful…*

Marcus knew in his heart of hearts that he had grabbed hold of the Lord with both hands and not let go. He could trust, then, that God would faithfully guide him. And yet, the fears that beat around inside his chest like manic butterflies offered no peace. He'd never felt so weak in the face of temptation before or seen so clearly the potential for harm.

* * *

Marcus set aside his sermon notes, aimed the remote at the music system and lowered the bass, head tilted to catch the shrill, discordant note that had bothered him for several seconds. The phone rang, and it was only then that he realized the sound was not part of the music that he routinely listened to on Saturday night as he made the final preparations for his Sunday sermon. That's what came from turning the sound up so loud.

Chuckling at himself, he switched off the system and reached with his right hand for the cordless phone resting on the table beside the chair. At the same time, from sheer habit, he checked the watch on his left wrist.

Nine forty-one on a Saturday night. It could be a social call, but not likely. He looked at the readout on the tiny screen in the telephone receiver. The name Archer had him suddenly sitting up straight.

For a moment he considered not answering, but then he shook his head in self-disgust. Of course he would answer. The Archers were now part of his flock, even if informally, and he truly cared about their welfare. He wouldn't allow his inappropriate feelings for Nicole to derail the right and proper functions of his office as her pastor. He punched the answer button with his thumb just as the phone rang again.

"Hello."

"Marcus, it's Nicole."

He leaned forward to brace his elbows on the arms of the chair, recognizing panic in the tone of her voice.

"What's wrong?"

"Is Beau there? Have you seen him? Have you spoken to him?"

"Whoa. Back up. Tell me what's happened."

She began to sob. "Beau's gone! I thought it would be all

right. Like I told you, Dad often stays out all night on Saturdays. There's this bar he likes, these guys he knows there. So when my work called me to come in for another server, and Beau said he didn't mind, that he'd be all right on his own for a few hours…I thought…I thought…I shouldn't have left him!"

"Your father came home early," Marcus surmised.

"I don't know what happened!" she wailed. "Dad's obviously been in a fight, and Beau's gone!"

Marcus closed his eyes, sending up a brief, silent prayer before saying, "Let's think this through. Where might Beau go, besides here?"

"H-He has a buddy named Austin, but I didn't get any answer when I called his number. I guess he could try to get to Ovida in Fort Worth, but I don't really think he would. You're the only other one I could think of!"

"There has to be someplace else we could look," Marcus insisted. "Where's his favorite place, someplace he talks about?"

For several heartbeats he heard only sniffing on the other end of the line, but then she gasped. "Tahlequah, our grandparents' old place in Oklahoma, but he wouldn't try to go there."

"Where you used to spend summers," Marcus said. "Yes, he's spoken of it to me. Are you sure he wouldn't try to get there?"

"The old cabin is barely livable," Nicole murmured, "but he is saying all the time how we could go there to get away from Dad. Y-You don't think he'd try something so foolish, do you?"

"I don't know," Marcus muttered, thinking quickly, "but it's all we've got. How far is it?"

"I'm not sure. Four, five hours by car."

Marcus rose to his feet and started gathering up his coat, wallet and keys, the telephone receiver trapped between his ear and shoulder. "Tell me how to get there. Maybe I'll come across him on the way."

"I should go with you," she insisted. "I can show you the way and keep an eye out for him at the same time. I'll meet you at the parsonage."

Marcus didn't argue. He knew it was the best way, but he didn't want her driving that old car in her state.

"I'll come to you." He stuffed his wallet and keys into his pocket and threw on his coat, heading for the front door because he'd left the sedan in the drive earlier. "I'm on my way now."

"Marcus," she whispered brokenly, "what if we don't find him?"

"We will," he assured her. "I promise you, honey, somehow we'll find him."

She was silent for a long, puzzling moment, but then she whispered with silky, unnerving certainty, "I knew I should call. I knew you were the one."

Before he dared ask what she meant by that, she hung up.

Chapter Six

Marcus tossed the telephone toward the couch and reached for the doorknob. Just then he heard the scuff of footsteps on the concrete stoop outside. Yanking open the door, he surprised Beau just as the boy was about to knock.

"Thank God!" Marcus exclaimed, reaching out to pull the boy inside. "Your sister is scared out of her wits!"

Beau hung his head and hunched his shoulders inside his oversize coat. "I'm sorry," he mumbled, "I had to get out of there." He swiped at his face, sniffling, obviously embarrassed by his tears.

Marcus led him into the living room, shedding his own coat and divesting Beau of his as they moved. "I have to call her. She thinks I'm on my way to pick her up."

He dumped the coats, located the phone and made the call. "He's here. He's safe. I'll bring him—" She hung up before he finished his sentence, having declared she was on her way over. He shut off the receiver and laid it on a shelf. "She doesn't have a cell phone, does she?"

"Too expensive," Beau muttered with a shake of his head.

Marcus frowned, thinking of her driving through the night in a panic in her old car with no cell phone in case of an emergency, not that he could do a thing about it. "Tell me what happened."

"He came home early," Beau said glumly. "Some guy called him a drunk, and they got into it, so they threw him out of the bar."

"Which means he also came home mad," Marcus surmised.

Beau nodded and wiped his eyes with both hands. "He was screaming and yelling about everything he'd been through in his life and how nobody understands."

Marcus took the boy by the shoulders. "Did he hurt you, Beau? Did he hit you?"

"No. He shook me, though. Called me an ungrateful little—" He broke off. "I just didn't want him to drink anymore," he wailed. "His face was all beat up, and I just wanted him to put some ice on it and not drink anymore. But all he cared about was having another drink, so I yelled at him that the guy was right. He *is* a drunk!"

"And that just made him madder," Marcus pointed out.

Beau nodded miserably, shivering. "I know I shouldn't have said it, but it's true!"

Marcus sighed inwardly, aching for the boy. "How did you get here?"

"Walked."

He turned Beau toward the sofa and pushed him down onto it. "No wonder you're still cold. I've got cocoa. Would you like me to fix you some?"

Beau shook his head and leaned forward, elbows braced on his knees, gaze trained on the floor. "I'm okay."

Marcus sat down on the coffee table facing the boy. "I'm sorry this happened. I know what it's like when a parent disappoints you."

"As long as Nic's around, it's okay," Beau said in a small voice.

"But she can't always be there," Marcus pointed out gently.

"She's busy trying to make a better life for us and keep everything together," Beau said defensively. He looked up, anger drying his tears. "That's what makes me so mad. He lays around getting drunk and moaning about his back while she's out there working and going to school and trying to make everything all right! He wouldn't even have a hurt back if he hadn't been drinking on the job!"

"I understand," Marcus assured him soothingly, "but what *you* have to understand, Beau, is that your father is sick. He's literally ill, and until he faces up to that, nothing will change. But it's not hopeless. God has changed harder hearts than Dillard Archer's, I promise you."

Beau shook his head, muttering, "You don't know my old man."

"I don't know him personally," Marcus conceded, thinking of the sermon he'd prepared for tomorrow. "I didn't know St. Paul, either, but I know that God changed him."

The light of interest suddenly ignited in Beau's eyes. "How?"

Marcus settled in to tell the story. "Paul lived at the same time as Jesus. He didn't believe in a Messiah who would give His life to pay the sin debt for everyone else in the world, and he didn't believe in the resurrection. So far as he was concerned, Jesus was dead. Period. And he hated those who believed otherwise so much that he made it his work to eradicate them, to wipe them out. Then one day he was going to Damascus to arrest Christians there, and he met Jesus on the road."

"Like actually *met* Him?" Beau asked skeptically.

"In a light so bright that it blinded Paul," Marcus confirmed. "But Jesus told him that a man would come and take away his blindness. When he did, Paul believed, and instead of persecuting Christians, he became the greatest missionary of all time."

"Just like that?"

"Just like that."

"So it was a miracle."

"Exactly," Marcus said. "But that same miracle takes place every day, Beau, every time someone commits his or her heart to Christ. And that often happens because someone else has been praying. I've been praying for you and your father and your sister, Beau, and I'm going to go on praying that God will work that miracle in your father's life."

Beau seemed to think about this for several moments before he said, "Back when my mom was alive and we used to go to church all the time, it seemed like my dad believed then."

"Maybe he did and his anger at losing your mom won't let him admit it. Or maybe he was just going through the motions to please her, thinking that was enough. The thing to remember, Beau, is that Paul's life didn't get easier after he committed himself to Christ. In fact, it got harder. But he tells us in his writings that he didn't mind, because in Christ he found the ability to cope with his difficulties and to find happiness, even joy, in doing so. Do you understand?"

"I think so."

They talked for several more minutes before clasping hands and bowing their heads in prayer. Marcus began, but Beau soon picked up and poured out his heart. Oddly, as Beau talked to God, his tears dried, but Marcus found his own eyes beginning to fill. He heard in Beau's softly spoken entreaties and confessions his own voice, the voice of the boy he had once been—confused, buffeted by life, lost.

When the door opened, he knew that Nicole had just entered

his house. Hearing her relieved gasp at the sight of her brother's bowed head, he glanced up and held out his hand in silence. She slid her small, cold palm against his. The silly woman had come out without her gloves. Bowing his head once more, Marcus tugged her close. Settling next to him on the coffee table, she gripped his hand tightly and bowed her head.

When Beau's conversation with God finally wound down, she said her own prayer of thanks, then slipped her arms around her little brother's neck. He groused a bit, but he did hug her back.

"I'm sorry, Nic! I shouldn't have gone off, but I just got so mad and I couldn't think what else to do."

"It's all right so long as you're safe," she told him, rising to her feet and taking him with her.

"Was Dad really mad when you got home?" he asked, pulling back.

She shook her head. "He was too drunk for that, but when I saw the bruises on his face and you were gone, I can't tell you how scared I was."

"I didn't do that to him," Beau quickly vowed.

"He got into a fight at the bar and came home angry," Marcus explained. Then he turned to the boy. "Beau, the next time that happens, I want you to call the police."

Beau cast a troubled glance at his sister before addressing Marcus. "But that'll just make him madder," Beau said uncertainly.

"And Child Welfare could very well step in," Nicole added skeptically. "I'd rather he do exactly what he did this time. Un-unless you don't want him coming here anymore."

"It's Children's Protective Services," Marcus corrected, trying not to sound exasperated, "and of course he can come here whenever he wants. That's not the point."

"I just don't see what good calling the authorities can do," Nicole argued.

"Nicole, this thing is just going to continue to escalate," Marcus warned. "Can't you see that? In the short time I've known you, your father's gone from saying hurtful things to getting into fights. The next time he uses his fists, it could be on one of you. I don't want to see that happen."

"But calling the police just makes it more likely to happen!" she insisted.

"Then call Family Services. They'll open a case file and—"

"No! They might take Beau away!"

Beau backed up suddenly, alarm rounding his eyes. "I'm not going anywhere!" he exclaimed. "I'm staying with you! Aren't I, sis? Aren't I staying with you?"

"Yes, of course you are," Nicole soothed, clamping a hand down on the top of his shoulder. "We said, remember? We promised Mom that we'd stay together, and we will. We are."

"It's only one more semester after this one," he told Marcus desperately. "Then Nicole will graduate and get a regular job, and we're going to move out into our own place, aren't we, Nic?"

"That's right," she answered soothingly. "Then once we're on our own, we can try to get Dad some help." *From a safe distance* were the unspoken words understood by all.

"And what if he doesn't let you take Beau?" Marcus asked softly, looking down into her upturned face. "He's the custodial parent, you know."

She looked like a deer caught in the headlights for a moment, wide-eyed and frozen with fear. He saw how truly young she was in that instant, little more than a child. But with such responsibilities! Then her expression hardened. Her mouth compressed into a tight line, and her chin rose, eyes flashing fire.

"We'll make it work," she said. "Even if we have to leave here, go far away where he'll never find us, we're going to do just what we've planned. It's the only way."

Marcus shook his head, truly fearing for both their sakes, and moved to the side, hoping to improve his perspective somehow. They still looked like two frightened kids doing their best in an uncertain and potentially dangerous situation. Both seemed downtrodden and weary. In fact, Nicole hardly looked like herself at all.

Maybe it was the subdued clothing. She wore blue jeans and a pilled gray sweater beneath an olive-green corduroy coat, her dark hair caught in a loose ponytail at the nape of her neck. Only the red leather shoes looked like something she would normally wear. Marcus sort of missed the color and vibrancy that he associated with Nicole. Then he saw the stamp of weariness around her eyes and mouth, and knew that arguing would only do more harm than good at the moment. Bringing his hands to his hips, he nodded in defeat.

"Do you think it's safe for you to go home tonight?"

She waved a hand dismissively, saying, "He's out like a light by now. He probably didn't even make it to bed. Trust me, when he's that drunk, he rarely does."

Marcus sighed. "All right. Then you'd better go. It's getting late, and I want to see you both in church tomorrow."

"We'll be there," she promised, turning Beau toward the door and giving him a little shove before looking up into Marcus's face. "Thank you. Again."

"Yeah, thanks," Beau chimed in from the entryway.

"I didn't do anything," Marcus protested, getting snared in those chocolate eyes.

"You always help when we need you," Nicole said softly.

"Of course," Marcus retorted impatiently, "but, Nicole,

there's an old saying. God helps those who help themselves. And sometimes that's how it is. Sometimes we have to do the hard thing, take the difficult path, to get where we need to be."

"I understand, but just because it's difficult doesn't make it the right thing to do, Marcus."

He didn't know what to say to that. She was entirely correct and very possibly wrong. Either way, he was frightened for her, for them. He'd told himself long ago when he'd first found God that he would never deny his faith by being frightened again, but he hadn't realized then that he could be frightened for someone else. If only he could make her understand.

"The time may come when you don't have a choice," he warned her.

"But right now I do. In fact, since I met you, I have more choices than ever before. God bless you for that, Marcus."

She placed her hands on his shoulders then, rose up on tiptoe and pressed a kiss on his cheek at the very corner of his mouth. By the time his head cleared and he could get air back into his lungs, they were gone.

"It wasn't that troubles did not come into Paul's life," Marcus said, his voice ringing solid and true from the pulpit. "Indeed, the path Paul chose led to greater difficulties, but it also led to more joy. And Paul learned, as we must, to depend wholly on God for the answers to our problems, for there is not one detail of our lives that does not concern and interest our Lord."

Nicole looked down at the Bible in her lap as Marcus went on, his words calling to mind the troubles that her mom had known. Suzanne Archer had possessed a deep faith that had grown only deeper with her illness. Dillard, on the other hand, had always been somewhat ambivalent, and his ambivalence had hardened into anger as his wife's illness had progressed. Nicole vividly remembered his anguish on the day that they had received the diagnosis.

"Why you?" he had demanded.

Her mother's serene reply had been, "Why not me? Why should others be stricken with cancer and not me?"

Nicole could understand that sentiment. This life was not meant to be all good times and ease. That would be heaven, as Marcus had just pointed out. Looking at her own life, Nicole was even willing to concede that he was right about God providing solutions, too, even if sometimes the solution was simply to endure for another day or week or month or year. Thankfully, sometimes the solution was immediate.

Take the gas bill, for instance. She'd been so worried about paying it. February had been colder than usual, and their old house seemed to leak at every joint and corner. The bill, which was due next week, would undoubtedly be astronomical. But she'd prayed about it, and twice now she'd been called in to work extra shifts, and on weekends, too, when the tips were best. Catastrophe averted.

Even the fiasco with her father and Beau had turned out better than it might have. She shuddered to think what her impulsive little brother might have done if Marcus hadn't been available to him.

Crashing Marcus's birthday party was turning out to be one of the best mistakes she'd ever made. In fact, she was beginning to think that it might be part of God's plan for her life.

Her mom had believed completely that God always has a plan and a purpose for the lives of His children, and Nicole was starting to believe that, too. Except she still could see no purpose behind her mother's death, and the more she thought about that, the more it bothered her. Instinctively, she knew that this one question must be settled to her satisfaction before she could move forward, and she could think of only one place where she might find the answers she needed.

Immediately after the service she went straight to the pastor. "I need to speak with you."

"All right. About what?" He folded his hands and widened his stance as if settling in for a long conversation.

"I guess you could call it a spiritual matter."

"I see." Marcus nodded solemnly, his gaze flickering over those waiting to shake his hand. "Perhaps we'd best make an appointment then."

"An appointment." She was a little surprised by that, but the idea certainly had merit. "Yes, that will work."

"You can call the church office, and my secretary will find a convenient time for you."

At first she was taken aback by the formality, but then she realized that his office would be as private as his home or anywhere else they might meet. "Certainly. Good. I—I'll see you soon then."

She went out with a smile on her face, feeling as if a burden that she hadn't even known she was carrying had been lightened a bit. It was good to have someone to share things with, someone other than Ovida, who was good and kind and dear but who had her own family and concerns. If it should become more than that between her and Marcus someday, if he should come to see that he could depend on her, too, that they could be something more than friends, well… Prayers were answered every day, weren't they?

Marcus couldn't help feeling a certain excitement along with the trepidation that was fast becoming part and parcel of his dealings with Nicole Archer. He told himself that it had

A Love So Strong

to do with his deep desire to help the Archers, but he couldn't be so dishonest as not to admit that it had more to do with his attraction to her and that kiss on the cheek, innocent as it had been. Something about Nicole intrigued him, which was, of course, a large part of the problem and exactly why he needed to inject a little formality and distance into the equation.

It was one thing to befriend the girl—which, he kept reminding himself, was exactly what she was—and another thing entirely to lead her on, even unintentionally. He meant to have a word with her about that, whatever the topic of discussion at this meeting.

Surely, that was why he felt as if insects were crawling beneath the surface of his skin and why the day seemed to creep by at a snail's pace, until suddenly he looked up and it was almost at an end. Alarmed, he rushed out into the reception area.

"Carlita, we do have Nicole Archer in our appointment book for today, don't we?"

"Five o'clock. Last appointment of the day," Carlita said, looking away from her computer screen. "I told you that on Monday afternoon."

"Right. I, um, I forgot."

He pinched the bridge of his nose between his thumb and his forefinger, feeling like an absolute idiot. For perhaps the thousandth time, he wondered what Nicole had on her mind. A spiritual matter, she had said. Such counseling was part of his job, and by some accounts he was actually good at it. Still, he sensed that he was courting disaster here. Gulping, he dropped his hand, becoming acutely aware of his secretary's furrowed brow.

"She's a young lady with a lot of adult responsibilities," he announced, wincing inwardly at the defensive tone of his voice. "I hope the appointment time is convenient for her."

Carlita rolled her black eyes, muttering, *"El loco!"* She

pushed away from her desk, jabbed her fists into the indentation of her waist, and fixed him with her why-do-I-put-up-with-you glare. "What? You think I chose the time at random and kept it a secret. Of course, the time is convenient for her! That's the whole point of an appointment, isn't it?"

Marcus held up a hand, saying, "All right. Okay. I was just checking."

Carlita pulled her chair closer to the desk with a hand clamped onto the edge of the heavy, wood top, conceding, "She may be ten or fifteen minutes late because she has to get her little brother to the community center for a guitar lesson. I told her not to worry about it."

Marcus nodded and scrubbed a hand across his face. "I don't mean to be difficult. It's just that she's a sweet, troubled kid—"

"With an alcoholic father and a little brother who depends on her too much," Carlita said. "I know. Haven't you said it so many times already?" She smiled, adding gently, "But with your background you're just the one to help her."

Marcus tapped the tip of a forefinger against the edge of her desk, saying, "I pray so. I guess I do identify pretty strongly with her situation, although, by the time I was her age, my folks were both long gone."

"God prepared you in this, eh?" Carlita said. "So don't worry. It's not like you to have such worry."

She was right. It wasn't like him to worry. He hadn't worried like this since Connie had gone to jail, and he'd thought he'd learned the futility of the exercise then. If only Nicole would let Family Services take a hand with her father, he wouldn't *have* to worry. He could understand why she didn't want to, but it was almost the only way he could see for her and her brother to live safely. Almost.

There actually was another solution, one he couldn't help thinking about even though he didn't want to. The fact was that if Nicole had a husband, someone mature and sensible and settled, he could stand up for her and Beau. He could provide a stable home for them. If Nicole had a husband. Something he couldn't let himself think about.

"Sorry to bother you," he muttered, turning away from his secretary's desk and heading back to his office.

It wasn't difficult to keep himself busy for the next hour. Between the needs of the church and the day care center, the demands on his time had always been significant. The state licensing and oversight process of the day care center alone was almost a full-time job.

Nevertheless, he had always made counseling a priority, which was why he dropped what he was doing at precisely five o'clock and returned to the outer office. He was just in time to hear Carlita exclaim, "*Caramba!* I *like* this outfit."

A trill of bright laughter followed, and Marcus knew even before he clapped eyes on her that Nicole had outdone herself. Smiling, she stood with her arms outstretched, showing off the wide, pointed sleeves of the filmy, V-necked, madras print tunic that she wore over a purple turtleneck and bell-bottom jeans. Green platform sandals and purple socks encased her feet, while her long, sleek hair flowed straight from beneath the ribbed cuff of a bright yellow stocking cap with a hot pink silk flower pinned to the front.

She looked like something left over from the 1970s, with a touch of skater and a dose of shabby chic thrown in for good measure. Somehow it worked for her. In a funny way, Nicole was like walking, breathing art, and just looking at her never failed to make him smile, which was why he stood there now grinning like a blooming idiot.

She glanced up and caught him at it, beaming his smile right back at him. Marcus cleared his throat and made a show of checking his watch. "I, um, I understood you might be late."

"We got away from the house earlier than usual."

"I hope Beau wasn't inconvenienced."

She strolled toward him, stopping close and rocking up onto her tiptoes, as if barely able to contain her enthusiasm. Marcus had to remind himself to breathe.

"No, he likes a little extra time to set up," she said, her smile stretching even wider.

Marcus was having trouble following that. "I, uh, uh, set up?"

"For the lesson."

"Right. I—I knew he had an interest in music, but I didn't realize he was taking lessons."

"Oh, he doesn't *take* guitar lessons," Nicole said, tilting her head to one side. "He *gives* them to kids at the community center."

"Oh! That good is he?"

"Absolutely. It brings in a little extra spending money for him, too, though he doesn't charge nearly as much as an adult teacher would."

"I wonder if he's thought of trying out for the praise band we're putting together?"

"I'm sure he'd love that."

"I'll be sure to mention it to him then," Marcus said, pleased. Only then did he realize that he had rolled up onto *his* tiptoes in a copy of her exuberance. Abruptly, he slammed his heels onto the floor again and shot out an arm.

"My, uh, office is this way. First door on the right."

Still smiling, Nicole moved forward. Marcus swiftly

stepped aside, catching sight of Carlita as she hunched her shoulders in question.

Nicole slipped past him into the hallway, allowing Marcus to address Carlita. "What?"

"I thought you said she was a child!" Carlita hissed.

Marcus glanced over his shoulder in time to see Nicole disappear into his office. Frowning, he turned back to his secretary. "I didn't say she was a *child.* I said she was young, which she is."

Carlita put her hands on her hips. "There is young, and there is *infancia.*"

"She's not even twenty-one," he protested through his teeth.

Carlita threw up her hands, exclaiming, "I was a mother twice before twenty!"

"Will you keep your voice down?" Marcus insisted in a harsh whisper.

The hands went back on the hips, accompanied by a narrowing of the eyes. "You really are *loco.*" With that she turned away, snagged her omnipresent coffee cup from the corner of her desk and stalked off toward the tiny break room, where they kept the coffeepot.

Marcus turned toward his office, muttering to himself, "I am not crazy. She's too young."

Nicole swiveled in her chair as he entered the small office, asking, "Who's too young?"

Had he actually said *too* young? "Oh. Um."

Blinking, he seriously thought about lying to her. That was not his way, though. In the end, he just shook his head and averted his gaze, edging past her to slip by the bookcase and around the desk in the corner. As he dropped into his chair, he glanced out the window at the church across the way, reminding himself why he was there. Somewhat more composed, he folded his hands at his waist and turned to face Nicole.

"Now then," he said in his best minister's voice, "what can I do for you?"

Nicole tilted her head and looked down at her hands, smoothing the hem of her tunic. "I want to ask you a question."

"All right. Shoot."

He was ready for any number of topics. Privately, he hoped that she was ready to talk about calling in Family Services to help her deal with her father's alcoholism. What she ultimately came out with, though, threw him for a loop.

"Why did my mother die?"

Initially, he must have looked like a blank slate sitting there. The subject was so unexpected that he couldn't seem to think beyond the obvious. He spread his hands. "I—I understood that it was cancer."

She gave her head a tight little shake and slid to the edge of her seat, leaning forward to lay one arm on his desktop. "That's not what I mean." She slumped forward, seeming to gather her strength as well as her thoughts before she looked up again. "On Sunday you said that God is concerned about every detail of our lives."

"Yes, I believe that's so."

"Well, it got me to thinking about something that my mom used to say."

"And that is?"

"My mom believed that God always has a plan, that there are reasons for everything that happens to us."

"I agree," Marcus said, leaning forward so that he, too, could brace his arms atop the desk. "I believe that God is intimately involved in the lives of His children, that He has a plan for each and every one of us. Now, of course, we also have free will, and we can choose to do things that are contrary to God's plan, and sometimes those choices have consequences that must be endured, at least in this life. But that, too, is a result of God's overall plan for us in that He created us with free will for a reason."

"That's what I'm talking about." She sat back and folded her arms. "I mean, if He has a reason for everything, then what reason could He have for letting her die?"

Now they had come to it.

Marcus nodded and linked his fingers together atop the desk blotter. "Let's be clear about something, Nicole. God did not cause your mom's illness."

"That's what Mom always said, too. Dad would get mad, you know, and she would tell him that God didn't give her cancer."

"That was a product of this world we live in," Marcus agreed. "But God does have power over life and death."

"And He chose to let her die," Nicole said simply. "I need to know why."

Marcus tried to decide how best to answer her, but in the end he could give her only one answer. Almost certainly it wasn't what she wanted to hear, but he could only give her what he had to give her and pray that it was enough.

"I don't know."

She looked stricken and disappointed at the same time.

Something welled up in him that he hadn't known for many, many years. Funny how something rooted so far in the past could feel so immediate and so familiar. Suddenly he remembered all the times he'd felt this way as a child, watching his mother sob over not being able to pay the bills or some boyfriend dumping her. Just as bad had been watching her manic elation when she'd embarked on some new romance and knowing that he and his sisters would once again be taking a backseat to her obsessive search for ever-elusive love.

But Nicole was not his mother. She was, in many ways, the exact opposite of his mother, and he was no longer that powerless, ignorant little boy.

On pure impulse, he reached across the desk and gripped her hand. Even as tears gathered in her eyes, a smile slowly curved her lips, and in that moment all his worry fell away. He knew that God had brought her here for this reason.

He was called to this, and he must not, could not, would not, fail her.

Chapter Seven

"I don't know," he said again, releasing her hand and sitting back. Words flowed into his brain. With them came the confidence that the Spirit upon Whom he relied was at work. Purposefully, he let the words leave his mouth. "There could be any number of reasons, Nicole, some of which we may never know, but I assure you, that it was not so your father could drink himself into an angry stupor every night. That is his choice, Nicole, his alone."

"I get that," she said softly. "What I don't get is what it was *for?*" She bit her lip, and when she spoke again, her voice quivered. "If I could believe there was a purpose for her dying o-or even that something good would come from it, then somehow I think I could…"

"Let it go?" he ventured gently. "Start to get over her loss?"

Nicole swallowed. "Maybe. Maybe it's just that it would make it easier to go on. Easier to *trust*. You know?"

"Well, then, let's look at it. Let's look at you."

"Me?"

"You." He spread his hands. "I was talking about you

earlier when I said, 'She's too young.' And you *are* too young for the responsibilities you bear. On the other hand, I don't know anyone else your age who cares for someone more than you care for your brother. Certainly, I know of no finer example of sisterly love than you."

She brightened. "Really?"

He was grinning again, and couldn't do a thing about it. "Most twenty-year-old college girls are busy partying and chasing boys," he went on. "You're making a home, working, caring for your family, getting an education, trying to do the right things. Maybe you wish you could be that carefree party girl, and I would certainly wish an easier life for you, but who you are is just a delight. And I have to wonder if you'd be that if you hadn't had to take on a more responsible role."

She sat there for a moment, just staring at him. Then she whispered, "Wow."

Pure joy beamed straight into his heart. "And there's Beau," he said earnestly. "Would your relationship with him be what it is if your mom had lived? Most brothers and sisters argue and feel a little jealousy even when they really love each other, but you and Beau… I've never seen siblings who were closer. Even my sisters and I weren't able to be that close."

Nicole leaned forward slightly, her beautiful eyes sparkling. "I'll tell you a little secret," she confessed. "When he was about three until he was maybe nine, I thought Beau was the biggest pain who ever lived."

Marcus chuckled. "And I'm sure it was mutual."

"Oh, yeah!" She wrinkled her nose. "I guess I was a little spoiled back then." Suddenly, a look of wonder came over her face. "You know, I really wouldn't want to be that girl again." As the realization settled over her, she put her head back and laughed.

Marcus enjoyed her pleasure, but he wasn't disturbed when she sobered and a thoughtful expression once again overtook her face.

"When Mom got sick," she said, "Beau became so precious to me. It's awful that it took that, isn't it?"

"It's just the way it is," Marcus said. "I'm glad that Beau was there to fill a place in your heart, because I'm sure your father grew more angry and distant."

"Yes, he did. But he used to be a good dad, you know."

"Maybe he will be again, if he can get past being angry at God."

She bowed her head as if in contrition. "I guess maybe that's part of the reason I'm here. I think…" She sighed, then forthrightly admitted, "I was pretty mad myself for a while. Then I sort of got over that, but I just…I don't know…pushed God away, I guess."

"And now you're ready to renew your commitment," Marcus surmised gently.

"*Now* I am."

A great sense of satisfaction swept through him, and he rocked forward in his chair to address her. "Would you like to know how to start that process?"

"Yes."

"You start with confession. You start by telling God what you've just told me."

"That's it?"

"That's how you start. After that, it's a matter of making God a real priority in your life by daily taking time to pray and read the Bible and worship. It's like anything else you want to change. You have to behave your way into a closer relationship with God."

She nodded her understanding, and then she sucked in a

deep breath. He noticed a certain softness about her, a new sense of ease, and his soul rejoiced because he felt that he had given her, or at least led her to, what she needed.

He reached across the desk for her hand again, asking, "Would you like me to pray with you?"

She clasped his hand tightly. "Yes, please."

They spent some time talking to God, first him and then her, and then him again. Afterward, she rose to leave, wiping happy tears from her eyes. He came around the desk to walk her out, but she stopped him before they reached the door, a hand on his shoulder.

"You know something else, something I'm really, really thankful for?"

"What's that?"

"You," she said, holding his gaze with hers. "I'm just so glad that you're a part of my life now."

He smiled, and somehow his hand found hers. "I'm glad, too."

"You've made a real difference for us, Marcus."

"That's what I'm here for. I want to help. That's the only reason I suggested you contact the authorities concerning your father."

She squeezed his hand. "I know." The hand on his shoulder slid around his neck as she leaned into him, going up on tiptoe to press her face into the curve of his shoulder and hug him. "Thank you for caring."

He couldn't seem to speak past a sudden lump in his throat, and he was literally unable to stop his free arm from curling lightly around her waist. After a long moment, she lowered herself to her heels, loosening her embrace, and then he was gazing down into her face, a face that seemed to come closer and closer, even as it tilted back, her chin lifting.

Suddenly he realized that he was about to kiss her!

Galvanized, he jerked back, cracking his elbow against the bookshelf behind him. White-hot pain flashed up his arm all the way to his shoulder.

She reached for him, exclaiming, "Are you all right?"

He jerked even farther away. "Ow! I mean, sure. Uh…" He grabbed the tingling joint in question, desperately searching for rescue from his own folly.

"Beau!" he exclaimed. "Wh-what time do you have to pick him up?"

Nicole stared, goggle-eyed, for several seconds before reluctantly checking the cheap watch with its worn leather band on her wrist. "Yeah, I have to go, but are you sure you're okay?"

"Of course!" he insisted too brightly, forcing his hands to his sides, though one of them felt disturbingly numb still. "I'll walk you out."

She wrinkled her brow, but then she turned and moved through the door into the hallway. Marcus intentionally lagged a step behind, relief and dismay mingling within him.

What on earth was wrong with him? Had he lost what little sense he'd had? And where were his ministerial ethics? He couldn't go around kissing, or even almost kissing, those who came to him for counseling!

He managed to keep a straight face as Nicole took her leave, but he avoided Carlita's all-too-perceptive gaze, heading at once back to his office. Closing the door, he walked around his desk and sank into his chair, squeezing his eyes shut. Sighing richly, he bent forward and rested his forearms on his knees, dropping his face into his hands.

"Lord, forgive me," he said, and what followed was a long confession of unruly desires, envy for those happily married, indulgence in self-pity and a lack of control. He would do better, he promised, if only God would remove the temptation from him.

When Carlita tapped on his door to say that she was leaving for the day, he didn't open it, only called through it that he would see her tomorrow.

"Tomorrow's your day off," she reminded, the door muffling the volume but not the sternness of her voice.

A day off, he thought. Maybe that was what he needed right now. It certainly wouldn't hurt. Maybe he'd even get a little perspective.

"Monday, then."

"Right," she muttered doubtfully, but she went away, and he went back to his problem.

The hour was bordering on seven before he came to some unsatisfactory conclusions. One: Obviously he couldn't be trusted around Nicole Archer! Two: Until he got these ridiculous impulses under control he simply couldn't minister personally to the family. It wouldn't be prudent.

That concession made him sick at heart, but what else could he do except keep his distance from the Archers? He wouldn't abandon them completely, of course, but hereafter someone else would have to fill the role of personal rescuer.

Ovida Cutler was the logical choice. Her relationship with the Archer family went back for many years, decades, even. He didn't know what he was thinking to have interfered in the first place. He'd been warned in seminary about the tendency of many ministers to try to save or aid everyone who crossed their paths, the result being burnout or ethical lapses. Though often born of a genuine desire to serve others, the overinvolved minister sometimes began to serve his own need to be of service rather than the needs of others. Marcus felt that he might be suffering from a touch of that.

Certainly he was overstepping the bounds of good, effective ministry.

Time to back off. Definitely. He saw no alternative. What had almost happened today could not be repeated.

Glum but resolved, he went home to his lonely little house and a cold, solitary evening.

"Hello."

Nicole smiled at the sound of his voice. "Marcus! I thought for a moment that Carlita was mistaken and you weren't at home, after all."

"I, uh, I'm doing some cleaning."

"Ah. The dreaded housework," she teased. "I know how you guys hate anything remotely having to do with actual neatness. I, on the other hand, actually enjoy straightening up—when I get the opportunity to do it, which admittedly isn't often." She sighed. "Oh, well. In a way, that's why I'm calling. I have to go in early to the restaurant again. Would you mind picking up Beau from school? He'd love to hang out with you again, or 'kick it,' as he would say."

A short pause followed, then, "Nicole, I'm sorry. I'm afraid I can't. Why don't you call Ovida? I'm sure someone in the massive Cutler clan would be happy to have Beau this evening."

Surprise and disappointment made her pause to actually look at the telephone receiver, as if that might tell her why his voice sounded so odd. Carefully placing the receiver against her ear again, she asked, "Marcus, are you all right?"

"Oh, yes. Just busy."

Impersonal, she decided suddenly. That was the tone she was hearing. Or might it be distraction? Of course, if he was very busy, that would be it.

"Okay. I understand. Thanks anyway."

"Goodbye, Nicole."

"Bye."

She barely got the word out before he hung up. Nicole slowly replaced the receiver in its cradle on the kitchen wall, her lip clamped between her teeth. Then she shook her head.

No matter what was going on with him just then, she could trust in Marcus's intentions. If he couldn't help them out, then he undoubtedly had good reasons. So he had sounded odd. So what? Whatever the problem was, she was sure that it was important. She and Beau weren't the only people in the world with troubles, after all. In fact, compared to some people, their troubles were small, indeed.

Picking up the phone, she dialed Ovida's number. Unfortunately the phone rang and rang without answer. Finally, the machine clicked on. Nicole left a brief message, and then began dialing other Cutler numbers. After several calls, she reached Donna.

The baby could be heard wailing in the background, and Donna herself sounded exhausted. It seemed that the Cutlers had been hit by a twenty-four hour stomach virus that had spread through the family like wildfire.

"One of the drawbacks of being a close family, I guess," Donna said with a chuckle and a sigh. "Vince is so worried about Jolie getting it that he's planning a little jaunt down into the hill country over the weekend with Connie and Kendal and their kids."

Nicole kept her voice light as she asked, "Any idea when they're leaving?"

"This afternoon, I think."

Grimacing, Nicole conceded defeat. "Well, I hope y'all get better real quick. Tell your mom not to worry about us. We'll be praying for you."

Donna thanked her and got off the phone. Nicole dropped the receiver back into its cradle, idly watching the old-fashioned cord coil and knot as she tried to decide what to do.

Beau had a couple friends whose parents she might call, but one of the moms worked and Nicole had no idea how to reach her at her job. The other friend didn't exactly have a stellar home life himself. His parents seemed to scream and argue all the time, and they didn't care who was around to witness it. As she chewed over the problem, her father came into the room.

"What's going on?"

Nicole straightened away from the wall. "Oh, uh, I've got to go into work early."

"That's good. Little extra money won't hurt, will it?"

"No, it sure won't."

He flattened a hand against his belly, and she noticed that he was wearing a clean T-shirt. His hair looked freshly shampooed, too, although he could use a good shave.

"Well, don't worry about us," he said. "I'll scramble up some eggs or something for supper."

Nicole bowed her head, trying to think her way around the immediate problem. True to form, Dillard had been easing up on the booze lately. She guessed they were cycling out of the bad phase and into a good one. In fact, they'd passed a pretty pleasant night the evening before. It had almost seemed like old times, everybody sitting around the television for an hour or two.

Usually, after she and Beau retired to their individual rooms, Dillard would sit up late into the night, watching television and drinking himself into a stupor. Last night, however, he'd shut off the television well before midnight.

She knew because the sudden silence had actually awakened her. She'd sat up in bed, blinking at the clock and thinking that it must be time to get up until she'd heard him on his way to his room.

Maybe her dad was on the upswing again. If so, surely he could be trusted to spend one evening with his own son. It wasn't as if Beau needed constant supervision, after all. This might even heal the breach that had opened the night that Beau had fled to Marcus.

Nicole took a deep breath. "Okay, Dad. Um, actually, there's some mac and cheese in the pantry. You might try that with the leftover chicken in the fridge."

Dillard shrugged. "Yeah, whatever. Don't worry about it."

"All right. I'll just get my things and take off then."

"Hey," he said as she slipped past him.

Nicole froze, suddenly tense. "What?"

"Don't you have a class this afternoon?"

Relaxing, she wheeled around to face him. He really was more sober than usual. For a moment there, he'd actually sounded like a real dad.

"Yeah," she said. "But it's an easy A for me. I can skip without hurting my grade average, and the money's more important right now."

He just nodded and turned back into the kitchen. Feeling suddenly lighter than she had in some time, Nicole hurried to her room and gathered up her things. Then she stopped by Beau's room and penned a quick note, which she left on his desk, suggesting that he concentrate on his homework that night instead of putting it off until Sunday evening. That ought to keep him out of his father's way. Just in case.

Confident she'd done the best she could under the circumstances, she went out to the car and headed off to work.

* * *

Dillard was sitting alone in front of the TV in the darkened living room nursing a drink when Nicole came in later that night. She figured Beau had already turned in or simply stayed out of their father's way. Dillard did little more than grunt at her when she walked past on her way to her room, but she saw the dirty dishes in the sink and knew that he'd made them some sort of dinner, at least.

She was tired, and her feet hurt, so she peeked in at her sleeping brother and went on to bed herself. In the morning, she rose and wandered out into the small hall bath that she shared with Beau. She was washing her hands and looking for the towel that normally hung from the ring next to the sink when she saw the hole in the wall beside the door.

Gaping, she backed up a step. Only when water dripped from her hands onto her bare feet did she jerk and actually start to think. Quickly she turned off the water and went back to studying the hole in the wallboard. It only took a moment to realize what had happened. Just to be sure, she curled her hand into a fist and slipped it into the jagged hole.

Oh, Lord, what have I done?

She tore out of the room and down the hall, practically falling into Beau's bedroom, the doorknob grasped firmly in one hand. "Beau!"

He rolled over, then sat up, grumbling, "What time is it?"

"I don't know." Swiftly crossing the room, she dropped onto the side of his narrow bed. "Are you all right?"

He hung his head.

Going up on one knee, she clamped her hands onto his upper arms. "Answer me, Beau! Are you all right?"

Silently he pulled his hand from beneath the covers and presented it to her. Nicole gasped. The knuckles were skinned, bruised and swollen. She had no doubt now who had put that hole in the bathroom wall. Tears blurred her eyes.

"What happened?"

Beau suddenly yanked his hand away and flopped back on his pillow, declaring, "I hate him!"

Nicole picked up his injured hand and cradled it in her own. "Don't say that, Beau. Hating him hurts you more than him."

"I don't care! I hate him anyway. I wish he had died instead of Mom!"

"Beau!"

He yanked away from her again and rolled onto his side, weeping as she hadn't seen him do since shortly after their mother's death. "I don't care," he wailed in a small voice, repeating it again and again.

Grimly, Nicole insisted, "Let me see your hand again."

Beau scrubbed his uninjured hand over his face and shifted onto his back, presenting the injured knuckles.

"Can you move your fingers?"

He made a fist, then straightened his fingers out flat.

"At least it's not broken. Does it hurt?"

He shook his head, and Nicole breathed a sigh of relief.

"Did you do anything for it last night?"

"I put some antibiotic cream on it," he muttered sullenly.

Nicole nodded approval. "Okay. Well, let's try some ice and a couple aspirin, then, but first I want to know what happened."

Beau folded his arms, but after a moment he started to talk. He'd wanted to watch a certain music program on TV, but Dillard had been intent on watching some "stupid" movie that he'd apparently seen many times. The disagreement had escalated into a shouting match, and Dillard had resorted to the name-calling and put-downs that had become his norm. This time he'd sneered that Beau ought to stop dreaming about something that would never happen, specifically a career in music. He'd even degraded Beau's talent and intelligence. In frustration, Beau had locked himself in the bathroom and put his fist through the wall. Dillard had promptly drunk himself into unconsciousness. Not wanting to upset his sister, Beau had hopped into bed and pretended to be asleep when he'd heard the car in the drive.

Nicole mentally kicked herself, but she didn't let Beau see how upset she was. Instead she went into the kitchen, prepared breakfast and made an ice pack with a zipper bag and a kitchen towel.

They ate breakfast in Beau's room, while he iced his hand, Nicole entertaining him with an account of a precocious toddler who had dumped a bowl of salad on his head at the restaurant the night before. She left him to dress, moving into the kitchen to add their breakfast dishes to those already stacked in the sink and headed to the phone. Lifting the receiver from the cradle, she slipped out into the garage for privacy, leaving the door cracked to accommodate the cord.

Her first call was to Marcus, but he didn't answer, so next she dialed Ovida. Her mother's old friend answered on the second ring, and after ascertaining that Ovida was feeling better, Nicole began to tell Beau's story.

"Bless his heart," Ovida said after hearing the whole tale. "I understand his frustration, but Nicole, he can't go around punching holes in the wall."

"I understand that. I just don't know how to help him deal with his frustration in a healthier way."

"Of course you don't. He needs counseling, honey, professional counseling. You probably do yourself. I would in your position."

Nicole dismissed the part about herself. The only counseling she needed concerned how to help her brother, but she didn't bother arguing the point. "I don't know how to get him the kind of counseling he needs," she said. "You know we can't afford to pay."

"I'll ask around," Ovida said. "I know there are programs. I'm just not familiar with them. Someone at church has to know."

"Marcus," Nicole said. "He'll know."

"Yes, I dare say he will," Ovida agreed.

Nicole closed her eyes and sent up a silent prayer of thanksgiving, feeling that she was halfway to a solution already.

"Nicole," Marcus said, not quite able to meet her eyes as he moved toward the panel of light switches beside the sanctuary door, "forgive me, but I don't have time to visit today."

He'd realized that she was waiting for the building to empty so that she could meet with him privately, and he'd been racking his mind for a way to avoid her. It shamed—and in a strange way, angered—him that he'd just lied to her. And for nothing, apparently, as she simply followed him as he went about his routine for closing up the place after the morning service.

"I know you're very busy. I tried to reach you yesterday, but this is really important. I need your advice. About Beau."

He stopped in the middle of the center aisle and turned to face her. Advice he could give. If he'd known that was all she wanted, he'd have answered his phone yesterday. But he hadn't. He hadn't even turned on the answering machine. He'd just sat there with his head in his hands and stared at the caller ID, telling himself that he had to keep his distance.

"You remember that I called you on Friday," she began.

"Yes."

"Well, I called Ovida as you suggested. That is, I tried to, but the Cutlers were all sick. They've been passing around this stomach thing."

Marcus blinked. Before she'd left town, Jolie had said that a flu was going around, but he hadn't realized that it had laid low the entire Cutler family. The back of his throat began to burn. "Go on."

She did so, telling him how things had been with her father lately and why she had elected to leave Beau alone with him, and then how the evening had devolved into ugliness and, finally, the violence of a fist through a wall. Marcus listened in horror, guilt welling inside him. This was his fault! He'd let his own lack of control interfere with his ministry, and Beau had suffered for it!

"The thing is," Nicole was saying, "I don't know where to find it."

He shook his head, realizing that he'd missed something important. "I'm sorry. Find what?"

"Counseling," she said, tilting her head in obvious confusion. "Counseling for Beau."

"Of course." He gave himself a mental smack between the eyes.

"Like I told Ovida, we can't afford to pay, but she says there have to be programs available."

"There are," he informed her. "Our denomination provides psychological counseling for those in need on a sliding fee scale."

She rocked up onto her toes and back down again, a pleased expression on her face. "I knew you'd have the answer."

He couldn't look at her anymore. In her vivid green dress with its flounces and ruffles worn beneath a large, bulky shawl crocheted in zigzag stripes of rust and black and red, her dark hair braided and lying across one shoulder, she looked like a refugee from a vintage clothing store window.

Utterly adorable.

Completely trusting.

Guileless.

Unconsciously dangerous to his peace of mind.

Too young. Too *everything* for him.

Gulping, he gave her the unvarnished truth. "It may not be as simple as it sounds. Spiritual counseling and psychological counseling are two different things. As a minister, I can counsel Beau as long as your father does not expressly forbid it, but a psychologist will need written permission up front."

Nicole set her teeth and pressed her lips into a grimace. "I didn't count on that." She thought about it and finally shook her head. "I'm not sure I can convince Dad that Beau needs this."

Guilt and responsibility weighed heavily upon Marcus's shoulders. "I'll speak to him," he decided firmly.

"Oh. I—I don't know," she hedged. "That might not be such a good idea."

A part of Marcus wanted to accept that and simply walk away, but a larger, stronger part of him wouldn't, couldn't. "It's either that or inform Child Protective Services and let them get him the counseling he needs."

"How would they manage it without Dad's permission?" she asked warily.

Marcus worked his jaw side to side, wishing he could fob her off with evasions and half truths, but she deserved better than that, especially from him. "They'd have to remove Beau from your father's custody."

"Foster care."

"They couldn't leave him in the house with his abuser."

"Dad didn't bust his knuckles," Nicole argued. "Beau did that to himself."

"In reaction to your father's verbal abuse. The end result is the same, Nicole. Don't you see that?"

"But if Beau learns to control his temper, it won't happen again! That's the point!"

Marcus sighed. "CPS won't see it that way. They'll conclude, and rightly so, that the behavior will escalate on both ends until someone is seriously injured."

She backed away, shaking her head. "I can't let them take Beau! I promised my mom. It was practically the last thing I said to her! Don't you get it?"

"But if it's best for Beau—"

"It's not! Staying with me is best for Beau. Counseling would help, yes, but not at the cost of being separated." Her expression turned pleading, wounded, and Marcus saw in her achingly lovely eyes the girl who had lost so much more than a member of her family. Her mother's death had been the death of the family as a whole. "We're all either of us has," she whispered.

Marcus swallowed, unable to argue against that even though he knew intellectually that his way was best. "Leave it to me, Nicole. I'll do everything in my power to convince your father to allow Beau to receive counseling."

Doubt and fear stamped her face, but in the end she relented. "I'll be praying that you can convince him," she said forlornly.

Marcus linked his hands together to keep from reaching out for her. He wanted desperately to hug her close and give her comfort, but he didn't dare. He didn't trust himself to let it end there. How, he wondered, had he so completely lost his way?

"We'll both be praying," he said quietly.

Chapter Eight

Marcus placed the consent form in a black leather portfolio, checked to be sure that it also contained an ink pen and got out of the sedan. He carried the portfolio up the walk to the battered front door of the Archer house, sending up a prayer with every step.

Only a week or two ago the evening would have carried a decided bite. It was still cool, but he'd put away his overcoat in favor of a lightweight jacket. Tonight he wore jeans and a sport shirt with it.

He'd thought long and hard about the impression that he wanted to make, but without knowing Dillard Archer personally, he really couldn't make an informed judgment. He was prepared to be friendly but firm, approachable but authoritative.

Ringing the bell, he then knocked for good measure. The door opened a few seconds later, and Nicole stood before him, her pretty brow furrowed with worry.

"Marcus, I'm not sure about this."

"It has to be done, Nicole."

She leaned closer, whispering, "He's drinking."

"He's an alcoholic, Nicole. When he's not drinking, he's sick." She bowed her head, and he gently pressed on. "You asked me to wait until you were home. Then you asked me to wait until after dinner, but you can't ask me to wait until he's sober because he never is completely sober. You know I'm right."

"Just don't be surprised if he doesn't agree."

"I'll be surprised if he does," Marcus admitted, "but we have to try. *I* have to try. For Beau's sake."

Nodding, she backed out of the doorway and motioned for him to come inside. Marcus stepped up into a narrow, tiled entry.

A small, dark dining area lay on his right, separated from the tiny foyer by a halfwall. The polished rosewood tabletop gleamed in the gloaming light of a tall bay window that overlooked the front walk. On the left, the paneled living area could be seen through a short row of uniformly spaced spindles running from ceiling to floor. The heavy, old-fashioned, pleated drapes had been drawn, and as no lamps had been switched on, the only light came from the flickering television screen. Outside it was twilight, but in the Archer household it was already deep night, or so it seemed to Marcus.

Nicole led him toward the sagging recliner placed dead center of the floor in front of the TV. The rest of the furniture, with the exception of a small side table, had been pushed back against the walls. As he followed Nicole, Marcus glanced around at it, noting a mundane off-white sofa suite strewn with faded afghans and quilts.

"Dad," Nicole said over the sound of the television, her voice containing twin notes of studied nonchalance and ragged uncertainty, "there's someone here I'd like you to meet."

A large, squarish head swung around. "What?"

"Dad, this is Marcus Wheeler."

Archer pitched sideways in his chair, craning his neck, and staring at Marcus. He let out an undignified snort, lifted a beer can in salute and turned back to his television program.

"She doesn't have time to date," Archer announced loudly.

Astounded, Marcus felt heat flush his neck and face. Anyone with eyes in his head could surely see that he was too old to be dating Nicole. Wasn't he? Yes, of course, he was. Archer was just too drunk to know that, which didn't bode well for this mission. Embarrassed and deflated, Marcus dared not even look at Nicole.

"Dad, he's not here for that," she said in a cringing tone.

"I'm here about Beau," Marcus volunteered, stepping closer.

Dillard leaned forward, craning his neck again. "Beau?"

Marcus walked around in front of the recliner and went straight to the point. "Mr. Archer, your son needs psychological counseling."

Dillard's mouth cracked a wry smile. "Say what?"

Marcus wanted to sit face-to-face, but the nearest seat was a couple yards away. He had no choice but to stand. Holding the portfolio in front of him, he widened his stance slightly. "I'm concerned about Beau's level of frustration."

"Frustration?" Dillard scoffed. "Buddy, let me tell you about frustration. *I* have frustration. He's a kid. What does he know about frustration?" He shook his head and looked past Marcus to the television, muttering, "Frustration! Where do they get this stuff?"

"I understand that you're dealing with your own issues," Marcus said smoothly but firmly, "but my concern at this point is for Beau. I want your permission to take him for counseling. If you desire counseling, it can be made available to you, also."

Dillard glared up at Marcus for all of five seconds, then he calmly set aside his beer and rose to his full height, which was a couple inches taller than Marcus's own six feet. He was a big, beefy man going to fat but still strong enough to cause Marcus serious injury, although in that moment Marcus would have welcomed the excuse to try to pound some sense into the man. As coherent as he sounded, however, Marcus could now see that Dillard was well on his way to complete inebriation. The way he swayed slightly and the sour gust of his breath told Marcus that much. He wasn't the first sober-sounding drunk whom Marcus had encountered.

"Just who do you think you are?" Dillard demanded. "Coming in here spouting off about frustration, telling me my kid needs counseling! Who are you to be taking my boy any-where?"

"I am your son's pastor," Marcus said flatly, "and his friend."

Dillard glared for several seconds longer, but then he put his head back and laughed. The action toppled him backward into his chair, which rocked alarmingly. "His *pastor*," he sneered. "We got no use for your kind here, *pastor*. Go peddle your lies somewhere else."

"I'm peddling no lies, only genuine concern."

"Take your concern and stick—"

"Daddy," Nicole interrupted in a soft tone that Marcus was sure she'd perfected as a tool of distraction long ago, "Marcus is here to help."

"I don't need his help!" Dillard growled. "I don't want it!"

"This isn't about you," Marcus said heatedly. "This is about Beau!"

"Your god means nothin' to me!" Dillard roared. "So *you* mean nothin' to me! What do you know about me and mine anyway?" He grabbed the beer can and drained it, then shoved back in his chair. With a loud creak, the recliner flopped back, rocking wildly. Dillard seemed not to notice that the thing could collapse with him. He was too busy sneering at Marcus. "Your god's done nothin' for me, so I'm doing nothin' for you!"

Marcus clamped his jaw, trying mightily to moderate his tone. "This is not for me. This is for Beau."

Suddenly Dillard turned on Nicole, snarling, "Get him out of my face, girl, or so help me he's gonna regret it!"

She grabbed Marcus by the sleeve, tugging insistently, her big eyes imploring him not to argue further. Marcus sighed inwardly. Obviously he wasn't going to make any headway with Dillard tonight. He let Nicole lead him away. Dillard grumbled behind him, and when Marcus looked back over one shoulder he found the man fishing another beer from the cooler stashed beneath the side table, his chair tilting precariously side to side as he maneuvered.

Resigned to failure, Marcus quietly followed Nicole into the hallway that bisected this portion of the house. She made another quick turn into the kitchen, pulling him along with her. The lights blazing overhead were almost too bright after the gloom of the living room. Marcus glanced around, taking in the faded wallpaper and mottled green countertops.

The pecan cabinets were scratched and dull, the dinette set rickety and scraped. Nevertheless, the room possessed a cheery neatness. Yellow ruffled curtains hung over the window above the sink. The center of the small, round table held a pretty glass bowl of bananas, while a colorful set of canisters took center stage on the longest counter, and a red ceramic rooster looked down on it all from atop the refrigerator. A blue-enameled stew pot sat between the burners on the olive-green stove. This was Nicole's room, the heart of her home, and it evoked a certain longing in him that he was quick to suppress.

"Where's Beau?" he asked softly.

"I asked him to stay in his room. I haven't told him about the counseling for obvious reasons."

Marcus nodded grimly. "I haven't given up."

"Dad's not going to change his mind," Nicole warned, shaking her head.

"Maybe not, but God can change the situation, Nicole. You have to believe that."

"I know. I do know. That's what I'm counting on."

"If you were to call Family Services," Marcus pressed carefully, "they would see to it that Beau and your father both get the counseling they need."

She was shaking her head long before he got through the sentence. "We've been through this. I can't risk them taking Beau into foster care."

"But, Nicole, something has to change. You can't go on living like this."

"Better like this than separated from my brother!" she hissed.

A door opened somewhere down the hallway. Nicole lightly touched Marcus on the forearm, warning him with a glance. He nodded and pasted a smile on his face. Beau entered the room a few moments later, carrying an empty glass. His eyes widened at the sight of Marcus.

"Hey! What are you doing here?"

Marcus clapped a hand on his shoulder in greeting. "Talking to your sister."

Beau's gaze slid from Marcus to Nicole, clearly speculative. "What about?"

Nicole ruffled his hair, saying glibly, "Mind your own business. Want some more milk?"

Beau grinned, and Nicole widened her eyes at him in some silent message. "Yeah, if it's got banana and chocolate in it."

Nicole rolled her eyes, but she took the glass from him and motioned him toward the table. "Sit down." She moved to the cabinets. "You, too, Marcus."

Beau went around the table and pulled out a chair, plopping down into it with no obvious concern for its stability. Marcus followed suit, but a bit more gingerly. Nicole took down a blender and went to the refrigerator.

"We call it a poor man's milk shake," she told Marcus, carrying a tray of ice back to the counter. "It doesn't keep very well, so you'll have to help us drink it."

Marcus watched her walk toward him, noticing for the first time that she was garbed rather mundanely in jeans and a splotchy blue sweatshirt, her sleek, dark hair held back by a white knit headband. It was something of a disappointment. He sort of missed the more interesting costumes that she usually wore.

"Okay," he said.

As she drew near, she laid a hand on his shoulder, then leaned past him to pluck a banana from the bowl. Peeling it, she carried the fruit back to the blender. When she went to the pantry for cocoa powder, he made himself focus on Beau, asking lightly, "So, how have you been?"

"Okay."

Marcus quickly searched his mind for a sustainable topic of conversation and came up with, "Tell me about these guitar lessons."

Beau launched into his favorite subject, ignoring the noisy whine of the blender. Beau taught three kids, one of them as old as he was. None had access to guitars of their own and shared Beau's old acoustic model. It was basically a tale of poor kids, Beau included, eager for a chance just to indulge the dream of escaping hardship through music and fame.

"My friend Austin's got an electric," Beau went on happily, "and, man, I can make that baby sing. When Nic and I get out on our own, I'm gonna get me one. I am so crunk about it."

Marcus laughed. "I'd love to hear you play." He didn't have to ask twice. Beau was already on his feet and heading for the door.

Nicole carried three glasses of light brown slush to the table, saying, "Now you've done it."

"No, really," Marcus said, eyeing his glass warily, "I'd really like to hear him play."

She took the chair to his left, her own beverage in her hand. "We have a straw if you'd like."

A straw, Marcus mused, wondering if she literally meant one straw. He reached for his glass. "No, that's all right." The first sip surprised him. He lifted an eyebrow and went back for more. "Not bad."

Nicole laughed and leaned back, her feet braced against the spanners between the legs of Marcus's chair. He fought the urge to slip his hand down around her ankle.

"Mom always put vanilla extract in it," Nicole told him, wrinkling her nose, "but it's too expensive."

"I like it this way," he said, taking another drink.

Beau reentered the room just then, a blond guitar strung around his neck with a leather thong. It was obviously old. The wood had lost much of its original luster, and the brand name was partially worn away, but his eagerness was palpable. He took his chair, paused long enough to gulp down about half of his drink and began strumming.

"I tuned her up earlier," he explained. Nevertheless, he made a tiny adjustment before downing another long swig of his drink, wiping his mouth on his shirtsleeve and setting to work.

Marcus saw that the knuckles of Beau's right hand were scraped and scabbed, but it didn't seem to hinder his playing. In fact, Marcus required only moments to realize that he was in the presence of true talent. The boy's nimble fingers flew over the strings. Closing his eyes, Beau poured his heart into the music, which filled the room and those in it with unexpected richness.

It wasn't a song that Marcus recognized, but he knew he would never forget so much as a note of it. Indeed, they seemed to swell inside Marcus until he felt ready to burst with the ethereal beauty of the sound. When the last chord was strummed and faded into memory, Marcus felt himself wanting more. Then suddenly Beau launched into a rollicking, bluesy number that put a smile on Marcus's face. This one he recognized as a classic.

"My word," Marcus breathed, sharing a glance with Nicole, who smiled with supreme satisfaction.

He found his feet tapping along in time with Beau's. And then the sound morphed into the riffs and rills of solid rock. This, it became obvious, was where Beau's heart lay. The boy shifted to his feet and moved with the execution of the music, dipping and swaying, forward and back, gliding side to side as the music took him where he made it. When he was done, Beau dropped into his chair with a plop, as if his strength had left with the music.

Marcus was dumbfounded. He couldn't find words to express his appreciation, but his mind whirled with possibilities. Finally a coherent thought crystallized and popped right out of his mouth. "I have to introduce you to Leanne."

Beau slid a knowing look at Nicole, asking, "That the lady who plays the piano at church?"

"Leanne Prist, our director of music," Marcus clarified, nodding. "She's going to want you to provide special music and, of course, join the praise band we're putting together."

Beau shrugged and picked up his glass, sitting back. "Sure."

Marcus grinned. His time here hadn't been wasted, after all.

He looked at Nicole and caught his breath. Her brown eyes glowed with some emotion that shimmered through him, tingling in his extremities and clogging his throat. For a long moment, he literally could not look away. Then Beau rose, stretching and saying that he was going to bed. He started toward the door, and Marcus realized that in another moment he would be alone with Nicole.

He could not, dared not, allow himself that luxury. How long, he wondered, even as he planned his getaway, would he have to carry this cross before God took these dangerous feelings from him?

Marcus glanced at his watch. "I'd better be going, too," he said smoothly, picking up his glass for a final swallow as he rose to his feet.

Nicole slipped out of her chair and placed a stilling hand on his shoulder. "I'll walk you out. Just hang on a minute, will you?" With that she quickly left the room.

Beau met Marcus's gaze openly. "She wants to be sure Dad's out of it before you go. Does he even know you're here?"

"Yes," Marcus answered tersely.

"I had my headphones on," the boy said matter-of-factly. "Did he yell at you? Tell you to get out?"

"We had a few words."

"Don't take it personally. He's like that with everyone."

Marcus nodded. "I'm not worried about that. I am worried about you. Your sister said you put your fist through the wall."

Beau's gaze slid away, and he shrugged. "No big deal. He made me mad is all. Said I've got no talent, only stupid dreams."

"He's wrong," Marcus declared quietly. "You have great talent, but you can't go around busting up things, Beau. You'll destroy your hands, if nothing else. Think about that. How will you play with busted fingers?"

Beau grimaced and whined, "I know, but I can't help it."

"Beau, listen to me," Marcus said urgently. "You and your sister need assistance, professional aid from people trained to deal with these types of situations. I'm sure if you asked her to call Family Services she would."

"It'll just make everything worse," Beau insisted. "I won't punch the wall anymore, honest."

"That's not the point, Beau."

"Dad's out of it," Nicole said from behind Marcus, adding sternly, "and we've already had this discussion."

Marcus sighed. Why couldn't they see that he just wanted to protect them? This was no way to live, tiptoeing around a sharp-tongued drunk. Perhaps he hadn't resorted to physical abuse yet, but Marcus did not doubt that he would unless something changed.

He bid Beau a final good-night and followed Nicole from the room, racking his brain for some way to convince her that his way was best. As they passed the living room, Dillard's snores could be heard over the sound of the television. Marcus marveled that Beau's music hadn't awakened him. Obviously the man was far drunker than he'd realized.

They reached the front door, but instead of standing aside, Nicole opened it and walked through, obviously angry. He had a pretty good idea what was coming, so he merely followed her out and pulled the door closed behind him. Folding her arms against the chill, she stepped out of the shadow of the eaves and turned on him.

"That was low, Marcus, trying to turn Beau against me."

"I wasn't doing that. I just need to make you two understand the reality of your situation."

"Don't you think I know! I live with it every day. Every day. I'm just trying to make the best of a bad situation here, and so far we haven't done too badly."

"So far," he tossed back at her, "but what if next time your father takes his fists to your brother? What then?"

She seemed small and vulnerable, standing there with her head bowed. "We'll just have to cross that bridge if we come to it," she muttered. Then she lifted her chin to a stubborn angle. "But so far we haven't, and I intend to keep looking for a way around."

Marcus put his hands to his head. Couldn't she see that she was running out of options? How could he protect them, he wondered bleakly, if she wouldn't let him?

Perhaps he should call the authorities himself. Even if she never forgave him, at least she and Beau would be safe. How he would live with their anger and disappointment, he didn't know, but what else could he do?

And it might even be for the best.

If she never spoke to him again, he couldn't give in to these inappropriate impulses. If he was going to fail, he might as well fail safely.

"Everyone fails sometime," he told himself, not realizing he'd spoken aloud until he heard the scuff of feet as she shifted closer, reaching out a hand to place it gently against his chest, over his heart.

"Please don't," she begged softly. "You did your best, and truly I didn't expect any other outcome."

With a groan, Marcus closed his eyes, fighting the need to drop his arms around her and pull her close. "I'm not the one in need of comfort here. I'm just sorry that I couldn't help."

She laid her head against him, tucking it neatly beneath his chin. "We just need to find another solution is all."

There is another solution, whispered a small voice in his mind. *And it meets everyone's needs.*

Startled, Marcus let the thought come. She needed someone who could legally stand up for her, someone to help her shoulder responsibilities that would have crushed a lesser individual by now, someone CPS wouldn't hesitate to recommend as a guardian for her brother. A husband.

Someone like Marcus, who himself needed a wife.

Appalled, he shook his head. She was not the wife he needed.

True, it could be done. So easily. She was over eighteen and wouldn't need permission to marry any more than Marcus would. He could convince her. He knew he could. Marriage to him would get her and Beau out of this house and away from Dillard. She could finish college without working herself half to death. Marcus wasn't wealthy by any means, nor would he ever be, but he could provide her and Beau with everything they would ever need. They would be a real family. Marriage would solve everything. For her.

There was nothing to prevent them from marrying. Except his commitment to live in God's will.

He was a minister. He had a calling that he could not doubt. He needed a woman called to be a minister's wife, a spiritually mature, sedate, retiring individual to whom his congregation could relate and look for guidance and aid. He needed a woman who understood the challenges and limitations of his position, a partner in ministry. A young, ebullient, quirky almost to the point of eccentric *student* would never fit the bill, however much he might want her to.

He couldn't escape the fact that Nicole Archer was not the woman for him. No matter how beautiful she was or how much she lit up his heart simply by walking into the room, no matter how much she needed and deserved rescuing, no matter how much he wanted to be the one to do it, marriage between them just wasn't appropriate. And he couldn't believe he had to tell himself that!

Suddenly he wanted desperately just to walk away. Run, truthfully, so far and so fast that he could forget he'd ever met Nicole Archer and her brother. But he couldn't do that, either. His calling demanded otherwise. He couldn't give up, not on Nicole and Beau and not on the ministry to which he was called.

Now all he had to do was figure out a way to manage one without destroying the other.

After a moment, he gently extricated himself and took his leave, but there would be no escape from the fearful ideas that crowded his mind. Not now. Not for him.

God help him.

Nicole closed the door to her bedroom and put her back to it. The red shawl that she'd draped over the lamp on her bedside table cast a dim, rosy glow over the cheap French Provincial furniture. It corresponded fittingly with the warm glow around her heart.

She ought to be steaming, considering what Marcus had done tonight, urging Beau to call the authorities the minute her back was turned, but she couldn't stay angry with him.

He tried so hard to do what was best, and like most men he couldn't conceive that what he thought was best might not be. Her mother used to say that her father couldn't help it if he saw the world through the eyes of a man. That's why they needed wives, after all. And Marcus was no exception.

Because he considered every situation carefully—she never doubted that he prayed diligently over every issue—Marcus naturally assumed that the first answer he hit upon was necessarily the right one. He didn't understand yet that her perspective was every bit as valid as his.

She knew that in Marcus's world calling Family Services and letting them deal with her father was only reasonable, but in hers it was tantamount to dumping her problems on them when she'd vowed never to do so. It wasn't that she didn't see his point or that his point didn't have validity. It wasn't even that she couldn't see a time or a circumstance when his solution would make more sense than hers. It was just that they hadn't gotten there yet, and God willing, they never would.

That didn't mean that Marcus wasn't the sweetest, dearest man on earth anyway for trying so hard to help them.

She peeled off her robe and dropped it over the chair beside the door wandering over to the bed and plopping down. Tired, she fell back against the pillows and stacked her hands beneath her head, considering. If her life wasn't so complicated right now, she'd go after Marcus Wheeler so hard he wouldn't know what hit him, even if he did think she was too young.

Wrinkling her nose, she rolled onto her side, tucking her hands beneath her cheek.

She wasn't too young. She understood why he thought that, though. A minister had to be a sober, responsible sort, which just meant that he needed brightness and childlike enthusiasm in his life more than most others did. He wouldn't see it, of course, precisely because he was sober and responsible. Nicole, on the other hand, made a concerted effort to seek brightness and hold on to all the innocent enthusiasm she could for as long as she could.

She wished she could give that to Marcus.

"He's a good man," she whispered, only realizing at the last moment that she was talking to God. "He deserves all the good things in this world, and I'd give them to him if I could, but I can't, so You'll have to do it. Please."

After a few more moments, her prayer fell back into its usual pattern, filling with her concerns for her father and her brother and the knife-edge of ruin against which her family seemed continually to dance.

"Just help me hold it together a few more months," she pleaded. "I'm not asking for miracles, just a few more months. Then Beau and I can head out on our own."

What would happen to her father then? she wondered.

"He's the one who needs the miracle," she said. "Save it for him, if You please. All I need is just a few more months."

It never occurred to her to ask for more than time or that anyone else would be asking for more on her behalf.

She slid beneath the covers and snuggled down to sleep, remembering what it had been like to lay her head on Marcus's strong shoulder, if only for a moment.

Chapter Nine

"**I**'m not having any of your charity or anything else!" Dillard Archer exclaimed. "And stay away from my daughter!" With that he slammed the door in Marcus's face.

"Charity!" Marcus fumed, whirling away to stomp toward his car. He was offering the man psychological counseling, not alms, for pity's sake.

No wonder Beau was putting his fists through walls. Dillard was as stubborn as he was unreasonable. The man considered it *charity* to get his son the counseling that he so obviously needed!

After much prayer and thought, Marcus had come back here today on his lunch hour hoping that he'd have a better result by speaking with the man when he was sober, albeit hungover. He'd felt that he had to give it one more shot before he took the next step. He should have known that he would fail. Again. But desperate men took desperate measures.

And even if it is charity, Marcus thought angrily, *his pride shouldn't trump Beau's emotional pain.*

But Dillard seemed incapable of thinking of anyone except

himself: *his* pride, *his* loss, *his* prejudice, *his* anger. He wouldn't even let Marcus into the house to plead his case.

As for staying away from his daughter, Marcus had already come to the same conclusion. Again. Which both simplified and complicated the matter greatly.

Nicole needed help. The Archers needed help, the kind of help that only Family Services and the weighty authority of the state could give them. How was he to convince her to take the necessary steps, though, if he couldn't even trust himself to sit down in a quiet place with her?

Marcus knew he'd run out of options. The ridiculous notion of marrying the girl aside, it had become painfully clear that Dillard could not be moved to do what was best for his children, not by an individual, at any rate. What was just as painfully obvious was that Marcus wouldn't have to worry about getting too close to Nicole if he availed himself of the only viable solution he could see.

He didn't kid himself. The personal consequences of taking such an action would be grim, but it would be best for everyone all the way around. Given another choice, he'd have gladly taken it, but he couldn't put his own considerations ahead of what was best for Nicole and Beau. That would make him no better than Dillard.

Besides, he thought bleakly, if Nicole never spoke to him again, that would remove temptation from him as nothing else could. Accepting her anger and disappointment as the price he paid for doing what was right could well be the most loving thing he could do for her.

After unlocking the driver's door, Marcus tossed the portfolio containing the unsigned permission waiver onto the bench seat of his sedan and followed it inside. He gripped the steering wheel with both hands, steeling himself for what he was about to do.

"Lord, if this is what it takes, I'm more than willing, but if it's possible, for her sake more than my own, let her forgive me. Help her understand why this is necessary. I don't expect her to look at me ever again with that hero worship in her eyes, but that's just as it should be, surely. Amen."

He reached into his breast pocket and took out his mobile phone. As he thumbed through the preprogrammed numbers, he took in a deep breath. He had tried it her way, and it hadn't worked. He could only assume, then, that the one remaining credible option was the one he should take.

The name for which he was searching popped up. Jonathan Bertrand was a friend from seminary who had found his calling with the offices of Child Protective Services. Having grown up in the CPS system, Marcus was all too aware of how difficult a career in social service must be, and he had long admired his friend's dedication in the face of thankless tasks, red tape and heartbreaking situations. He was grateful that he had this resource, sorry that he had to use it.

Grimly resigned, Marcus dialed the number and waited for the answer, expecting to leave a message on Jonathan's voice mail. Instead, he reached Jonathan himself.

Having risen through the ranks of CPS caseworkers to a position of supervisor, Jonathan was uniquely placed to take immediate action. After hearing Marcus's version of the Archers' story, Jonathan was prepared to send one of his field agents to make an unannounced visit to the Archer home the very next evening. Satisfied, Marcus ended the call.

If his stomach felt tied in knots as he drove back to the church, he bore it with as much resigned grace as he could muster. What point could there be, after all, in holding out against the inevitable? Whatever befell he was bound to reap a whirlwind in this situation.

The confirmation of that dreary fact came almost forty-eight hours later. He was heading back to the office from the day care center via the covered walkway that connected the buildings when Nicole's car turned the corner in front of him.

She didn't park outside the administration building. She didn't even bother to put the car in a space, let alone turn it head in. Instead she simply swerved to the curb next to him, threw the transmission into park and bailed out with the motor still clanking.

She was dressed in black from the jaunty beret parked atop her head to the boots on her feet, including a turtleneck sweater of thin knit and a gauzy, ankle-length skirt composed of ruffled tiers. The color perfectly portrayed her mood.

"How could you?" she cried, her hands fisted at her sides. "You knew we didn't want CPS brought in!"

Marcus didn't bother pretending that her accusations were unfounded. Neither did he defend himself.

"I made sure they came when you would be there. I didn't want them talking to Beau or your father without you."

"Oh, they came, all right, some silly little woman with excruciatingly good manners and no idea when she was being snowed!"

Marcus's heart filled with dread. "What do you mean?"

"You spoke to him," Nicole pointed out sharply. "No one who doesn't know him will even realize he's drunk unless he gets up and starts bumping into things! How was she to know that he'd keep his cool until she'd gone?"

Marcus winced. She was right. He should have thought of that. He should have warned Jonathan that Dillard could maintain precise speech even when scarcely conscious.

"What happened?"

She parked her hands on her hips and glared at him. "He exploded. He smashed Beau's stereo for punishment!"

Marcus briefly closed his eyes. "Was Beau hurt?"

"Physically, no. But Beau doesn't know when to keep his mouth shut, so I wound up between him and Dad's belt!"

Suddenly Marcus was too angry to breathe, but he didn't know who he was angrier with, Dillard or himself. Finally, he got out what felt like the most important words he'd ever spoken. "Did he hit you?"

She looked him square in the eye. "No."

"Did he touch you at all?"

Her gaze dropped. "Just to try to shove me out of his way. When I didn't budge, he backed off."

Marcus forced air into his lungs, held it until his heart slowed and expelled it again. "I'll buy Beau another stereo," he vowed, but Nicole dismissed that with a slash of her hand.

"What's the point? Dad will just smash it the next time he's angry. I had to hide the guitar to keep him from destroying that, and he tore up *my* room looking for it!"

Gulping, Marcus said, "I'll talk to him. I did this. His anger should be directed at me, not you. I'll make him see that."

She folded her arms, her chin set at a stubborn angle. "You will not. He already suspects it was you who turned him in, and if he finds out for sure he'll forbid us to attend church. He probably will anyway."

Marcus shook his head, confused and contrite. How could this be? Had he sacrificed her goodwill, her friendship, even his ministerial position in her life for nothing? Calling CPS had been for the best. Hadn't it? It had to be.

"They have a case file now. The next time they won't be

fobbed off so easily. It'll work out in the end," he promised, but the look on her face smashed him to bits inside. It was like a hot poker in the chest.

Her big eyes welled with tears, and her stubborn little chin began to quiver while the rest of her features remained wooden.

"Yes, it will," she agreed in a thin, trembling voice. "But there won't be any next time, Marcus. I promised my mom, and I'll do whatever it takes to keep that promise." She stomped her foot then. "But none of that has anything to do with the fact that I trusted you and you betrayed me!"

Marcus closed his eyes. "I had no choice."

"And for what?" she went on. "It didn't change a thing."

He popped his eyes open. "It would have if you'd told them the truth. But you pretended everything was fine, didn't you?"

"What else was I going to do? Hand my little brother over to them, forget every promise I've ever made?"

For nothing! he thought. He couldn't have done this for no good at all. And she hated him now. Was that what it had been for, so she would hate him because he wasn't strong enough to ignore the way she looked at him? "I didn't know what else to do!" he said helplessly.

She was already sliding back into her rattletrap car, as if she hadn't even heard or just didn't care anymore. The tires screeched as she whipped a U-turn and left the same way she'd come in.

Marcus put his head back, sheer agony writhing inside his chest.

"I didn't know what else to do," he repeated, which was no comfort at all. All he could do now was try to put it right somehow.

He pulled his cell phone from his pocket and quickly found

Jonathan Bertrand's number. This time he did have to leave a message, and nearly an hour passed before Jonathan returned the call. He explained that he'd taken the time to speak personally with the investigating agent. She'd reported that the Archer home seemed safe, clean and comfortable despite its slightly run-down condition.

"God knows she's seen much worse," Jonathan commented, and Marcus knew that was solely because of Nicole's efforts.

Jonathan went on to read aloud the caseworker's notes. She had found Dillard Archer lazy, self-involved and somewhat crude but neither abusive nor dangerously inebriated. She'd written that Nicole obviously had assumed a major role in the life of the family, and that since Nicole seemed trustworthy and responsible, Beau was of an age to assume some personal accountability and neither of them had made any complaint concerning their father's behavior, it was the caseworker's opinion that no further action on the part of the county or state was necessary. Jonathan concurred.

Feeling sick, his heart pounding with dread, Marcus explained what had happened after the caseworker had left the Archer house.

"Will she swear to that?" Jonathan asked. "Because if she will, I'll send my agent back out there right away. I expect she would at least recommend anger management classes for Mr. Archer."

Anger management classes would be a start, Marcus admitted, but only that, and he knew without a doubt that Nicole wouldn't cooperate.

"Beau might under the right circumstances," Marcus speculated aloud.

Unless one of them did, Jonathan's hands were tied. Marcus groaned inwardly, thanked him and got off the phone.

He was in no mood for the agitated mother of two who greeted him the moment that he stepped foot back into the office, but it was his job to deal with such minor problems as a toddler with a tendency to bite, and he did so with as much patience and diplomacy as he could muster. Only later did he have time to sit down, bow his head and beg God to show him where he'd gone wrong.

After much more prayer, he decided that he'd been somewhat precipitate, that he'd done it as much for his own sake as Nicole's or Beau's. He still believed that involving the authorities was best for them and that he'd had a responsibility as a member of the clergy to report the abuse, but his motives had been selfish.

At least he'd accomplished one thing. Neither Nicole nor Beau would likely ever speak to him again. That might well have been the point of the whole exercise. Perhaps that was what God intended.

He'd prayed to have the temptation removed, after all, and so it had been. He didn't have to worry about a romantic relationship developing between himself and Nicole anymore. If ever she'd had a crush on him, that was surely finished. He should feel relieved.

He felt as if he'd lost his best friend, as if color had drained out of the world, leaving it a pale, pallid version of what it might have been.

It was best, no doubt, but it wasn't happy, and he couldn't help feeling that he ought to try to make amends. If he and Beau could just remain friends, he might still be able to help.

It was the only recourse he could think of and little enough, considering how it had turned out. Sick at heart, he accepted this half measure as all that was left to him, and for the first time in more years than he could even remember, he had to fight back tears.

* * *

Nicole looked at the brown paper bag that Beau had dropped in her lap and folded her arms. The bag should have been empty, but obviously it wasn't. Unfolding the top, she checked inside. All the original contents were there, with the exception of the cookies. Sighing, she handed the bag back to him and fixed him with a questioning glare.

"Care to explain to me why you only ate cookies for lunch?"

Smiling smugly, Beau dug into the bag, removed the peanut butter sandwich and began peeling back the plastic wrap, clearly preparing to eat it. "I didn't eat cookies for lunch," he said cheekily. "I ate them in study hall."

"So you skipped lunch," Nicole surmised, quickly seizing the wheel and driving forward as the line of cars ahead of her moved.

"Nope. I ate a chili cheese dog, onion rings and a side salad with buttermilk dressing." He bit off a huge chunk of the sandwich and apparently swallowed it whole.

"Chew your food," Nicole instructed automatically, looking both ways before pulling out into the street that ran in front of the school. "And where did you get the money to buy a chili cheese dog, let alone onion rings and… You ate a side salad?"

"Mmm-hmm. Wi bu-urmil drezin."

"Don't speak with your mouth full," she scolded mildly. "Now answer my question."

He gulped, smacked his lips and said, "I had lunch with Marcus."

She brought the car to a stop at the red light on the corner and turned her head to gape at her brother. She still hadn't forgiven Marcus for calling the authorities, but deep down she knew she wasn't going to hold it against him forever. He'd only done what he thought was best. The fact that he was wrong, at least to her mind, did not negate his intentions, and she couldn't deny the relief that she felt at knowing he hadn't completely abandoned them to their fate.

"So Marcus came to the school for lunch," she said, looking away again.

"Yep, and brought lunch with him."

Nicole faced forward and lifted a hand to her hair, trying to appear nonchalant. "What did he have to say?"

Beau finished the sandwich and reached into the bag for the pretzels she'd packed for him that morning. "He's worried about us, and he feels bad about my stereo." Beau turned big, pleading eyes on her. "He'll replace it if you'll let him."

"Beau."

"I know. It's not really his fault Dad broke it, but if I wait for Dad to replace it I'll get old and grow hair in my ears before I can listen to my music again."

He started crunching the pretzels, and Nicole found herself on the verge of smiling. She quickly disciplined her pleasure as she pulled away from the light.

"Marcus shouldn't have called CPS."

"I know. I told him that."

"And what did he say?"

Beau poked around inside the paper bag for a moment, long enough for her to know that he was stalling.

"Beau, what did Marcus say when you told him that he shouldn't have called CPS?"

Beau looked up and reluctantly said, "He wanted me to tell CPS what Dad did after that lady left. He said if I would, they'd probably send Dad to anger management classes."

Nicole rolled her eyes. "Anger management. Like that'll help the next time he's too drunk to see reason. You told Marcus you wouldn't do it, didn't you?"

"Sure I did."

"If he bothers you about it again, I want to know."

"Aw, Nic. He's just trying to help," Beau said.

She shifted in her seat. "Yes, well, he always tries to help. He just has to learn that we sometimes know best. Not everyone fits the standard protocol."

"What's that?"

"Never mind."

Shrugging, Beau worked on the pretzels for another block or two. Then he reached into the bag for the apple. Lightly polishing the apple on his pant leg, he asked, "Think I could go to youth group at church tonight?"

Nicole bit her lip. "I don't know, hon. Dad's liable to be home and sober enough to notice."

Beau sighed. "Yeah, that's what I figured, too. Think we'll be able to make it on Sunday?"

She'd thought about not going at all or finding another church, but once her anger had subsided somewhat, she'd known that she would do neither. Still, things could get a lot trickier now.

"Maybe. I can't promise, though."

Beau nodded his understanding. "I can meet the music director some other time, I guess."

Sadly, Nicole couldn't offer more hope than that. Dillard could stop them from going to church if he really wanted to, and she had no doubt that he would if he were sober enough to think of it. They'd have to be very careful from now on.

She watched Beau bite into the apple, wishing that she could give him the same carefree, untroubled life that other boys seemed to experience. At least she could keep his life from getting any worse, and that's what would happen if she lost him to the foster care system. Couldn't Marcus see that? Didn't his own experience tell him that was the case?

On one hand, she wanted to be angry with Marcus. He'd had no right to call CPS, knowing how she and Beau felt about it. On the other, she knew that he'd done it because he cared about them. That was something she couldn't forget. She only hoped that with time things would get back to normal. In the meanwhile, she'd do the best she could.

Seemed as if that was what she'd been doing ever since her mom had died.

One more semester to go, she told herself.

Surely they could hold out for that long. Maybe she shouldn't skip the summer, though. She'd meant to work full-time in order to scrape together the tuition for her final semester, but maybe she could manage full-time work and summer school, too.

She shook her head. The summer semester was short, and Beau would be out of school. She dared not leave him on his own every day in the house with their dad. They'd just have to keep on keeping on as they were—and pray for the best.

Marcus clasped the hand that Nicole offered.

"I'm so very glad to see you," he said, casting a glance around the church foyer. He nodded at someone behind her, and his manner grew slightly more formal. "We've missed having you and Beau at services."

She let her hand fall, knowing that they were being observed. They had nothing to hide, she and Marcus, but she was astute enough to realize that it wasn't wise for Marcus to show more interest in one member of the congregation than another. Besides, she wasn't quite ready to completely forgive him.

Still, it was wonderful to see him. She smiled, realized that she was standing on her tiptoes and quickly lowered herself again.

"It's been difficult to get away lately," she told him, sure he would understand.

"I'd like to talk to you about that if you have time," he said meaningfully, glancing down the line of those waiting to shake his hand.

She knew what he was asking her to do, and despite everything she would have liked to hang around until they could speak privately, but she dared not. Her father had stumbled in and fallen into bed around four in the morning, but he'd wake up when he got hungry. She and Beau were already taking a chance just by being here. If their father woke before they got back home, he'd know where they'd been, and while he hadn't specifically forbidden them to attend church, he suspected that Marcus was the one who had called CPS.

They couldn't give him the slightest pretext to lower the boom. She shuddered to think what he'd do if ever he knew that Marcus had been meeting Beau regularly for lunch at school.

"I'm sorry," she said, leaning in close. "I just can't. Not yet. Maybe in a few more weeks."

"This is the first time you've been here in a month," Marcus whispered urgently. "Beau won't tell me what's going on, and I can't help worrying when you don't show up for church."

The woman behind Nicole nudged her slightly, and she straightened away from Marcus saying loudly, "Wonderful sermon. I look forward to next time."

Marcus nodded stiffly and reached out for the other woman's hand. Nicole strode swiftly for the exit, signaling Beau to leave his acquaintances and join her. They hurried around the church, across the street and between the administration and day care buildings to the car parked at the curb on the street beyond. The church parking lot had a tendency to bottleneck, and they didn't have the time to spare.

In truth, it had been foolish of her to take the time to greet Marcus personally when she could have slipped out another door, but she hadn't been able to resist. Now they had to rush. She broke speed limits getting home, holding her breath all the way, only to walk into the kitchen and find her father sitting at the table. He held his head in one hand, nursing a cup of coffee with the other.

Dillard jerked at their sudden halt, as if the squeaks of their shoes on the worn vinyl flooring pained his head. Nicole reached out a hand to keep Beau in his place, her heart in her throat. Dillard slid a narrow-eyed glance over them and turned back to his coffee in glum silence. After a moment, he spoke.

"So did you make plans for lunch or what? I'm starving here, or don't you care?"

Nicole handed Beau her purse and Bible and motioned for him to leave them. At the same time that he slipped from the room, she walked across the floor to the counter and the slow cooker atop it. The spaghetti with meat sauce that she'd put into the freezer last week had gone into the cooker as a solid lump before she'd started dressing for church this morning. With luck, it would just about be ready. She'd intended to put together a salad, but opening a can of green beans would be quicker, and at this point, quick was definitely the better option.

A few minutes later, when she set Dillard's plate in front of him, he looked up and growled, "Don't think I don't know where you've been or that I can't put a stop to it."

She said nothing to that, merely asked, "Have you taken anything for your head?"

Dillard closed his eyes, muttering, "I forgot to get the

aspirin before I sat down." He opened his eyes and looked up at her beseechingly. "Will you get them for me, baby?"

Nicole's heart turned over. He was a pathetic loser drunk, but he was still her dad, and no matter what, she loved him. She'd take the first opportunity to get away from him, but that didn't mean he wouldn't always be her dad. For today, at least, that seemed to matter.

"Sure, Daddy."

Absently patting his shoulder, she went to get the painkillers, silently breathing a sigh of relief. Maybe things would get better for a while again. As Marcus had said in his sermon today, God really did have the power to change lives, and maybe, just maybe, He was already beginning to change her father from the inside out.

Chapter Ten

Nicole hung up the phone, carefully assessing the situation.

It had been a couple weeks of relative peace and normalcy. Dillard hadn't again threatened, even obliquely, to forbid her and Beau from attending church. In fact, he'd said nothing at all about it. He'd had little to drink, gone to bed at a decent hour and been downright pleasant most of the time, sometimes even joking and teasing with them. As a result Beau was content and relaxed. Still, she wasn't quite ready to trust that all would be well if she left Beau and her father alone together again.

Beau shambled into the kitchen just then, his backpack slung over one shoulder, humming as he fingered an invisible guitar. Catching her pensive expression, he stopped.

"What?"

Nicole smiled, thrilled to see him so happy. But how long, she wondered, would it last? Another day? A week? She dared not hope for forever at this point, but didn't that demonstrate a lack of faith on her part? She'd been thinking a lot about that. Only last Sunday Marcus had said from the pulpit that asking God to fix your problems and then not trusting

Him to do so was tantamount to denying His ability and right to direct our lives.

She missed Marcus deeply. He hadn't tried to talk to her again since she'd rebuffed him a few weeks ago, and his greetings, while perfectly polite, were strictly impersonal. He continued to spend time with Beau, but if he even thought about her, she certainly couldn't prove it. Nevertheless, she trusted his teachings. Perhaps it was time she stepped out on faith.

"I've got another chance to work a few extra hours," she said to Beau. "The restaurant just can't keep fully staffed on Fridays." Some people, it seemed, actually had social lives.

"That's cool," Beau commented offhandedly, walking over to the counter to pick up his lunch bag.

"You think it'll be all right then, even after last time?"

Beau turned and met her gaze. "Don't worry," he said. "It'll be fine. Besides, don't we need the money?"

"You know we do."

"Well, then."

She bit her lip. Old habits died hard. "I could call Ovida and Larry Cutler. You haven't seen them in a long time."

Beau made a face, complaining, "You know I'm not as tight with them as you are. They're old folks, and besides I'm not some little bitty baby anymore."

"Marcus, then. You've been eating lunch together a couple times a week. I'm sure he wouldn't mind."

"Listen," Beau said emphatically, "it's okay." He lowered his voice, adding, "And I don't think Dad would like it if we called Marcus."

"Has he said something?"

Beau hitched up one shoulder. "Not really. But the other night when you got up and left the room, he asked if you were still seeing Marcus."

"Seeing? As in *dating?*" Where, she wondered, had he gotten an idiotic idea like that? It must be more obvious than she realized how much she liked Marcus—and less obvious how little he thought of her.

"That's what it sounded like," Beau confirmed. "I sort of blurted that I was the one Marcus was having lunch with all the time, and Dad looked—I don't know—hurt, I guess. Then I thought he was going to get mad, but instead he got, well, nicer."

Nicole lifted her eyebrows. "Really? Hmm." It almost sounded as if their father was a little bit jealous of Marcus. Perhaps he regretted having alienated his son. Was it really possible that God had begun to soften his heart? "So you think it'll be all right if I go on to work and leave you two here alone together?"

"Yeah, I think so. In fact, I want you to. It could be fun, just us guys. You know, the way it used to be when you and Mom would go off together. If Austin's mom can't give me a lift after school, I'll even catch the bus home."

Nicole widened her eyes comically. "Now that's a first."

The bus ride was long and monotonous, and some kids chose to entertain themselves by picking on others. Beau had been an occasional target, so they tended to avoid that particular district service. Beau was older now, though, better able to avoid trouble and defend himself if the need arose.

"I'm not saying I'll make a habit of it," he warned.

Nicole suppressed a smile, put away her fears and gave in. Her little brother was growing up. And maybe it was time not only to exercise her faith but also to give their dad the benefit of the doubt. She picked up the drawstring bag that contained the things she'd need for the day and slung it over one shoulder.

"Well, what are you waiting for?" she demanded teasingly. "Or maybe you want to ride the bus *to* school."

"No way!" Beau exclaimed, heading for the door.

Nicole laughed and followed him out. Maybe, just maybe, the long, gloomy winter of their lives was finally coming to an end.

Nicole heard the shouting the moment she got out of her car. In an instant the hopeful dream in which she had passed the day vanished like so much smoke in a gale. Dropping her bag on the garage floor, she darted through the narrow laundry room and into the kitchen, discerning at once her father's voice coming from the living room.

"I am your father!" Dillard roared. "And I'll teach you to watch your mouth!"

A loud, sickening *thwack* followed, and Beau cried out. Gasping, Nicole lurched for the doorway, only to draw up when the horrific sound came again. She had no doubt what was transpiring. Her father was taking his belt to Beau. She knew as well that she could do nothing to stop it, not physically anyway.

In hopes of defusing her father's anger, she called out cheerily, "I'm home!"

"Stay out!" Beau screamed, as the leather belt whistled through the air again.

"Disrespectful little idiot!" Dillard bellowed.

Nicole ran for the phone. For an instant, her finger hovered over the key pad as she wondered frantically whom to call. Marcus was her first thought, but she greatly feared that would only incite Dillard to greater violence. Besides, Marcus's solution would be to call the cops. She realized in that instant that Marcus had been right all along. She had only one real option now. Perhaps it had always been so, and she just hadn't wanted to face it. Sobbing, she punched in the numbers 9-1-1.

After choking out the reason for her call and answering what seemed like endless, pointless questions, she hung up and rushed to the living room, which had gone eerily quiet. For a moment, the heap of bodies on the floor seemed as still as death, but then Beau gasped and began to struggle beneath the much greater weight of their father.

Nicole lurched forward, seized Dillard by the shoulder and tipped him sideways, literally rolling him off her brother. Dillard groaned and muttered something unintelligible. Apparently he had passed out. Beau pushed up into a sitting position, drew his knees close and rested his forearms atop them, dropping his head into his hands.

"I'm sorry!" he wailed. "I'm so sorry. I didn't mean to argue with him!"

Nicole went to her knees and pulled his hands away from his face, which showed clear signs of bruising. The marks of a belt were visible on his forearms and the backs of his hands. He gasped out the details of his fight with their father.

Dillard had wanted to go out for dinner, but he'd been drinking steadily for hours, and Beau had known that he was in no shape to get behind a steering wheel, so he had refused to get into the truck with him. The argument had escalated from that to this.

Nicole cast a despairing glance at her father, who had begun to snore as if comfortably tucked into his bed. Thank God he'd passed out when he had. Otherwise, she shuddered to think of what damage he might have done.

At least Beau hadn't gotten into that truck with him, but why, oh, why had she trusted in the fragile peace that had arisen within her crippled little family? She had the awful feeling that things were only going to get worse before they got better. Her instincts were proven right not a minute later when the police arrived. They were not alone.

As soon as two uniformed officers had swept into the house and declared it secure, a tall, slender gentleman with prematurely gray hair entered and went straight to Beau, looking him over with a practiced eye. An African-American, Linus Eversole introduced himself as the local police department's Child Advocate. Though probably only somewhere in his late thirties, Mr. Eversole had an air of caring, world-weary wisdom about him, and he quickly assessed the situation with self-assured expertise, asking a few, seemingly casual questions and listening with focused intent.

Emergency medical technicians arrived in an ambulance and one pair promptly carted off her father, while another made a thorough evaluation of Beau's injuries. Eversole quietly conferred with the officers before firmly but gently steering Nicole into the hallway, where he explained that her father was being transported under arrest to an Arlington hospital where it would be determined if his blood alcohol level was sufficient to be toxic. Beau would also be leaving, with Mr. Eversole himself.

"I'll follow you," Nicole said, looking around for her bag and only belatedly remembering that she'd dropped it in the garage.

Linus Eversole laid a consoling hand on her arm and looked her square in the eye. "I'm sorry," he said, "that won't be possible."

The bottom seemed to drop out of Nicole's stomach, but she refused to accept the inevitable without an argument. "Wh-what do you mean? How will he get home?"

"Beau won't be coming home, Miss Archer, unless or until this can be proved a safe environment for him."

"B-but it is safe!"

"Circumstances have proved that is not the case, I'm afraid."

"You don't understand," Nicole argued frantically. "I've been taking care of my brother since our mom died! A-and with Dad gone, everything will be fine."

"I'm sorry," Mr. Eversole said again, "but even if your father is remanded to treatment, which I expect to be the case, he'll eventually return here, and that could place your brother in danger once again. So I'll be taking Beau to an emergency shelter. In a few days he'll be placed with a foster family until such time as the court can ascertain—"

"No!" Nicole cried, but Eversole went on calmly.

"If your family can be reunited." He patted her shoulder kindly, adding, "Reunification is always our ultimate goal."

"When?" Nicole demanded. "How soon?"

"A few months, most likely," he hedged carefully.

Nicole put her hands to her head. It was her worst nightmare come true, the very thing that she'd most feared. Beau would feel crushed, terrified and betrayed. And her father! She knew how angry he would be and whom he would blame. How had this happened? What about the promise she'd made her mom?

"But why can't he just stay with me?" she begged. "I won't leave him alone again, I swear."

"Miss Archer," the Child Advocate interrupted, "let's be frank. You're twenty years old. If you were thirty, after what's happened here tonight I'd still remove Beau from your care."

"But later?" she asked tremulously.

Eversole adopted a milder tone. "Please understand that Beau's welfare must be our only concern. Should your father prove unfit even after treatment, he would still be free to return to this house. Therefore, Beau must not."

"We'll go somewhere else," she promised.

"I'm afraid you'll have to meet a very high standard of proof to convince a court that you are capable of giving Beau the guidance and support he needs," Mr. Eversole told her, shaking his head.

She stared at him, horrified beyond words. He patted her shoulder and bowed his head to look into her tear-ravaged eyes.

"Do you need medical care? Were you injured?"

She couldn't seem to do anything more than shake her head.

"You'll be safe here tonight," he told her, "but you may not want to be alone in the house. Maybe you have a friend you can stay with?"

A friend? she thought. The first person who came to mind was Marcus. She knew there were others, but in that moment, she couldn't conjure up a single face or name besides his, and suddenly she wanted desperately to see him.

"You'll want to speak to your brother before he leaves," Linus Eversole said, turning and walking back into the living room. Nicole followed him robotically.

The EMTs had gone. Only one police officer remained, a woman with long blond hair fashioned into a thick plait at the nape of her neck. She held Beau by one arm as if to prevent his escape, but her eyes showed a sort of steely compassion.

Nicole went straight to her brother, took his hands in hers and cleared her throat, but her voice still trembled noticeably when she said, "You have to go with Mr. Eversole, Beau. I'll see you tomo—" She broke off and amended, "Soon. Very soon."

"I don't want to," he insisted, sounding panicked. "I have to stay with you!"

"I know," she said, trying and failing to smile. "We'll be together again soon. I'll talk to Marcus. He'll know what to do. But right now you have to go with Mr. Eversole."

Murmuring words of encouragement, Eversole steered

Beau through the door with both hands. At the last moment, Beau turned his head, looking over his shoulder at Nicole with both fear and accusation in his eyes.

"It's going to be okay," she whispered, tears rolling down her face, but Beau was gone, and she was not at all convinced that her own words were true.

The officer stayed behind to ask her more questions, all of which Nicole answered, but then she had one of her own.

"What if we don't press charges? What will happen then?"

She was told that it was out of her hands. The state would press charges against their father on Beau's behalf. Apparently, having given statements, neither Nicole nor Beau had anything more to say about that part of it, which meant that Beau was now a ward of the state. Nicole was still crying about that when the other woman pressed a card into her hands, promised that someone would be in touch and took her leave. The moment the door closed behind her, Nicole ran to her car in the garage, just one thought in mind.

She had to see Marcus. Now.

In some ways the trip to the parsonage seemed to take forever, and in others it passed in the blink of an eye. She couldn't remember afterward how she'd actually gotten there, only that she seemed to have been traveling for a very long while. As she ran up the walk to the steps, she didn't think about the lateness of the hour or the possibility of being turned away. She only thought about Marcus and the need to see him. She didn't even wonder what help he might have to offer her or whether he could offer her any help at all. She only knew that in this moment of acute distress his was the face she most wanted to see, and she didn't bother to even wonder why.

Nicole ran to him without question or forethought, like a

homing pigeon winging its way back to safety by instinct and nature alone. Despite her anger at Marcus in the past, despite the fact that she hadn't shared a single private word with him in weeks, her need of him was the most real thing in her world at the moment.

Marcus had just set aside the novel he was reading and turned out the bedside lamp when he heard the sound of a car in the drive. Telephone calls at this time of night were not terribly unusual, given how many medical emergencies seemed to arise after 11:00 p.m. Visitors were. Not much thought was required to realize that something was wrong.

He was out of bed, hastily but decently clad, by the time the first blow fell on his door. Flicking on lights as he passed through the house, he threw the dead bolt and opened up without even checking the peephole to see who was on the other side. It didn't matter who was there, only that someone needed his help. Unsurprisingly, that someone turned out to be Nicole, who literally fell into his arms, sobbing incoherently.

Every protective instinct he'd ever possessed rose swiftly inside him. Wrapping his arms around her, he guided her quickly into the living area, kicking the door closed behind them.

"What's wrong?" It didn't take much imagination to figure that her father was involved. "Did he hurt you?"

She was shaking her head when he dropped onto the sofa with her. "B-Beau," she gasped. "They t-took him!"

"Who took him?"

"P-police! E-Eversole."

Marcus knew Linus Eversole well, and just the mention of the name told him much. Linus was a dedicated advocate for children, a stern but caring man with excellent judgment who routinely tended to err on the side of caution.

Letting out a breath that he'd been holding much too long, Marcus tucked her head beneath his chin and gently rocked her, crooning comfort and gradually pulling the full story out of her. As she spoke, she calmed. By the time the facts had been disclosed, it was obvious that her very fine brain had started to function with its usual sharpness again.

"This is exactly why I didn't want to call the authorities," she stated hotly, emphasizing the thought with tiny pecks of her forefinger against one knee as she sat facing him on the end of the couch.

"You did the right thing," he assured her. "Your father didn't give you any other choice."

She brushed that aside with a sharp shake of her head. "The important thing now is getting Beau back. Tell me how."

Choosing his words very carefully, Marcus outlined what was going to happen and how she could petition the court for physical custody of her brother. "In other words," he summed up, "you have to prove that, as family, you are the most capable supervisor of your brother's welfare, despite your youth and this incident. I, of course, will speak to Child Protective Services on your behalf."

She reached for his hand and squeezed it at that, saying, "I'll do anything. I'll drop out of college and get a full-time job, if I have to."

"I'm not sure that's the best approach," he told her, unable to resist the urge to reach out and smooth back a strand of hair that had fallen forward and tangled in her damp, spiky eyelashes. It slipped through his fingers like dark silk. "You're too close to the end to think of quitting now, and I suspect that CPS would be better impressed if you got that degree."

"But I can't leave Beau with strangers that long!"

"You may not have to," he argued gently. "Listen, if worst

comes to worst, I'll have myself certified as a foster parent and get Beau placed here."

Crying out, she literally launched herself at him, throwing her arms around his neck and rocking him back. His own arms closed around her reflexively.

"Thank you! Thank you! Oh, Marcus, I love you! I'll love you forever!"

He heard those final words with horror. Her declaration of love necessarily brought any expression of affection, however innocent, to a screeching halt. Marcus wasn't at all sure just how "innocent" his affectionate feelings were, anyway. Desperate to put distance between them, he all but shoved her away. Leaping to his feet, he tucked his hands safely into the rear pockets of his jeans.

Nicole's brow furrowed. Then understanding sent her warm chocolate gaze to her lap. She nodded as if to say that she'd gotten his message loud and clear. He felt an instant of relief, but when she lifted her head again what shone in her eyes made his breath catch in his throat. It was his worst nightmare and his fondest dream, and he felt immediate recoil along with the sharpest yearning imaginable.

"Nicole, I—"

"It's all right," she interrupted, giving her head a truncated shake. "I understand."

"I'm not sure you do," he began determinedly. "You're a lovely young woman, operative word here being young."

"I'm not *that* young, Marcus. I know how I feel."

He let that pass, pressing on with what had to be said. "It's not just your youth, Nicole. It's…" This was more difficult than he'd realized, but he took a deep breath and plunged on. "A minister has to be careful who he loves, Nicole, r-romantically, that is. He just can't casually involve himself with anyone."

"No one said anything about involvements, casual or otherwise," she pointed out, just an edge of testiness in her tone.

"What I'm trying to say is that a minister's spouse is called by God just as surely as a minister is. A-And there are certain…*qualifications* necessary to the calling."

"Qualifications I obviously don't have," she said, lifting her chin and waving a hand as if completely unconcerned by this.

Marcus hurt for her, but he couldn't deny that he believed her correct in this. He licked his lips, trying to find words that wouldn't bring her greater pain.

"You're a lovely, vibrant—"

"Too vibrant, you mean," she put in, darting a glance at him.

"In ways, perhaps," he said carefully, "not that I'd have you change for the world. It's just, you are who you are, who you should be."

"And not for you," she murmured, looking away. "Yeah, I get it."

"I'm sorry," he whispered.

She swiped a hand across her eyes, huffed a deep breath, and shot a bleak smile at him. "No apology necessary."

He wanted to cry for her, and he wanted her out of there before anything else was said that they'd both surely regret.

"It's late," he said softly, pausing to clear his throat. "You need to get home and rest."

Nodding, she rose to her feet and slowly moved past him toward the door. It was only then that he realized she was wearing a hooded purple sweatshirt with the sleeves cut out over a red T-shirt and stirrup pants tucked into yellow galoshes. He was quite certain that it hadn't rained in days; yet he found the getup strangely charming. Nevertheless, it only pointed up the fact that Nicole Archer was not the woman for him. Imagine a minister's wife who wore yellow galoshes as a fashion statement!

He walked her to the door without actually walking *with* her. When she paused and whirled around to face him, he literally skittered backward, his heart thumping.

Her gaze searching his, she quietly asked, "Aren't we going to pray?"

He couldn't believe he'd had to be reminded. "Of course! Absolutely." Bowing his head, he linked his hands together and put forth what he hoped was a pointed, eloquent prayer for peace of mind and healing, as well as guidance for those whose decisions could reunite brother and sister.

Nicole added her own spoken prayer to his, pleading for her brother's quick return home. She asked, too, that her father's alcoholism would be dealt with successfully, and she finished by thanking God for Marcus and all that he had meant to the lives of her and her brother. Marcus felt a stab of guilt at the latter. His mind was still reeling, and he was beginning to understand that he might have made a rash promise earlier.

It was much heavier of heart that Marcus returned to his solitary bed a few minutes later.

Nicole let herself into the darkened house and tiredly slung her bag onto the kitchen counter. She didn't bother to turn on a light. The dark suited her mood better, and she could navigate her childhood home with equal ease day or night, but the house now felt strangely alien, as if her presence alone was not enough to make it home. She stood a moment simply to gather her thoughts before she began the journey to her bedroom.

Two conclusions stood out. One, when she'd picked up that

phone and dialed 9-1-1, she really hadn't had any other option.
Even if she'd known that her father would pass out before he
could do Beau any further harm, she'd still have made the call.
That didn't mean she was happy with the results. She could say
the same thing about her second conclusion, which was that,
despite everything, she loved Marcus Wheeler with all her
heart.

Sadly, Marcus didn't feel the same way about her. That
much was painfully obvious, but it changed nothing, really.
No matter what he felt—or didn't feel—for her, she loved
him. Deep down, she'd known it for some time, but in the
back of her mind she'd assumed that he would discover it for
himself when the time was right. Now she knew there
wouldn't be a right time for them.

It hardly seemed to matter at the moment, but she knew
that the numbness overlaying her heartbreak wouldn't last
forever. She was right about that. After falling into an exhausted, uneasy sleep, she woke sobbing hours later. Curling
into a fetal position, she wept for every loss—her mother, her
brother, Marcus, even her father. Grief literally swamped her.
At length, she began to fear it would drown her. That was
when she began to cry out to God.

Day came. She didn't even think about getting up or going
to class. Instead, she sprawled on her face and spoke into the
mattress as if she were speaking straight into God's ear. Eventually, she began to hear—sense, really—His answer.

There was no going back from here. All she could do was
deal with what she had. Like it or not, keeping her promises
now meant dealing with the state, so that's what she would
do.

She faced a few other unhappy facts. For one thing, she
and Beau might have to live apart for some time. That didn't

mean she would abandon him. Quite the opposite. She'd work every moment for reunification, and in the meantime she'd spend every possible minute with him.

Loving Marcus was another fact of her life, unchanged by the knowledge that Marcus didn't love her. So be it. She felt how she felt; his feelings were his business. She happened to think that she'd make a fine minister's wife, so long as that minister was Marcus, of course. But what difference did it make when he didn't feel the same way? He owed her nothing, least of all an emotion he didn't possess. On the other hand, she owed him much. Not only had he done his best to help them, he'd been proven absolutely right in his arguments and warnings.

She had what she had, and she had to learn to deal with it. She came to one other conclusion, then, and this one at least gave her some comfort. What God willed, He would give her the strength and acceptance needed to live with. All she could do was to go on fighting for what was left of her family, knowing that the outcome rested solely in God's hands.

Marcus tossed and turned throughout the night, deeply troubled. No matter how he looked at it, he couldn't convince himself that following his heart was right. Nicole was not the woman for him. Oh, he could see them together well enough, with entirely too much ease, in fact, but he couldn't see Nicole as a pastor's wife.

As he'd told her, it wasn't just her youth, which time would remedy soon enough. It was her exuberance, her flamboyance, her eccentricity, none of which he would see changed. Nicole was who she was, perfect and whole as God had made her, but not right for the difficult role of a minister's wife. Therefore, it only stood to reason that she couldn't be for him. He'd known it all along.

He couldn't help asking himself what would happen to her fledgling faith after this, though. Would she blame God as her father had blamed God for her mother's death? Marcus couldn't bear the thought of that. Yet, what could he do about it?

No one could sustain another's faith. That, ultimately, was the personal responsibility of every individual. But, as an old seminary professor of his had used to say, a pastor could go a long way toward destroying the faith of another. He very much feared that he had become just such a pastor to her.

It seemed to him that whatever he did, he was bound to fail in this situation, and he supposed that was just recompense for his inability to control his wayward heart. By offering to take Beau, he had put himself into a no-win situation. He couldn't depress her hopes for the two of them and at the same time maintain a close personal relationship through his care of her young brother.

How could he bring Beau into his house and deny Nicole easy, frequent access? Yet, under the circumstances, how could he maintain any but the most cursory contact with her? He thought of the past lonely weeks when he'd tried to do just that, and something inside him shriveled with dread. It came down to this: rescind his promise to take Beau or risk becoming more involved with Nicole than was wise for either of them. Either way, his ministry suffered.

Morning came with Marcus no closer to resolving the debate with himself. He finally concluded that he would have to go outside himself for another perspective. Perhaps a female perspective was what was needed here. Fortunately, God had given him excellent resources in that regard.

As soon as it was decently acceptable to do so, he called his sisters and invited himself to breakfast at Jolie's house.

Chapter Eleven

Marcus shoved a hand through his hair. "I can't believe I let it come to this."

"Hey," Jolie said, reaching across the table to clasp his hand with hers. "You haven't done anything wrong."

"That's right," Connie added, returning to the kitchen table with a fresh cup of coffee. "All you've done is try to help and be yourself."

"That doesn't matter. What matters is what I do about Nicole."

"What do you want to do?" Jolie asked.

Closing his eyes, Marcus sighed richly and said, "The right thing." He didn't say what he wished the right thing could be.

"Do you know what that is?" Connie asked softly.

Marcus looked down at his hands. "Yes. That is, I—I think so. The real problem is that I just don't see how I can possibly take custody of Beau and derail this...this..." He couldn't bring himself to say the word *infatuation*. What he'd seen in her eyes last night deserved something more than that, which made it all the worse.

"I don't think you can," Connie said after a moment. "If you take custody of Beau, you're just going to wind up hurting Nicole even more in the long run."

"I agree," Jolie said. "Unless, that is, you *want* to encourage her."

Marcus shot her an appalled look, exclaiming, "No! No, of course I don't *want* to encourage her." At least he didn't want to want to encourage her.

"Then I think you have to back out of your offer to take Beau," Jolie said gently.

"I know that you've given your word," Connie added, "but in this case, it's only wise not to invite more misunderstanding."

Reluctantly, Marcus agreed. "You're both right. It's the only solution, but I feel so guilty because I know she'd rest easier if he was with someone she could trust, someone she's familiar with."

"Let me talk to Ovida and Larry," Jolie suggested. "I'm betting they'll offer to step in, but if they don't, I'll ask them to consider it."

"That sounds like a reasonable solution," Connie said brightly.

Marcus thought about it and really couldn't see any better answer. Finally, he nodded. "I'd appreciate it if you wouldn't say anything about my situation to the Cutlers though. I don't want to embarrass Nicole. She doesn't deserve that."

Jolie glanced at Connie before aiming an understanding smile at her brother. "Sure. Don't worry about it. I'll be very circumspect."

That, Marcus realized, was all he could really do for Nicole in this. He only hoped that she and Beau would be more enthusiastic about this idea than he felt himself.

* * *

Jolie absently rubbed her distended belly, specifically that spot where little Aaron Lawrence liked to kick his mommy. As May approached, with the baby's delivery scheduled for late June, it was getting very crowded in there, but Jolie wasn't thinking about that at the moment. What she was thinking spilled from her lips the moment Connie walked back into the room, having seen their brother on his way.

"Do you think we gave him the right advice?"

"I think we gave him the only advice, and I think he knows it, too."

"That's it, though," Jolie said, wrinkling her nose. "Marcus knew perfectly well what he had to do, yet he came to us for affirmation. Makes me wonder if he really wants to do it."

"Well, of course, he doesn't *want* to do it," Connie said.

"Yes, but what if he doesn't want to do it because he cares for her more than he wants to admit? I mean, what if she's the one?"

Connie stared at her as if she'd grown a second head. "The one? For Marcus?" Folding her arms, she pursed her lips in consideration. "I don't see it. A minister's wife must be sedate and mature. Nicole is…well, Nicole. I mean, she's adorable, but she's just not *suitable*."

Jolie leaned back, trying to ease the tingle in her rib where the little rascal had gotten in a particularly smart blow, and looked up at her baby sister. "You said that about someone else not so long ago, as I recall. You."

Connie shrugged helplessly. She *had* thought that about herself. Of course, she had. How could an ex-con—no matter that she wasn't guilty of an actual crime—be a suitable wife for an upstanding man like Kendal Oakes? Yet, she no longer doubted that God Himself had picked her for Kendal and vice versa. Still, Kendal was a financier, not a minister.

"I trust," she said, "that God will work it out. Don't you?"

Jolie smiled. "Yes. You know I do. All I'm saying is, don't be surprised if it doesn't work out like we think it should."

"I'm sorry," Marcus said, standing in the middle of her living room. "I should never have made that promise."

Nicole looked stunned. Her eyes were swollen and red, her mannerisms listless and slow. She wore drab sweats and her hair hung in a tangle down her back. He wanted nothing so much as to take her in his arms and tell her that everything would be okay, but instead he slid his hands into the pockets of his pleated slacks, cringing inwardly with shame for having gone back on his word.

What else could he do, though? He'd prayed and prayed for an alternative solution, and he just couldn't see anything between risking romantic involvement with Nicole and this difficult course of action.

"But I've already told Beau that he would be with you," she said in a small, perplexed voice.

"I'm sorry, Nicole," Marcus said again, feeling helpless. "I'm just not comfortable with the arrangement now."

"Because I'm in love with you," she surmised softly.

For a moment Marcus couldn't seem to breathe. He felt splintered, one part glad, one part appalled, one part proud, one part frightened, one part certain, one part doubting. He couldn't think what to say at first; then he simply said, "Yes."

"I know you don't feel the same," she told him, beseeching him with her gaze. "I don't expect anything from you."

Except that I keep my promise, he thought miserably. All her expectations, it seemed, were for Beau, and that almost convinced him that moving Beau in with him wouldn't be courting disaster. Then she showed him the folly of that with one whispered thought.

"Of course, if you should change your mind then—"

He brought a hand up swiftly, cutting her off. She bit her lip, and he used the hand to bracket his temples with thumb and forefinger, swallowing. "It's best if we limit our contact, I think. You and me, I mean. I want to be here for Beau. I intend to be here for Beau, but…"

"You'd rather not see me," she said for him.

Something clinched inside his chest. He looked down at his feet. "I think that's best."

Nicole sighed, walked over to the sofa and collapsed onto it. Marcus hesitated, then went over and lowered himself onto the edge of the love seat that now sat perpendicular to the end of the sofa in the middle of the living room floor. Leaning forward, he braced his elbows against his knees and clasped his hands together.

"I know you're disappointed," he said, "but we've worked out a solution to keep Beau from going to a foster home that you don't know or trust."

"We?"

"Myself, a fellow named Jonathan Bertrand, who's a supervisor at CPS, and the Cutlers."

Nicole sat up a little straighter. "Ovida and Larry?"

Marcus nodded. "They've volunteered to get themselves certified and take Beau."

Nicole swallowed and nodded. "At least I won't have to tell him that he's got to stay with strangers."

"I'll speak to him about it if you prefer," Marcus offered, but she shook her head, slipping him a glance from the corners of her eyes.

"Better let me."

"You think he'll be angry?" Marcus surmised.

"He's already angry."

"Angry with me, then," Marcus clarified.

She carefully avoided his gaze. "I—I'd just rather he didn't know about…"

Marcus swallowed, the back of his throat burning. "I understand."

She looked up sharply. "Do the Cutlers know why you backed out?"

Marcus shook his head. "No, only that Beau needs a place to stay and that you and he both would feel better if it was with someone you know and trust."

Nicole seemed relieved about that, and he was glad that he could give her that much, at least. He glanced around the living room, commenting, "You've moved the furniture."

"Yes, among other things."

"I like it."

"I still have work to do before the official home visit," she said, lifting her chin. "I called Julia Timmons first thing this morning and asked her advice about that."

"Julia Timmons?" he asked, curious.

"She's the caseworker who came by that time you called CPS."

"I see. I hope she's been helpful."

"Yes."

"I'm glad. I've felt bad about that, but maybe it was for the best, after all."

"Maybe so. I like to think that God's working everything out, you know, and that she's part of it, even though it didn't seem that way at the time."

Marcus heaved a great, silent sigh of relief. "I'm so glad

to hear you say that. I may have failed you, Nicole, but God never will."

"You haven't failed me," she insisted, leaning forward and copying his position. "It's not your fault that you don't feel the same way I do."

It was as if a hot poker prodded him. He shot up to his feet without even realizing he was going to do it. "Please don't try to absolve me from responsibility!"

"There's no responsibility to be absolved from," she declared. "It's no one's fault, Marcus. It just *is*. I would change it if I could, you know, for Beau's sake, if nothing else, but I realized a long time ago that what can't be changed has to be endured."

Endured, he thought, twisting with an emotional agony unlike any he'd ever felt before. How much was she supposed to go through in her life? That he had given her one more disappointment to be suffered was a pain that *he* would have to live with, which seemed both just and at the same time terribly unfair.

"I'm sorry," he told her. "I—I really just have to go now."

She rose to see him out. He fairly bolted for the door. Once there, though, he found he couldn't leave without offering her something in parting.

"You must know," he said, standing in her open doorway with one hand firmly gripping the knob, "that I wish you only the best." She managed a weak smile, and his chest tightened. There was a heaviness behind his face that he didn't immediately identify with tears until he turned his back on her. "You'll be in my prayers," he told her, and then he walked resolutely away.

"Goodbye, Marcus," she whispered, pushing the door closed behind him. His face was wet with regret by the time he reached his car.

* * *

The first day of May was gloriously beautiful with the kind of perfect weather that made sunlight seem crystalline and the air as soft as velvet. The vegetation had turned a green so deep and rich that it hurt the eyes, and the sky was the clearest blue. Birdsong could be heard even where there were no trees, and the great Metroplex area of Dallas-Fort Worth seemed to be at peace with itself. It seemed ironic that such a day should be the stage for one of the most horrific moments of Nicole's life.

She sat beside her brother in the small, informal courtroom and bit her lip as he threw himself facedown over the great blond table and sobbed his heart out, while the judge, a kindly middle-aged woman who wore a lace collar with her black robe, swept from the room.

"It really is for the best," Julia Timmons said gently about the judge's decision to place Beau with Larry and Ovida Cutler until Dillard was judged to be a fit parent or Nicole finished college and was employed full-time.

Short and plump and somewhere in the vicinity of thirty, Mrs. Timmons stood in her ill-fitting suit, clutching her brief-case in one hand, and offered Nicole a crumpled tissue. Until that moment, Nicole hadn't even realized that she was crying, too. All that had happened had left her so numb and drained that she was barely even aware of her surroundings anymore.

Logically, she had known that she was taking a risk by pressing for a quick decision, especially since she couldn't afford legal representation, but Beau was so unhappy with the situation that she'd felt she had no other option. It wasn't as if the Cutlers hadn't done everything in their power to make him comfortable in their home. It was just that it wasn't his home. Except that now it had to be.

Ovida was trying to comfort Beau, and he was ignoring her, ungrateful brat that he had become lately. But Nicole couldn't really blame him. Their lives had been turned upside down and inside out. She'd be angry, too, if she could muster the energy. Sighing, she leaned forward and slipped her arms about her brother's torso, tugging him back into an upright position in his chair.

"It's all right," she said softly, keeping her mouth close to his ear. "It isn't as if we aren't going to be seeing lots of each other. We're both safe, and you're getting the counseling that you need."

"I don't want stupid counseling," Beau grumbled, sniffing and wiping his eyes with the back of his hand. "What does that guy know anyway?"

"More than you think, I'm sure," Nicole told him. "Besides, it won't be that long. This semester ends in a couple weeks, and the new one starts in a month. I'll be finished by the end of the summer."

Provided I can come up with enough money to get enrolled and don't flunk anything, she added silently. Fearing this very outcome to today's proceeding, she had arranged to take more than a full course load during the short summer semester. Instead of taking the summer off to work, she would instead finish her degree early, provided she could come up with the tuition, didn't fail any of her classes and could find an internship.

It was going to be a formidable amount of work, but she dared not cut back on her hours at her job. Things were tight financially as it was. Nevertheless, there were only so many hours in a day. She didn't know how she was going manage, but she had to try, for Beau's sake. The sooner she was out of school, the sooner she could convince the court to name her as his guardian.

If she could find an internship that paid, that would help immensely. If not... She couldn't bear to think of disappointing Beau again, but all she could do was her best and trust God for the rest. Meanwhile, Beau was safe with the Cutlers, if not happy, and her father was drying out, by mandate of the court and courtesy of the state of Texas, in a hospital in Terrell. At least she didn't have to worry about him right now.

If only Beau could be reconciled to living in the Cutler home, everything would be easier, but he complained that he felt lost amongst the multitude of Cutlers and that Larry and Ovida were "too old." Worse, he'd had to change schools, so he didn't even have his two best buddies around anymore. He even complained that the Cutlers' church was too big.

Nicole knew exactly how he felt. Truthfully, she still felt like a stranger in the big Fort Worth church where she went with the Cutlers on those Sunday mornings when she could manage it. She was at fault, she knew. The services were fine, better than fine, really. She just didn't belong. She belonged where Marcus was, and she suspected that Beau felt the same way. Marcus Wheeler seemed to have left a huge hole in both their lives.

It hurt terribly that he hadn't come to the hearing today, but she shouldn't have expected it. She'd told herself not to expect it. Yet, somehow she had.

Beau didn't understand why Marcus hadn't taken him. Nicole had tried to explain that it was her fault, but because she hadn't given him any of the details, Beau was not exactly accepting of that. She didn't know what she could do about it. She didn't know what she could do about anything anymore.

Sometimes she felt like snapping at Beau that her life was no picnic, either. She hated being alone in the house. She missed him. She missed Marcus. She missed church. Oddly, she missed her mother more than before. She even missed their father.

It was so bad that at times Nicole worried that if Beau did adjust to his new surroundings, they would grow apart. Of course, she wanted him to be happy, but Beau was all she had, and she was beginning to understand that she wouldn't have him forever.

Beau would grow up. One day he'd even get married. Nicole felt suddenly as if time was running out, but how could that be when autumn still seemed so very distant?

The month of May was nine days old when Marcus could no longer stay away. He didn't dare go to Nicole, but he couldn't convince himself that he didn't bear a certain responsibility to the Archers, either. So he went to Beau.

When Ovida let him into her chintz-upholstered house, he could hear the television playing softly in the den. The Cutler siblings had banded together to purchase a big-screen set for Larry the Christmas before last, the very Christmas when Vince had proposed to Jolie, and it had become the family joke that Larry really liked to demonstrate his appreciation for that gift.

Marcus wondered if Beau found as much to like on TV as his foster father did. Apparently not, since Ovida walked him back to the boy's bedroom.

"How's it going?" he asked on the way.

She shrugged, frowning. "I know we're a couple of old fuddy-duddies compared to Nicole, but he won't even give us a chance." She sighed, adding, "Ah, well, it hasn't been that long. The counselor says some anger and bitterness is to be expected at this stage."

"I hope you know what a good thing you're doing," Marcus told her.

"Well, our intentions are good," she conceded wryly, "but we'll have to wait and see what the results are."

"God has a plan," Marcus assured her.

"He surely does," Ovida replied. "Now if we can just keep from mucking it up."

Marcus felt that he'd already done that.

They stopped in front of a closed door. Ovida tapped with her knuckle, then opened up and stuck her head inside.

"You have company, hon."

"Nicole?"

The desperate sound of it tore at Marcus's heart. Marcus knew just how the boy felt.

He hadn't been able to keep from looking for her on Sunday, even though he'd known she wouldn't be there. They must keep a certain distance, but the thought of never seeing her again was alarmingly painful. He'd tried to convince himself that in a few more weeks or months her feelings would fade and they could begin to gradually rebuild their friendship, but he didn't really believe it. He knew somehow that they would never be simply friends, which meant that they would never be anything again. That, undoubtedly, made his being here pretty stupid, but he couldn't figure out how not to be.

"Hello, Beau," he said, pushing the door wider.

For an instant, hopeful welcome lit the boy's eyes, but it quickly dimmed, leaving him sullen and resentful.

"What do *you* want?"

"Beau!" Ovida scolded mildly.

Sensing that would do more harm than good, Marcus sent her a loaded smile, asking, "Could you excuse us?"

Reluctantly, she nodded and went on her way. Marcus didn't wait to be invited in, he simply stepped into the room and closed the door behind him. It was rough going for the next hour or so.

Fort Worth wasn't so far away from Dalworthington Gardens, but it might as well have been the moon. Beau complained about school and having to leave his friends and not being able to give guitar lessons at the community center anymore. Nobody at the immense youth group at the Cutler's church was friendly, he claimed, and who wanted to watch sports all the time or play golf or dominoes or do any of the other stuff that Larry and Ovida Cutler did?

"At least my granddad played the guitar and went fishing," Beau huffed, folding his arms mulishly.

"And it doesn't matter to you at all that Larry and Ovida have opened their home so you don't have to live with total strangers?"

"They wouldn't have to if you had," Beau accused. Then suddenly tears filled his eyes.

Marcus took that as his due. He sat down next to the boy and looped an arm around his shoulders, knowing how lost and confused Beau must feel. Marcus remembered so well how he'd felt after he and his sisters had gone into foster care. The adjustment had been agonizing but unavoidable.

Yet, there had been other options for Beau. If Marcus had taken him, he could have stayed in his old school and carried on with his life pretty much as usual.

"I'm sorry, Beau," Marcus said earnestly. "I let you down."

The boy turned his face into the hollow of Marcus's shoulder and sobbed, "Why did this have to happen?"

Marcus couldn't answer that, so he talked to Beau about his own problems in adjusting to life without his mom and sisters. He spoke, as well, about Jolie's rebellious cynicism and Connie's neediness, which had landed her in an abusive relationship and, eventually, jail.

"What's that got to do with anything?" Beau wanted to know. "Me and Nic aren't you and your sisters. We're old enough to take care of each other."

Nothing Marcus said, no correlation that he was able to draw, made any difference with Beau. Finally, Marcus simply advised Beau to give his own situation time, but he could tell that didn't go over very well, either. Thirteen was too young to appreciate the fleetness of time, and Beau's judgment was heavily colored by his anger. He had a lot to be angry about.

"Yeah, I know," he grumbled. "Wait until Nicole gets out of school."

"You don't think you'll go back home after your dad gets out of rehab?" Marcus asked.

Beau just rolled his eyes. "He doesn't care about us, and I'm not giving him another chance to beat me."

Marcus couldn't blame the boy for feeling that way, but he was praying that Dillard would get sober and realize the value of being a father before it was too late. That, it seemed to him, would be best for everyone, but only God and Dillard could make it happen. Marcus chafed at his own helplessness. Right now, praying seemed to be about the only thing that he could do, and for the first time it didn't seem like enough. But it was either that or inflict his rejection on Nicole daily. Or marry Nicole and take Beau into the house with them.

He was shocked by how appealing that idea was.

Appealing but completely inappropriate.

He could see it quite clearly, the three of them in his little house, Beau in Connie and Russ's old room, he and Nicole in his. He smiled, thinking about what she must go through to get herself dressed in the mornings. How did she ever come up with those outrageous costumes?

His smile died, because though he could so easily envision making a place for Nicole and Beau in his house and heart, he couldn't see Nicole standing next to him at the sanctuary door, demurely shaking hands as people filed past them.

"How is she?" he heard himself ask, fearing that really might be why he'd come.

Beau shrugged. "How would I know? She's working and in school all the time, and when she does come over, she doesn't tell me nothing because she doesn't want me to worry. I guess I might as well get used to not seeing her, 'cause she's trying to finish up early by going to school this summer. Then in the fall, we'll get our own place."

The more he talked about that, the more Marcus realized that Beau was holding on to the picture of what he wanted the future to look like, not realizing how it resembled the past he'd described to Marcus.

"Me and Nic could go to Tahlequah," he theorized, "and live on the river. It wouldn't take much to fix up that old cabin, I bet."

Marcus didn't bother explaining how unlikely such a move would be, especially if the courts did not deem Nicole an adequate custodian for her brother. Instead, he promised to return soon, prodded Beau into joining him in a short prayer, and left before Ovida could invite him to stay for dinner.

Marcus didn't think he could handle that. He probably deserved to sit across the table from a determined-to-be-miserable Beau, but he just didn't have the heart for it.

Lately, Marcus grimly admitted to himself, he just wasn't very good at his job. But he would do better. He had to. Otherwise, what was the point in anything?

Please, God, he prayed, *help me do better.*

It had become his personal litany, and it was starting to take on the feel of desperation.

Chapter Twelve

Big whoop, Nicole thought morosely, sitting across the desk from her academic advisor. That pretty much summed up Nicole's enthusiasm about the possibility of landing one of the two—count them, one, two—paid internships remaining on the advisor's list of unfilled summer positions.

They were the same words that Beau had used about the end of the school year, which was exactly one week away. He hated the Fort Worth school, but apparently he hated the prospect of a "do nothing" summer even more.

Nicole figured Beau's chances of having an exciting summer were far stronger than her chances of landing one of those internships, but she had to try. Besides, as she'd often reminded herself lately, anything was possible with God.

"This one's a plum," the advisor said. A brusque, sixty-something woman with short, steel-gray hair and ink-stained fingertips, she slid a sheet of paper across the desk for Nicole. "It's only minimum wage, but because they have a preschool and kindergarten they offer classroom as well as day care experience. I can't imagine why it's still open, frankly. It's usually one of the first to fill."

Nicole leaned forward hopefully. Classroom and day care experience, as well as a paycheck. *Please, God,* she silently prayed. Then the words printed on the top of the page leaped out at her: First Church Pantego Day Care. She sat back with a stifled gasp, closing her eyes.

"What is it, hon? Something wrong?"

"No, um, I know that church, that's all."

The advisor reached for the phone, chirping, "Excellent! Familiarity always helps." She began pecking in numbers.

Nicole sat forward again. "Oh, uh, I—"

The advisor stalled her with a lifted index finger, her attention centered on the telephone receiver pressed to her ear. After a moment, she smiled.

"Hello, Carlita! It's Linda Marsh, with the Early Childhood Development department at UTA. Any chance you're ready to start interviewing for that summer internship? I have a candidate who says she's familiar with your program." She nodded at Nicole, conveying Carlita's answer to her question, then went back to the conversation. "Her name's Nicole Archer. You know her? Excellent!" The advisor consulted Nicole's schedule and added, "She's available Thursday afternoons for an interview."

Mrs. Marsh covered the mouthpiece with the palm of one hand and addressed Nicole. "Is tomorrow good for you?"

"Yes, but—"

"Tomorrow at three," the woman said into the telephone, jotting the date and time on the top of the sheet of paper in front of Nicole.

Nicole felt her heart sink. It was department policy not to schedule more than one interview at a time in order to give everyone an equal shot at the positions available. Since there were always more applicants than paid internships—half a dozen early childhood development students waited in the outer office at that very moment—it was only fair, but in this case it undoubtedly meant that Nicole had just lost her best shot.

"Now," Mrs. Marsh said, hanging up the telephone and folding her arms against the top of the desk as she swept her gaze over Nicole, "let's talk about the interview. Wardrobe is one of the best ways to make a good impression."

Nicole made a pretense of paying attention as the adviser droned on about what not to wear, which pretty much covered everything Nicole owned, but she was only listening with half an ear. What difference did it make when the pastor at First Church Pantego was only going to take one look at the name of the applicant and strike it from the list? Still, she reminded herself as she folded the paper and tucked it into her bag, she had to show up for the interview. Otherwise, she wouldn't get a chance at an internship next semester. Those were the rules.

Maybe Marcus didn't have anything to do with the hiring at the day care center? Besides, chances were she'd at least catch sight of him while she was there. It was embarrassing how much she missed just looking at him. Meanwhile, her hopes for finishing her degree this summer and gaining custody of her brother by fall were melting. Her only hope now was that the judge would take into consideration that the internship was just a formality and accept her finished transcript as proof of her degree.

If that didn't work, she'd file for custody when she turned twenty-one in October. That was better than having to tell Beau that it would be at least the end of the winter term before he could come home with her.

It would work out, Nicole told herself. She had to believe that God was in control of the situation. Because she hadn't found any other way to cope.

* * *

Marcus laced his fingers behind his head and leaned back in his desk chair, smiling at Nina Upconn, or "Miss Up," as the day care staffers fondly referred to her. Marcus could never be sure if the nickname referred to her cheerful attitude or the short, dishwater blond hair which always stuck up somewhere, giving one the impression that she'd fallen out of bed the very moment before meeting.

At thirty-nine, Nina was not a Miss. Indeed, she was married and the mother of two teenagers. She was also a cheerful improvement over the last director of the day care center, whose negative attitude toward his niece, Larissa, and her admittedly challenging problems had led to a mutually agreed upon departure. Given, Nina wasn't the most efficient director the day care had ever enjoyed, but she was beloved by all, which was why Marcus tended to cut her a good deal of slack.

"I know I should have taken care of this already," she was saying about the hiring of a summer intern, "and I do appreciate you helping to expedite the matter by agreeing to simultaneous interviews."

"No problem," Marcus replied.

The usual routine was for the day care director to interview prospective interns on her own, weed out those she didn't like and arrange for Marcus to interview the front-runners. Then the two of them would make the final selection together. This way would work just as well, though.

They'd interview the prospects together over the next two days, compare notes and make a firm decision by Monday. With seven applicants so far, it made for two full days of interviews, but Marcus didn't mind. He'd always preferred keeping busy. More so now than ever. It helped keep his mind off other things. Like Nicole.

Why, he hadn't thought of her in, oh, maybe half an hour, Marcus realized ruefully. He'd begun to accept the fact that she would always be in his thoughts, but that brought him uncomfortably close to questioning God's intent. Or his own interpretation of it. As much from habit as conviction, he pushed the thought away and concentrated on the job at hand.

The two morning interviews went well enough if one discounted an irritating habit of smacking gum and a bad case of spring allergies. The first applicant after lunch was the lone male in the group. He was obviously more interested in the business end of things than the healthy development of children, but Marcus commended him for taking an in-the-trenches approach to learning the field before turning him down flat.

Then Nina handed Marcus the résumé for the next applicant and his heart stopped. For long minutes, he couldn't think, let alone digest the information printed on the sheet, but he didn't have to. He knew everything relevant there was to know about Nicole Archer.

True to form, she'd taken a unique approach to selling her abilities. The résumé was printed on vivid yellow paper with purple ink and a border of baby dolls and toy fire trucks against a background of rainbow stripes. Marcus quite liked it. The whole situation had a feeling of inevitability about it, and in one blindingly stupid and shockingly impulsive moment, he decided that if she walked in wearing anything approximating a normal outfit, he'd hire her on the spot.

She came in wearing red overalls, a tie-dyed T-shirt, candy-cane-striped socks and those ridiculous yellow galoshes, her hair up in pigtails. He could have wept. Instead he surprised himself by laughing and that seemed to put her at ease.

The happiest hour he'd known in weeks passed in the blink of an eye, and he knew Nina was going to pick Nicole before it was half over. He didn't have the heart to gainsay her, though he tried to talk himself into it that night, praying long and hard about the matter.

Friday's interviews were mere formalities. Marcus left it to Nina to inform Nicole of their decision and sternly told himself that his contact with her would be severely limited. He suspected even then that he lied. On Sunday at church, Nina informed him how ecstatic Nicole had been, and he couldn't help smiling at the day care director's description of the scene.

"I thought she was going to fly right out of the room. She sprang up on her tiptoes and threw out her arms. 'Thank God!' she exclaimed." Nina chuckled and then she sighed. "Now all Nicole has to do is scrape together four hundred bucks to cover the cost of her books." Nina shook her head, revealing a patch of hair that stuck out at a forty-five degree angle from just below her crown. "That sweet kid. Do you think we could use the two hundred dollars we have remaining in our scholarship fund to help her? I know it usually goes to a graduating high school senior, but I think need should trump age, don't you?"

Marcus reached into his pocket for his wallet, nodding in agreement. "Here's the other two hundred," he said, marveling at how impulsive he'd become of late. It was his personal benevolence fund, the money he kept on him specifically for those in need whom he came across in the normal course of things. "Just don't tell her it came from me personally."

Nina literally snatched the cash from his hand, beaming ear to ear. "I like that kid!" she exclaimed. "I can't wait to work with her."

Me, too, thought Marcus. *Me, too.* Yet, he'd never stood on more dangerous ground ministerially.

Or was it that things were finally going right? Had he been

wrong about this all along? Was that why God had suddenly thrust her back into his life like this?

He'd prayed repeatedly these past weeks that God would remove his feelings for Nicole and bring him someone else, someone more suited to his position, and he couldn't figure out why that wasn't happening. He was trying to be patient about it, and really, in an odd way, he was in no hurry.

He'd come to realize that his feelings for Nicole would not be easily dismissed, and some part of him so treasured those feelings that he was reluctant on several levels to let go of them. Yet, he sincerely wanted God's will in this. Anything less would be sheer disaster. He just didn't know anymore what God's will was.

He wasn't as certain now as he had once been that Nicole wasn't who God intended for him.

True, she didn't fit his idea of what a minister's wife should be, but was his interpretation of what God wanted in a minister's wife truly God's ideal? Or was it something he, Marcus, had made up from assumptions and arrogance? He didn't know anymore.

What he did know was that God is not a god of confusion. He never sets out to perplex and frustrate His children. Besides, Marcus seemed to have done that well enough all on his own. Perhaps it was time to forget his assumptions, set aside certainty and simply wait for God to make His will known.

Marcus felt something then that he hadn't even realized he'd been missing for a while. Hope.

Nicole slipped the sales receipt into her wallet and picked up the shopping bag with the heavy textbook inside. This was the last one, and the only one she hadn't been able to find as a used book. Still, she had $7.74 left over, enough for a ticket to the movie matinee this afternoon and a treat from the concession stand. Beau could pay his own way with the allowance that the Cutlers were giving him from the monthly stipend they received from the state.

Nicole wished nothing but blessings on Larry and Ovida Cutler. Instead of using the rest of the state money to pay Beau's living expenses, as it was intended, they had opened a savings account for him, calling it his college fund. How Beau could remain so ungrateful and downright bratty she didn't understand, but so far as Nicole was concerned things were finally looking up.

Not only had Marcus not blackballed her, she'd landed the internship *and* a scholarship from the church to help buy her books for the semester. She'd already started the part-time job and loved the work, especially as it meant she saw Marcus every day.

Oh, it was only glimpses, to be sure. They hadn't actually spoken, and she didn't expect that they would. It was easier, frankly, if they kept their distance. Once she started classes again, on the first Monday in June, exactly one week from today, she wouldn't have very much time to think about him, so it was a good thing that she'd be carrying such a heavy load. Yes, she could definitely see the hand of God at work.

If only Beau could be happier about his situation, she could face the grueling summer ahead with an almost light heart, but he wouldn't even try. As she drove them both to the theater that afternoon, she remarked that they had never used to go to the movies. Beau grumbled that he didn't care about that, though he seemed to enjoy the movie itself well enough. Still, he whined when she dropped him off at the Cutlers' house.

"You're juicing me, Nicole. Don't you see that?"

Nicole sighed. "How have I 'juiced' you, Beau? Where's the betrayal in this? Things are going according to plan, if you haven't noticed."

"Something will mess it up," he grumbled, yanking on the door handle. "We'd be better off in Oklahoma."

It had become a recurrent theme with him. They could run off to Oklahoma, live in their grandparents' tumbledown old cabin and hide from the state of Texas indefinitely. How he expected them to support themselves, let alone get him enrolled in school, was something he dismissed out of hand. Shaking her head, Nicole watched him trudge up the walk to the Cutlers' neat, boxy house. Ovida appeared in the doorway. Nicole waved and drove away, determined to be optimistic.

When she pulled into the driveway at home, she was struck by something odd. Her father's old rattletrap truck, which still sat nose-in almost against the garage door, seemed to be parked a few inches farther to the right than she remembered, but she dismissed the notion at once. The thing couldn't have moved by itself, after all.

Since it was warm out, she left the car parked next to the truck and let herself into the house through the front door, carrying her purse and the heavy textbook in its plastic shopping bag. She dumped everything on the kitchen counter and went to the refrigerator for a drink of cold water from the pitcher that she kept there during the warmer months.

The pitcher was empty. Only her father ever emptied the pitcher without refilling it before returning it to the refrigerator. Her heart skipped a beat, and that was when he spoke.

"You moved my furniture."

Nicole jumped and whirled around. Her father stood in the

doorway to the hall, leaner than she'd last seen him and cleanly shaven. She clapped a hand to her chest, trying to still her galloping heart. One part of her was pleased; another was horrified.

"Daddy."

Dillard folded his arms and put his back to the door frame. "Long time no see, Nicole."

She ignored the razor sharpness of his tone. He was her father. She wanted to be glad to see him. "You look well."

"No thanks to you," he said bitterly. "Do you have any idea what they put me through? Does it matter to you that I have a record now?"

"Daddy, please," she began. "I had no other choice."

He threw up one hand, exclaiming, "No other choice but to have me arrested! How's that?"

"You took a belt to Beau!" she pointed out.

"I didn't know what I was doing," he argued, as if that were an excuse. "And he wasn't even hurt. I asked, and they told me he had some bruises." He mimicked someone else then, saying, "'But that's not the point. Sobriety is the number-one goal.' They made me out to be some kind of monster!" He pointed a finger at her. "You made me out to be a monster. This is all *your* fault."

For the first time in a very long while, she lost her temper. "This is *your* fault, Daddy! I didn't pour alcohol down your throat and put a belt in your hand!"

"No, you called the cops!" he roared. "Now your brother's living in some foster home, and I'm branded a child abuser for the rest of my days! How do you think your mother would feel about that, Nicole Suzanne?"

"No better than she'd feel about you drinking yourself into oblivion and abandoning us!" she threw back at him.

"I never abandoned you!" he roared.

"Yes, you did!" she shouted right back. "Every time you opened a bottle and crawled inside it!"

He looked stunned, as if she'd struck him, but then his anger hardened into resolve. "Well, then," he said, suddenly as cold as he'd been hot the moment before. "You sure as shootin' don't want to be sharing a house with me."

Nicole felt the air leave her lungs in one sharp *whoosh*. "What do you mean?" He couldn't mean what she thought he did—except that he did mean it, of course.

He folded his arms again, saying calmly, "Your brother's not here and not likely to be for some time, so it seems to me you don't have any right to be here, either."

"You're throwing me out?"

He hung his thumbs in his pockets and glared at her. "Isn't that what you did to me? Or tried to. But you forgot that this house and everything in it belongs to me."

She stared at him, barely able to believe it. "You're throwing me out." It was a statement this time, a statement he didn't refute.

After a long moment while the world turned upside down, Nicole numbly picked up her purse and the shopping bag. She saw the rest of her textbooks sitting in a neat stack on the kitchen table. She lurched over to them, gathered them up and turned blindly for the door, knowing that whatever happened this would never again be her home.

Her impulse was to go straight to Marcus, but the moment she realized where she was heading, she turned the car in another direction. Realizing that it would be upsetting to Beau, she didn't even consider going to the Cutlers in her present state. Instead, she just drove around until she could get hold of herself. It was some time before she could even begin to think rationally. When she passed a gas station, she realized that she was wasting precious fuel and pulled over. Calming finally, she tried to take a dispassionate look at things.

It shouldn't have surprised her that her father had come home. She'd been told that the program to which he'd been sent would last four to six weeks. It was thirty-five days since that awful night, exactly five weeks.

She had expected that he'd blame her. Yet, for some reason she'd convinced herself that once he was sober he'd actually be reasonable again. The anger was still there, though, and she'd begun to realize that until he dealt with his anger toward God, he would never be able to face life. That was one lesson she supposed she ought to thank him for teaching her. At the moment, however, she was having a difficult time thanking him for anything.

Pushing away the hurt of his rejection, she rubbed her forehead and tried to take stock of her options. They were extremely limited. In the end, she went to her friend Kattie.

Kattie, short for Katrina, was a server at the same restaurant as Nicole. Two years older, she'd worked for a while before starting college and was able to afford a small studio apartment in an aging building near the campus in Arlington. At various points in the past, she'd tried to convince Nicole to share a larger apartment with her, but Nicole had always refused because she'd had Beau to worry about.

Kat was surprised to see her. Nicole didn't often stop by. As soon as she heard her story, Kattie offered to let Nicole camp out with her. She only had a twin bed to sleep in and was locked into a lease for another five months, but she offered Nicole her broken-down old couch. Nicole took it. What else could she do?

She couldn't bring herself to impose further on the Cutlers. They hadn't taken both Beau *and* her to raise. Going to Marcus was out of the question. Besides, she found that she didn't want anyone else to know what had happened just yet. Beau would have to know eventually, of course, but at the moment she was too embarrassed to talk about it. She was embarrassed for her father, embarrassed for herself and embarrassed for Beau. What kind of people lived the way they did?

It was time to live a different way. From now on, she determined, life would be lived on her terms. That meant with some dignity.

She wished she'd thought to pack some personal items before she'd walked out of her old life, but Kattie loaned her what she could. Kat's long, bone-thin frame didn't correspond too well with Nicole's shorter, shapelier one, but Nicole couldn't make herself go back to the house and beg her father for her own things.

For starters, she was afraid of what she might find. If her dad was drinking again, she didn't want to know. If he wasn't, that could be even worse. It was easy to justify and excuse the behavior of a drunk, not so easy to dismiss the considered words of a sober man.

She could make do. She was good at making do. Besides, she found much to be thankful for in this. At least she didn't have to worry about Beau. He was safe with the Cutlers, safer even than he had been with her. Meanwhile she would pray that her father would come to the Lord and keep going forward. She'd stick to the plan and trust God to work it all out. That, she realized, was what her mother would want her to do. One day, even Beau would see that the Lord God never abandoned His own.

* * *

Marcus stood outside the classroom door and peeked through the window set into the top half of it. Nicole sat cross-legged on the floor, holding a picture book open on her lap, while a scattered group of four-year-olds listened spellbound to every word she read. Suddenly feeling a presence at his side, Marcus stepped back, tempering his smile. Nina Upconn folded her arms knowingly. It wasn't the first time she'd caught him watching Nicole.

"Pastor," she said.

Marcus cleared his throat. "How is she? I mean, how is she doing?"

"Still doing fine," Nina told him, the glint in her eye said that she saw more than he wished her to.

He fought against blushing and adopted a caring, paternal tone. "She seems different lately. The clothes, I think."

"Mmm, more subdued," Nina concurred. She waggled an eyebrow. "Not her usual style."

So Nina had noticed, too. Well, of course she had. Who with functioning eyeballs wouldn't?

"Any idea why?" Marcus asked, faintly troubled.

Nina shook her head. "None. She just suddenly started wearing jeans and white T-shirts every day. Occasionally she wears something a little more colorful, but now that I think about it, it's always the same two or three things."

"Grass-green shirt, bright yellow tank," he said.

"Mmm-hmm, and once in a while a purple paisley print skirt."

"Sometimes she wears them all together," Marcus noted, smiling at the thought of her in yellow and green over purple paisley.

"And sometimes mixed with jeans and the white T-shirt," Nina confirmed.

"But always with the red shoes," Marcus murmured.

It was as if she only had the two outfits, but Marcus knew better than that. He'd never seen Nicole in the same outfit twice before the past couple of weeks. He knew because everything she wore was utterly unforgettable. Even now.

He wondered if he should speak to her about it, but the very thought made his heart pound and his palms sweat. It had been that way for some time, so he kept avoiding her, afraid of what he might say if he didn't.

"I've noticed you're dressing normally for a change. What gives?" Very endearing.

Or how about, *"I'm praying that I've been an idiot and misinterpreted God's will, but I'm still waiting to find out"?* Yeah, that would take care of everything.

Of course, he could always just declare the truth. *"I'm very much afraid that I've fallen in love with you, too. Now I'm trying to figure out what to do about it."*

He just wasn't ready for that. Yet. And he didn't know if he ever would be. Better to keep his mouth shut, which meant keeping his distance. Problem was, he didn't seem to be doing that very well, either, judging by the number of times he found himself standing where he was at the moment.

Even as Marcus took his leave of Nina and walked back to his office, he mused that it hadn't been so very long ago that he'd begged God for a wife, and now he was afraid to even think the word *wife*. Because when he thought about marriage, his next thought was invariably of Nicole. Maybe that was his answer. He just didn't know.

Whatever the answer was, Marcus was starting to think that God would have to smack him upside the head with it. Otherwise, how could he ever know that his own desires were not leading him astray?

* * *

"How've you been?" Marcus asked, keeping his tone bright.

Beau barely acknowledged his presence, shrugging as he picked out a desultory tune on the guitar. Stifling a sigh, Marcus tugged on the legs of his slacks and sat next to the boy on the sofa in the Cutler den. Ovida and Larry had gone into their bedroom and shut the door to give them privacy. Marcus didn't waste any time beating around the bush.

"Ovida and Larry are worried about you, Beau. You should have made the adjustment by now. Can't you see that they're doing everything they know how?"

Beau slammed the guitar down on the cushion beside him and slumped back. "I don't want them to do anything. I just want to go live with my sister!"

"Everybody understands that, Beau."

"Nobody understands anything!" Beau declared in a strangled voice. "Not even Nicole! We were always going to get our own place anyway, so why not now?"

Marcus shook his head. "You know that isn't reasonable, Beau. Even if the court would allow it, Nicole can't afford—"

"But she's already got her own place!" Beau complained, folding his arms sullenly. "It's supposed to be with me, but instead she's moved in with someone else, and she says they don't have room for me."

For a moment Marcus couldn't do anything but stare at Beau. What he'd said just didn't compute. "I don't understand. Why would she move in with someone else?"

"She can't stay at the house with Dad," Beau told him, spreading his hands.

Marcus caught his breath. "Your father's back?"

Beau glanced at him worriedly. "Yeah, and he's been coming around here, even though he's not supposed to."

Marcus blinked. "I see." And he really was beginning to. Nicole was wearing the same two outfits all the time because that's all she had to wear. He wondered if Dillard had even given her a chance to pack a suitcase before he'd tossed her out. He was on his feet before he even realized he'd meant to be. "I'm sorry, Beau," he said. "I have to go."

Beau threw up his hands. "Go on," he said. "What do I care?"

He cared. Marcus saw it in his eyes. "I'll be back soon," he promised. "Just try to be patient a little longer."

"But what if they give me back to him?" Beau whispered, his greatest fear revealed.

Marcus wanted to tell him that wouldn't happen, but he couldn't. Instead he said, "Everything's going to work out. You'll see. God has it all under control."

Beau snorted. "That's what Nicole always says."

"Does she?" Marcus smiled to himself. "Well, she's right. Maybe you should start listening to her."

Maybe they should both start listening to her.

Chapter Thirteen

"I have something for you," Marcus said. "Could you come by the house when you're through here?"

Nicole bit her lip. She'd counted on having an hour or so to read before class, but it wouldn't be the first time she'd gone to class unprepared lately. Besides, it wasn't like Marcus to seek her out, let alone invite her over to his house. It had to be something important. She nodded and glanced over her shoulder at the children on the playground.

"I'm done here at noon."

Of course, he'd know that. He smiled, nodded and walked away before she could ask what was going on. She supposed she'd find out soon enough. Part of her was thrilled that he'd taken this step; an older, wiser part knew better than to get her hopes up. Marcus was a friend, nothing more. She turned back to the children in time to stop a particularly precocious little boy from jumping off the top of the jungle gym.

The rest of the morning passed in a blur. Nicole was dimly aware that she wasn't firing on all cylinders lately. The lack of sleep was getting to her. The long hours at school, the longer hours on her feet waiting tables and the all-too-fleeting ones when she tried to study didn't leave much time for sleep. The utter lack of privacy and the uncomfortable sofa at Kattie's didn't help, either. Some mornings it was all she could do to drag herself out of bed in time to get to the day care center by six.

She yawned as she climbed the few steps to Marcus's front porch. The door opened before she got to it, and Marcus stood there looking at her with what felt like mild rebuke.

"What?" she asked, stopping where she was.

He waved her in, saying nothing as he turned away from the door. She followed, curious and now a little timorous. Was she in some sort of trouble? If so, she wasn't sure she could handle that.

He led her into the living area or, rather, to it. The space was filled by a number of large boxes, *familiar* boxes.

"My things!" she exclaimed, turning to him with a dozen unspoken questions.

"You should have told me," he scolded mildly, bringing his hands to his hips.

She shook her head. "That he put me out? What good would that have done?"

Marcus lifted a hand as if it should be obvious. "You'd have had your clothes for one thing."

Nicole looked around her again, touched but troubled. What did she do now?

"Marcus," she said, "I appreciate this. I really do, and God knows I'll be glad to have something else to wear, but I don't have anyplace to put this!"

He blinked at her. "What do you mean? Don't you have a place to stay? Beau said—"

"I have a place to stay," she answered quickly, "but it's tiny, just a studio apartment. I don't even have a closet of my own." She flapped an arm helplessly. "I can't take all this. Kattie would have a cow!"

"Katie is your roommate?" he ventured.

Nicole nodded. "It's her apartment."

"Ah, so she gets all of the closet?"

"What there is of it."

"Well, that is a problem," he said, folding his arms and lifting one hand to grasp his chin between thumb and forefinger. He shrugged. "Guess you'll have to leave it here."

"Oh, like you've got room for it."

"It can go in my garage. It was in your garage, I mean, your father's garage, until last night."

"Are you saying you have room for it in there?" she asked hopefully.

"For now. I don't put the car inside unless it's cold and wet. It's too small."

Nicole frowned. "Well, I guess I don't have a choice at the moment. I'll have it out before winter, I promise, even if I have to rent a storage locker."

"Don't worry about it," he told her. "Just take what you need for now, and the rest will be here when you're ready for it."

Nicole nodded, sudden tears welling into her eyes. She gulped. "Thank you for this, Marcus. I was afraid he might destroy everything or give it away."

"I don't think so," Marcus mused. "Oh, he seemed angry, yes. Gruff, certainly. But…I don't know…hurt, too, I think."

"Was he drinking?" she asked warily.

"I don't think so, but we didn't talk long. I told him I'd come for your things, and he led me straight to the garage, then he went back into the house, and that was it. I knocked on the door to tell him that I'd have to go borrow my brother-in-law's pickup truck to get everything, but he ignored me. He didn't answer the door again when I went back, so I helped myself and left again."

Nicole considered the information. "Larry Cutler doesn't think he's drinking, either. My dad's been going over there, trying to see Beau. Of course, the Cutlers haven't let him, but it worries Beau all the same."

"I know."

"Do you think he can get Beau back?" she asked worriedly.

Marcus bowed his head. "I don't know. Maybe. Not right away, though."

"How long do you think we have?"

He shrugged. "Six months, maybe. Don't hold me to that, though."

"Six months," she whispered, thinking that she'd be out of school and more gainfully employed by then. She closed her eyes in a quick prayer.

"I can ask," Marcus said, "try to get a better idea for you. I have friends at CPS, you know."

"Would you?"

"Absolutely."

"Oh, thank you, Marcus. For that and this." She flipped a hand at the boxes. Then she looked him in the eye and said what had needed saying for some time. "And thank you for the internship."

He shook his head. "Now that wasn't my doing. Nina does the hiring at the day care center."

"With your approval," she said. "Nina told me."

He inclined his head. "You were the best candidate. Nina saw that. I agreed."

"You didn't have to agree," she argued softly.

"Yes, I did," he responded simply.

Nicole looked away. No doubt he thought he owed her somehow, just because he didn't feel for her what she felt for him. It was nonsense, but she didn't argue with him; she was too grateful. Instead, she looked over the boxes, deciding which one to look in first. That was when she realized there were more boxes than there should have been.

"These two don't belong," she said, pointing out two smaller ones she'd never seen before.

"Funny you should say that," Marcus commented, "because I could swear those two weren't there the first time I looked in the garage."

"But they were when you came back with the truck?" she asked.

"Right."

Nicole shifted one of the boxes and opened it. Only moments were required to recognize the contents of the dresser and closet in her bedroom. It looked as if her father had dumped the dresser drawers one by one, but some care had been taken to create order with what had come from the closet. She was somewhat surprised. Dillard had never put himself out this much for someone else since her mom had died. Nicole sat on the floor, considering, but then she shrugged. What difference did it make? She had only to remember what had happened the last time she'd trusted that he'd changed.

Marcus crouched next to her. "Something wrong?"

"Nope." She indicated the two boxes from her bedroom, saying, "I'll take these two. They'll fit in the back of my car."

Marcus shifted, grasped the first box in a bear hug and rose. "If you'll give me your keys, I'll come back for the other in a minute."

"No need," she said, getting up to gather in the second box herself. "We'll get these in the car, then I'll help you move the rest out to the garage."

"Deal."

They carried the boxes out and stowed them in the tail of her hatchback. They just fit, which meant that her much-a-bused little car had now become a rolling closet. She just hoped it didn't become a closet broken down on the side of the road. Lately the engine coughed more than it chugged, but since she couldn't do anything about it, she elected to put it out of mind.

After helping Marcus shift the boxes from his living room to his tiny garage, she checked her wristwatch and saw that she just had time to get to class.

"I have to go," she said, heading back into the house.

"No time for lunch?" he asked, following on her heels.

She looked back over her shoulder in surprise. "No. Not today. But I hadn't planned on taking time to eat anyway."

He stopped her with a hand on her arm as she moved around the kitchen counter and toward the entry. "What had you planned on taking the time to do?"

"Read," she answered shortly, moving away again. "I'm behind. But I'm sure I'll catch up."

"Nicole, I'm sorry," he apologized, coming after her. "I didn't mean to usurp your time like this."

"It's all right, Marcus," she said, pausing long enough to smile at him. "Those things out in your garage belonged to my mother and grandmother. It's worth it to know they're safe."

"They'll be here when you're ready for them," he told her again, "and it doesn't matter when that is."

"Thank you, Marcus."

He shook his head. "I'm just glad to help. I want to help, you know."

"I know."

The fact that he hadn't brought Beau to live with him didn't change that. That Beau wasn't with Marcus now was her fault, not his. She understood, even if Beau didn't, that Marcus had only done what he thought best in that situation.

Marcus always did what he thought best. Sometimes she disagreed with him, but she couldn't fault him for following his conscience. It wasn't as if he just did the easy or convenient thing. He hadn't kept her from getting the internship, after all, and he certainly could have. Now he'd saved her things for her.

Where Beau lived at the moment would be a moot point, anyway, if the court sent Beau back to their father. She gulped, afraid to think what might become of Beau if that happened.

It wasn't that she didn't want to believe her father had quit drinking for good—nothing could please her more—but unless she was there to know for sure, how could she rest easily once Beau was back in that house with their father? Provided, of course, that Beau could even be persuaded to go back.

She very much feared what Beau would do if told he'd have to go back to live with his father. He'd taken off once already, and he talked a lot about how easy it would be for the two of them to get away now, openly advocating that they do so.

She prayed that Marcus was right about it taking six months or more for the courts to make a decision. Maybe by then she'd have a fighting chance to persuade everyone that she was the better guardian for her brother. If not... *If not* was too worrying to even think about.

* * *

Marcus found her the next morning sitting out in the empty playground behind the day school during her morning break. Perched atop the picnic table sheltered beneath the dubious shade of a pin oak, she had a textbook opened on her lap. She wasn't studying, however. Instead, she was staring off into space, her elbows resting on the knees of her folded legs.

Marcus noticed that she was wearing neon pink flip-flops and khaki capris under what appeared to be a straight, sleeveless, flowered sundress. She'd twisted her hair up on top of her head. Sort of. A great deal of it was falling down in wisps that floated around her face. He couldn't help smiling.

"Finally catching up on that reading?"

"What?" She turned her head to look at him, surprise quickly shifting to delight. "Not so you'd notice," she amended wryly, closing the textbook and laying it aside.

"Can I sit down then?"

"Sure."

She scooted closer to the edge of the table as he stepped over the bench. Straddling it, he sat sideways, the white elbow of his shirtsleeve resting on the edge of the table. He could see the question in her eyes.

"I talked to my friend at CPS."

She leaned back, bracing her upper body weight against her stiffened arms, palms flat against the tabletop. "And?"

He hated to give her this news, but she needed to know, and he'd rather do it than leave this difficult job to someone who might not try to reassure her.

"Your father's filed to regain custody."

She sat up straight. "Already? It's too soon, isn't it? Surely they'll need more time to figure out if he's going to stay sober."

Marcus nodded, reaching for her hand. "That's what Jonathan said. No one's rushing to judgment, Nicole. They want to be as certain as they can be that Beau will be safe with him. The thing is, though, he's likely to get visitation pretty soon."

Nicole caught her breath. "Beau isn't going to like that."

"I understand," Marcus said, squeezing her hand with his, "but he may not have a choice. Don't worry, though, the visitation will be supervised, at least in the beginning."

"You don't understand," she said, blinking rapidly. "Beau's liable to do something foolish when he hears this."

"Beau's already been foolish, if you ask me," Marcus commented, "not that you did. I just wish he wouldn't punish Ovida and Larry for how this has all turned out."

"I know." She stretched one leg over the bench where he sat and slid it to the ground before standing, adding, "especially when it's all my fault."

"It is not," he refuted instantly, rising to follow her as she wandered over to put her back to the trunk of the tree, her arms folded, head bowed. "None of this is your fault. How could you even think it? You've devoted your whole life to your brother's welfare since your mother fell ill. You know you have."

She swiped at her cheek with one hand, brushing back a strand of hair. "But I'm the one who called the police that night."

"You had no choice."

"But I'm still the one who did it," she insisted, digging her toe in the dirt. "And he blames me. I know he does, just as he blames me for him winding up with the Cutlers."

"We both know *I* am the one to blame for that," Marcus stated firmly.

She shook her head. "No, you wouldn't have had to beg off if I hadn't put you in a difficult spot." She sniffed, and that's when he realized she was crying.

He curled his fingers beneath her chin and tilted her face up. The tears streaming from her eyes clutched at his heart. He didn't know what possessed him to do it, but somehow it seemed like the only thing to do. He pulled her into his arms, and then she was sobbing against his shoulder.

"Hey, don't. Shh. It's all right."

"I—I know," she whispered brokenly. "I keep trying to count my blessings, you know, but I just feel so alone!"

"You're not! You're not," he assured her, holding her close.

She gulped, sniffed, and gulped again. Then she pulled back slightly and looked up at him.

There it was again, that look that always hit him like a sledgehammer. It humbled him, the love that he saw there behind those damp, spiky lashes, a love so strong that it could forgive anything: loss, abandonment, broken promises, dashed dreams.

The next thing he knew he was kissing her and her arms had stolen up around his neck.

He had never felt such trust, such rightness, and he was mentally kicking himself for everything he'd thought and said and done right up to this moment when she suddenly jerked away, clapping a hand over her mouth.

"Marcus, I'm so sorry!"

"Sorry," he echoed stupidly, the world whirling to a stop around him. She covered her face with her hands, and he tried desperately to marshal his thoughts, babbling, "No, no, I take full responsibility. I was—"

Kissing her. He'd been kissing her. He could hardly believe it.

"I don't know what happened!" she exclaimed.

He frowned. How she could've missed it, he didn't know, but just in case she had, he told her. "We kissed."

"I know that! I just don't know, er..." She closed her eyes, color flooding her face. "Marcus," she pleaded, "c-could you please just go away!" She turned her back on him then and bowed her head against the tree. "Please," she whispered.

He stood there for a moment, uncertain what to do or say. Then he realized that he was reaching for her and snatched back his hands. He racked his brain...and couldn't think of a thing to say. It was as if that single kiss had emptied his head.

After a moment, unable to think of anything else to do, he spun on his heel and walked away, straight through the building and out onto the covered walkway that led to his office. Every step of the way, he asked himself what he should do now.

Marry her.

As before, the thought rocked him right down to his socks. This time, however, it brought with it only a sense of certainty and relief, so that when he finally reached his office, he closed the door and went straight to God.

He'd already prayed about this until he was sick of his own thoughts, but he had no need to ask God to take these feelings from him now and no reason to think that he should. What he had need of now was confession, an apology even.

"Forgive me, Father. I just didn't understand. I admit I've been an idiot. It was my birthday. I asked for a wife, and Nicole walked through the door." He laughed, elated and appalled and hopeful and wary all at the same time. "It just seemed too easy. I—I guess I made it so difficult because... that's how my life's been." He closed his eyes. "I'm sorry. I should have known. What difference does it make how she dresses or how old she is in years when there's such goodness and sweetness and beauty and..." He spread his arms, looked up to the ceiling and said humbly, "Thank You."

After a moment, he walked around his desk, stood in front

of his chair and took a deep breath before letting it out again and sitting down. So now what did he do?

Ask her to marry him, yes, obviously. Or, more accurately, *convince* her to marry him. He didn't doubt for a moment that's what it would take at this point because no matter what he said now, after what he'd said before, she was going to think that this was about rescue, about making up for not taking Beau when he should have.

He shook his head. That kiss hadn't been about rescuing anyone, but he wasn't sure she'd realize that. She thought that kiss was her fault! As if fault even needed to be assigned.

No, he couldn't have her thinking that he would marry her out of pity or a misplaced sense of responsibility or for any other reason except that he loved her and she was the woman God had made for him. Nicole deserved better than to think— or to have anyone else think—that any man would marry her simply as an altruistic gesture.

So how did he convince her? He shook his head. Oh, man, if ever he'd needed a female perspective, he needed one now.

He was still trying to figure out how to explain this all to Jolie when he arrived at her house in west Fort Worth. He hadn't even bothered to call first or even to explain to Carlita where he was going when he left the office. He did ring the bell, but impatience quickly got the better of him, so after a moment, he simply opened the door and walked in, thanking God that she was obviously home.

"Jolie? Jo?"

Just as he got to the end of the entry hall, he saw her coming through the den toward him, her enormous belly leading the way. She looked ready to pop, though her due date remained almost three weeks away yet.

Jolie took one look at him and demanded, "What's wrong?"

"What's wrong?" He threw up his arms. "I'm an idiot, that's what's wrong! Correction. I *was* an idiot. Now I've got it figured it out. Mostly. Sort of, anyway. The thing is, how do I convince her?"

"Her?" Jolie echoed. Then she smiled. "I take it we're talking about Nicole Archer again."

"Who else?"

"Who else, indeed." She slid one supportive arm under her belly and placed the other hand on the top of it before turning to waddle back toward the couch and collapse upon it. "Okay. So what happened?"

"I kissed her," he announced, moving to stand in front of her. "To be perfectly fair, she kissed me, too."

"And since you don't want to marry her…" Jolie began, only to fall silent when he shook his head.

"I *do* want to marry her."

"But you don't think you should?" Jolie ventured carefully.

"I know I should," he corrected smoothly. "Like I said, I was an idiot before."

Jolie blinked. "I see. And the problem now is?"

"Exactly what I said. How do I convince her?"

"She needs convincing, does she? I thought she was in love with you."

"She does. She is. At least I think she is." He frowned, considering. Then he smiled, nodding. "Yes, she is, I'm sure of it. The problem is, after what I said before, she may not believe me when I tell her that this isn't about me feeling guilty and trying to fix all her problems. Although I do and God knows I would if I could."

"Well, why don't you then?" Jolie asked.

"Fix everything, you mean?"

"Sure, if you can."

He sat on the coffee table in front of Jolie. "I'm not sure I can now. It may be too late."

"You won't know until you try, will you?"

He leaned forward, wrapping his arms around as much of his sister as he could manage. "I love you," he whispered, "and that's one lucky kid in there. One very large kid." Grinning, he sat back again.

She made a face. "I love you, too, and I think we can safely say he takes after his father."

Marcus laughed. "At least sizewise."

"Let's hope in more ways than just the one," Jolie commented. Then she tilted her head. "Before you go running off to fix Nicole's world, can I ask you something?"

"Anything."

"Why are you so convinced you should marry her now? Before you didn't seem to think she would make a proper minister's wife."

"What *is* a proper minister's wife, Jo?" he asked. "Do you know?" She shook her head. "Neither do I," he admitted. "Maybe there isn't any such person. Or maybe it depends on the minister."

Jolie smiled. "That sounds right to me, but what about your congregation?"

"I don't know," he admitted, "and I'm not sure I care."

The truth was, he liked Nicole exactly as she was, naive exuberance, ridiculously flamboyant clothing and all. He could see himself all too easily at seventy, shaking his head over some outrageous pink-lamé-and-flowered-nylon nonsense. And loving her all the same. Because that was the fact of the matter.

He loved Nicole Archer. He loved everything about her, her devotion and her determination and her sweetness and her faith in God—and in him.

He should be so selfless, so slow to condemn and blame, so quick to forgive and excuse. Maybe the minister could learn something from that "unsuitable" young lady, such as not to jump to conclusions and be so quick to assume that he knew the mind of God.

Maybe his congregation could learn from her, too, if they'd just give her half a chance. Somehow he thought they would. In fact, he was pretty ashamed for not having realized it sooner. The congregation had never been the problem; it was always him.

But that was the past. The future was Nicole, and he had a pretty good idea now how to prove it to her, though it was going to take divine intervention to make that happen. Well, he knew Who to ask for that.

Marcus rose, bent to place a kiss in the center of his sister's forehead and straightened. Jolie winced and pressed a hand low against her belly.

"Something wrong?" Marcus asked, frowning.

"Yeah, I'm nearly eight-and-a-half months pregnant, and your nephew's dancing on my bladder," she cracked. She let her head fall back against the couch. "Only a couple more weeks to go!"

Marcus smiled. "Hang in there, sister mine. You'll be a mommy before you know it."

"I just have one favor to ask," she said. "Don't get married until after the baby comes. I simply cannot attend a wedding like this."

Marcus laughed and started for the door. "No promises, sis." He looked back over his shoulder and winked. "But I'll see what I can do."

"I'll say a prayer for you!" she called as he opened the door.

"Ditto!" he returned as he stepped through the doorway.

He closed his eyes and did just that. He'd like a healthy nephew brought into this world right away, please, and a wedding as soon after as he could manage it, but he'd settle for a solution to Nicole's problems.

Her happiness mattered more to him now than his own or anyone else's. And he knew who held that key. Whether or not he could pry it out of Dillard Archer's stubborn fingers was up to God alone.

Chapter Fourteen

"Someone to see you, hon."

Nicole looked up from her position on the floor, where she sat drilling a circle of four-year-olds on the alphabet via a game with flash cards. Beau stood in the doorway next to Millie, whom everyone referred to as "the gatekeeper" at the day care center. No unknown person got by Millie without proper identification or, apparently in this case, a very long face.

Nicole knew immediately that she wasn't going to like whatever was going on, starting with how her brother came to be standing in her classroom. Then again, this hadn't been the best of mornings so far, anyway. She hadn't slept well last night, despite being dog-tired. She just couldn't get that ridiculous kiss out of her head.

She still couldn't believe she'd kissed Marcus yesterday. Talk about dumb. Whatever she said or did after this, he was going to assume that she was throwing herself at him—and she wasn't entirely sure he'd be wrong.

Casting a wary look at her brother, she rose to her feet,

ruffled a couple of heads and asked, "Thank you, Millie. Can you watch this bunch for me? I'll be as quick as I can."

"Take your time," Millie said, moving into the room and leaving Nicole to shepherd her brother out into the hallway.

"What's wrong? How did you get here?" she demanded at once.

Beau shook his head, hissing, "We don't have time for that. We gotta go! We don't have a choice now."

Nicole folded her arms, saying, "You're not making sense, Beau. I can't leave. I'm working here. Then I have a class this afternoon and work again tonight at the restaurant. Now how did you get here?"

"I hitched a ride," he told her shortly, insisting, "I had to!"

"Beau! Ovida's going to be out of her mind. You can't just take off like this!"

"Dad came to the Cutlers' this morning," he said anxiously, grabbing her forearm. "He said he's going to get me back, no matter what. Then the caseworker called. He's going to get visitation, Nic. What's to keep him from taking off with me?"

Nicole leaned against the wall, momentarily closing her eyes. She'd known this would happen. "It's supervised visitation, Beau. You won't be alone with him."

"I don't care! It's the first step in sending me back to him. I heard what the caseworker said to Ovida. I was listening in on the telephone, and don't tell me I shouldn't have because I had to. Nobody tells me anything."

"That's not true."

"Yes, it is! Please, Nic, let's just go now before it's too late!"

"Had Dad been drinking when he came by this morning? Was he hungover?" she asked.

"I don't know! I didn't talk to him. Larry didn't think so,

but what if he stays sober just long enough to convince a judge to send me home again? What then?"

"That's a long way off, Beau. I know because Marcus looked into it. I'll have my degree well before Dad can regain custody. We can take off as soon as I graduate, if we have to."

"Let's just go now," he pleaded, "and you can finish your degree next semester the way you originally planned, just not here."

"It's not that easy to transfer, Beau," Nicole told him. "Now come on, we have to call Ovida and let her know you're safe." She took him by the arm and started down the hallway.

"No!" He planted his feet and yanked his arm free. "We have to get away before anyone finds out!"

"Beau, we've discussed this. I can't just pick up and leave everything I've worked so hard for now."

Beau folded his arms mulishly, muttering, "I thought you cared about me. I thought you were going to take care of me."

"I do! I am! But the best way to do that is to finish my education, get a good job and—"

"You care more about that dumb degree than you do about me," he accused.

"I do not! How can you even think that?"

"Just forget it," Beau said, turning away.

"No." She caught him by both shoulders and physically turned him back the way they'd started. "You're coming with me. We're going to talk to Marcus. Maybe he can convince you. But I'm telling you right now that we're going to be sensible and responsible and do all the right things. Do you hear me, Beau Leonard Archer? We're going to do this the way *Mom* would want."

That seemed to take the fight out of him, at least momentarily, but just in case, she didn't take her hands off him as she marched him down the hall, out onto the walkway and next door to the administration building. Even after they pushed through the heavy glass door into the outer office, she kept one arm around him.

"Hello, Carlita. We'd like to see Marcus, please, and would you call Ovida Cutler to let her know that Beau is safe with me?"

"Sure thing." Eyeing Beau with blatant curiosity, the plump secretary buzzed Marcus on the intercom. "Nicole's here."

Marcus appeared mere seconds later, a smile on his face. "Hi. You must've been reading my mind. I was just wondering—" He broke off when he realized that she wasn't alone. "Beau. This is a pleasant surprise." He glanced at Nicole, who had a hard time meeting his gaze.

She'd give anything if she could take that kiss back. Except that it was likely to be the only one they'd ever share and it had been rather nice. Oh, this wasn't helping at all!

"Maybe you'd better come into my office," Marcus said, and Nicole nodded.

They followed him, Nicole prodding Beau to get him moving. Marcus perched on the edge of his desk and waved the two of them down into the pair of chairs facing him.

"What's up?" he asked without preamble.

"You know that possibility we were discussing yesterday morning?" Nicole asked.

Marcus looked from her to Beau and back again. "I think so, yes."

"Well, Beau's heard it, too, and he did just what I was afraid he'd do. He took off."

"Ah." Marcus laid a fingertip against his nose.

"My dad's going to get custody of me!" Beau erupted. "And Nicole won't do anything about it!"

"That's not fair," Nicole and Marcus said at the same time.

Surprised, she looked at Marcus, only to find him looking at her. He switched his gaze back to Beau and bent forward slightly, bracing his hands on the edge of the desk beside his hips.

"Beau, I've never seen a sister as devoted as Nicole is to you. She's killing herself to graduate a semester early just because you don't like temporarily living with two perfectly nice people like Ovida and Larry Cutler."

Beau folded his arms and slumped until his chin was pressed into his chest, broodingly silent. Marcus sighed and shrugged apologetically in Nicole's direction.

"This isn't right, Beau," he went on. "You should be doing everything you can to ease your sister's mind, not worrying her like this."

Beau just folded his arms tighter and sank lower in his chair.

"Save your breath, Marcus," Nicole said, casting a look at her brother from the corner of her eye. "He wants what he wants when he wants it, and nothing else matters."

Beau grimaced and pushed up straighter in his chair again. "I just don't want to go back with him," he muttered.

"Not even if he's stopped drinking and is willing to do whatever it takes to put his family back together?" Marcus asked, looking at Nicole.

"Will he?" Beau mumbled, sounding half hopeful and half scornful.

Marcus switched his gaze back to the boy. "I don't know," he admitted. "Maybe someone should ask."

Nicole considered that. "I'm not sure it's a good idea. He can say anything now, but what's to keep him from starting to drink again once Beau's home with him?"

"What's to keep him from snatching me and disappearing?" Beau demanded.

Nicole couldn't quite imagine that. Their father had never shown that much interest in either of them. She didn't know if Beau was genuinely afraid of being abducted by his father or if he was using it as a scare tactic to try to get his own way.

"Has Dad said something to make you think he would do that?"

"You don't think he'd do it just out of spite?" Beau demanded. "What's to stop him?"

Nicole turned to Marcus, worried now. "Maybe it's time he left the Cutlers, went someplace where Dad wouldn't know to look for him. Could you arrange that with CPS?"

"No!" Beau cried before Marcus could answer.

Confused, Nicole sat back. "But if you're frightened—"

"I'm not going to strangers! You promised."

"With me, then," Marcus offered.

"Oh, I don't think that's a good idea at all," Nicole hedged. "I—I mean, nothing's changed that kept us from doing that to begin with."

"Everything's changed," Marcus said.

If he really thought that, though, then he was mistaken. Nicole knew better, and after what had happened yesterday, so should he. Before she could find a diplomatic way to point that out, Beau flatly announced, "I'm staying where I am."

Exasperated, Nicole threw up her hands. "What is this? First you can't wait to get out of there, and then you're staying no matter what!"

"At least I know what to expect there," Beau muttered, ducking his head.

"What's best for you, Nicole?" Marcus asked. "Where do you think he should be?"

Nicole sighed. "I'll never know for sure he's safe unless

I'm with him no matter where he is. At this point it would almost be easier if we could just both go back home, like before."

Beau stiffened beside her, but Marcus ignored him, asking, "Is that what you want?"

She glanced at Beau before admitting, "Not really, no. I mean, it's going backward, isn't it?"

"What *do* you want?" Marcus asked.

"A place of our own," she answered immediately, "somewhere safe. To be able to pay the bills. That's all."

Not all, she admitted privately, but it would have to do.

"Really?" Beau asked, turning toward her.

"That's what I've been working for all this time, Beau," she pointed out.

Beau looked down, seeming to think about that.

"I'd still like to speak to your father," Marcus said, "unless you object, not only to assess his intentions but also to let him know that there's someone else on your side."

Nicole thought about that. "I'm not sure he'll talk to you."

"Can't hurt to try. You never know. He might be reasonable at this point."

"Marcus," she said. "I know you want to help, but this isn't your problem."

"Oh, I disagree," he countered. "It's very much my problem."

"I don't see why."

He glanced at Beau, shrugged and said, "Still, I want to try to make him understand that it's best for you to care for Beau. If he's willing to let you, then maybe there's a chance to heal this family."

"I don't suppose it would hurt to know exactly where he stands," she said at last, "but frankly I don't hold out much hope that he'll listen to you."

"At least I'll have tried," Marcus said. "We can then go on from there."

Carlita tapped on the open door then and stuck her head into the room. "The Cutlers are here."

"Already?" Nicole said in surprise. "I didn't mean for them to come after him."

"I couldn't reach them by phone," Carlita explained. "Apparently they figured this is where he would go and had already started out."

It made sense. "Tell them we'll be right out, would you?" Nicole said.

Carlita nodded and left.

Nicole looked to her brother, prodding gently, "Beau."

Sighing dramatically, he got up and dragged himself toward the door. "Fine. Just remember what you said."

"About us getting our own place?" she clarified. "I haven't forgotten and I won't."

"We already *have* a place. You know, Grandpa's cabin," Beau said, "and we're going there when you graduate. Aren't we, Nic?"

"We'll see. I have to have a job, Beau. If it's not there, we'll find someplace."

Beau frowned, but he didn't argue, just set his jaw mulishly and went out to face the Cutlers. Nicole rose to go with him, but Marcus stopped her with a hand on her wrist.

"Before you leave, can I at least ask where you're living?"

"I'm staying with a girlfriend right now, but it's just temporary."

"I mean that I'd like the address."

She crooked up one corner of her mouth in a wry smile. "You already have it. I submitted a change of address right away. It's on my employee record."

Marcus nodded, shamefaced. "Nicole," he began, "about what happened yesterday—"

She winced and shook her head. "Let it go, Marcus, please. To tell you the truth, I've got enough on my mind just now without getting into that."

He subsided reluctantly. "All right, if that's what you want. For now."

Nodding, Nicole didn't tell him that if they never mentioned that kiss again it would be too soon for her. The last thing she needed was to humiliate herself like that again.

She also didn't mention that she could foresee a time and a circumstance when taking off with Beau might be the wisest course, but only if it began to look as though their father might actually regain custody. Until then, she'd stick to the plan, such as it was.

True, she was practically living out of her car—Kattie simply didn't have room even for the few things Nicole had taken from Marcus's—but at least she had a place to sleep. It was awkward, but she didn't think Kattie would toss her out, especially since she was paying a good portion of the rent now.

Meanwhile, Dillard had to know that if he had any hope of regaining custody of his son, he'd have to toe the line. She had to trust that. She had to trust that God wouldn't put her brother back into a dangerous situation without her being there to protect him. And this time she'd do a better job of it.

She turned toward the door, saying, "I have to see Beau off and get back to work."

Marcus didn't try to stop her again, and she told herself that she was glad. But glad or not, it was undoubtedly for the best. She just wished that for once what was best was not also what hurt most.

* * *

Marcus worked hard to cover all his bases before the week's end. He spoke to Jonathan at Child Protective Services again and then to a family law attorney recommended by his brother-in-law Kendal, who had arranged cross-adoptions for his and Connie's children.

He even convinced Beau's therapist to speak with him, shamelessly claiming the position of Beau's pastor. Since he'd recommended Beau for the denominational counseling service, he wasn't questioned on that. The psychologist was too ethical to give Marcus specific information, but he agreed that Marcus's proposal would be beneficial for Beau and willingly signed an affidavit to that effect.

Marcus had to wait for the attorney to draw up the necessary papers, and that was the most difficult part of his plan, but he used the time to pray diligently. Specifically, he needed to be very certain what he should say to Dillard Archer. He didn't want to threaten Dillard if he could help it. He had to consider the man's immortal soul, after all.

It was important to make Dillard understand that his best chance of healing his family was in letting Nicole take on responsibility for Beau. Marcus meant to help her do that by proving to the satisfaction of the courts that she wouldn't be shouldering that responsibility alone. Even if she wasn't convinced that marrying him was the right thing to do, he intended to make a commitment to her and Beau on paper. Financial support, legal support, emotional support, spiritual support—whatever it took.

Of course, Dillard could fight them in court if he chose, but Marcus intended to stack the deck against him by every legal and ethical means at his disposal. The optimum solution would be for Dillard to willingly choose what was best for his family.

Only then could he even begin to win back the trust and devotion of his children. Marcus's most solemn prayer, however, was that in making such a choice, Dillard would open his heart to God. True healing could come from no other source.

The restaurant where Nicole worked was one of a popular Mexican food chain that stayed open from 11:00 a.m. to 11:00 p.m. on Saturdays. Nicole spent almost every minute of those twelve hours on her feet. The tips, fortunately, were worth it.

Exhausted, she managed to drag her aching body back to Kattie's apartment before midnight, thanking God that it was on the ground floor of the aging building. She hadn't even taken time to change out of her work uniform, and once she reached the apartment she simply crashed on Kattie's lumpy couch in her black pants and white shirt. Kattie came in around three in the morning from a night on the town with some of the other girls from work. Nicole woke just enough to pull a pillow over head to block out the light and went back to sleep.

Bleary-eyed, she tried to make herself get up and dress for church when the alarm went off, but she just couldn't manage it and fell back asleep. She woke suddenly, sitting up on the sofa, half-dressed but somewhat refreshed. A glance at the clock told her that morning services were already underway. An urgent knock at the door revealed why she'd awakened at all.

Kattie mumbled from the bed, "You're closest, you have to get it."

Nicole got to her feet, wearing her wrinkled shirt from the night before and a chiffon skirt she'd put on for church when she woke earlier, and went to the door, expecting some chum of Kattie's. She did *not* expect to find Larry Cutler standing there. For a long moment, she wasn't sure that she just wasn't imagining Larry's broad, stocky form, wire-rimmed glasses and thinning gray hair. Then he spoke.

"We tried to call but figured the phone must be off the hook."

A sound had Nicole looking over her shoulder at the bed. Kattie gave her a sleepy, apologetic shrug as she groped for and found the cordless telephone receiver beneath the bedcovers.

"Sorry," she said, punching a button and dropping the receiver back into its charger.

A deeper concern had taken hold of Nicole, though. She looked back to Larry, who seemed distinctly uncomfortable standing there beneath the second-story balcony. Sheer terror threatened, pushing the fog from her sleepy brain.

"What's happened to Beau?"

"I guess that means he's not here," Larry deduced, frowning.

"Not here?" Nicole echoed, stepping closer. "Isn't he with you?"

Larry rubbed his furrowed forehead, saying, "He wasn't in his room when I went to get him up for breakfast, and we figured he most likely came here to you."

Panic sweeping over her, Nicole blurted, "I haven't seen him!"

"Where else would he go?" Kattie asked, tugging Nicole's attention her way again. She was sitting up now, holding a pillow to her chest. Shoving short, streaky brown hair out of her face, she asked, "Do you have any idea where to look?"

Nicole closed her eyes, imagining the worst. "What if Dad grabbed him? Beau's been afraid of that."

"I don't think so," Larry said. "The CPS caseworker came by yesterday afternoon. Apparently Dillard's doing everything they're asking of him. He's enrolled in parenting and anger management classes, and he's taking unscheduled tests every few days to prove that he's not drinking. Why would he do all that unless he planned to regain custody legally?"

Nicole beat back her surprise, sharpening her focus on the most pertinent facts. "Did Beau hear that?"

"Yeah, but I can't say he was reassured," Larry admitted dryly. "Kept saying that he didn't care and didn't believe it. He was so rude at one point that Ovida sent him to his room. Later, when I went in to say good-night, it was obvious that he still had a burr in his blanket. He doesn't trust your father, and I don't blame him, but it's not entirely rational. The counselor keeps saying to just give him time, but I'm not so sure that's going to work, frankly."

"Beau is more like Dad than he would care to admit," Nicole murmured, thinking. "Has anyone contacted Marcus? Maybe Beau went there."

"Marcus is in the middle of services," Larry pointed out. "We did try, but he'd already left the house, and his cell went to voice mail. We called Austin, that buddy of Beau's, but his mom says they haven't seen him."

Well, that about covered it. There could only be one other place where her stubborn, willful little brother would head, and Nicole knew as well as she was standing there that he'd taken off for Oklahoma on his own. He'd probably been planning this as a backup if she wouldn't go with him.

Of course! She snapped her fingers. That's why he'd been so desperate to stay with the Cutlers after these months of complaining about it! He wasn't reconciled to the familiar. He'd wanted to stay because he knew that he could get out of there whenever he wanted to. He'd proved that already by slipping away once before and hitching a ride to the church in Pantego. Now he was trying to get to Oklahoma. The little goof was forcing her hand.

"I think I know where he's headed," she said, turning back to Larry. "In fact, I'm sure of it."

"Where? Just tell me where. Better yet, come with me," Larry urged, holding out a hand to her. "Show me the way. We'll bring him back together."

Nicole stared him, her mind whirling. If they tried to drag Beau back here, he would hate them all, and next time he ran away, it wouldn't be to Oklahoma. Next time she wouldn't have a clue where he'd gone or any way to protect him.

Besides, what if their father did regain custody? That was looking more and more likely all the time. Even if by some chance she could be convinced that Beau would be safe with him, Beau would never be, not without a lot of hard work on her father's part. And one thing Dillard wasn't known for was hard work.

Whether he was forcing her hand or not, she had no choice but to follow Beau and try to make the best of it. Even if what awaited in Oklahoma turned out to be as difficult and unpleasant as she feared, she saw no other way now.

Maybe it was always going to come to this anyway. As badly as she hadn't wanted to admit it, she was falling farther and farther behind in school. Two jobs and a heavier than normal academic load were just too much for her under the present circumstances.

She thought of Marcus and knew that the farther away she was from him the better. What had happened the other day just proved it. Staying around would only leave her open for additional humiliation and rejection. She just didn't think she could take any more rejection.

Finally, she shook her head. "No. I'm sorry, Larry, but no. This is something I have to do myself."

Larry frowned, obviously troubled, and seemed to sink in on himself. "Are you sure?"

Suddenly she saw him as Beau might, aging and gray, his once-solid frame shrinking, sagging, his hair thinning and no longer dark. He was still a man to be trusted and admired, but he must seem as old as the hills to her thirteen-year-old brother, and certainly no match for their father who, despite his drinking, was twenty years younger and a bigger man.

She thought with longing of the possibility that her dad really was trying to turn his life around. He was doing what the courts said he must, in order to be the father he hadn't wanted to be before. But even if he did everything that everyone asked, it would be a long time before they could trust him again, if ever. Beau especially.

"This is the best way," she said firmly, "maybe the only way."

Mr. Cutler shook his head, saying, "I don't like the sound of this."

Nicole smiled with rueful understanding. "I know," she told him softly. "I know. But don't you see? It's out of our hands now."

Larry stared at her, his craggy face softening to resignation, and she knew that he understood what was happening here. "Ovida's going to be upset, but you've always had a good head on your shoulders. We know you'll do what's best."

"I'm sorry that we've been such a trial."

"It's just that we care so much."

"I know, and thank you," she told him with heartfelt sincerity. "You and Ovida have been wonderful to us ever since Mom died, and I'm more grateful than I can tell you. But you've done all that you can. Please try not to worry, and say a prayer for us, won't you?"

"Of course," he said. Then, "You'll be in touch?"

They both understood that this was goodbye. "As soon as I can."

He stood there for a moment longer before sliding his hands into the pockets of his khakis and turning away. Nicole closed the door and began gathering up her things, determined to find her brother and make sure that he was safe even if it meant turning her back on everything she'd worked for here.

God knew she couldn't have kept on the way she'd been going much longer anyway. Her weary, aching body told her that much. Besides, catching up with Beau was going to take the rest of the day, provided the little knucklehead had done what she thought he had. She wouldn't give up all hope of graduating just yet, but taking care of her little brother was her top priority. School would just have to wait.

She began to silently pray that Beau managed to make it to Tahlequah. Hitching a ride to Pantego from Fort Worth was one thing; making it all the way to northern Oklahoma was something else. Yet, she felt certain he would make it.

If she got to Tahlequah and he wasn't there, she'd be forced to call the police, but not yet. She'd done that once before and Beau still hadn't forgiven her. Besides, every instinct she possessed told her that he'd had carefully laid plans in readiness for some time now.

As she hugged Kattie goodbye and threw her few remaining things into the car, she told herself that she was doing the right thing.

Of course, Ovida or even her father might call the police. Even if that happened, though, she and Beau had a good chance of getting where they were going without being caught. After that…well, it was all up to God, anyway.

With a heavy but resolute heart, she stopped at the first ATM she came to and cleaned out her bank account. Armed with that and nothing more than a tall cup of coffee obtained via a drive-through, she set out.

By the time she reached Interstate 35 and aimed north, she was weeping, her thoughts having turned to all that she was leaving behind. She thought of the Cutlers, her friends at school and church and the day care center, neighbors, even her father. She thought of the diploma that wouldn't be hers at summer's end, family photos she might never see again, the house where she had grown up.

Most of all, she thought of Marcus, who had been so appalled at her unthinking declaration of love and yet had tried in every way possible to help her. She would never stop loving him, so it was undoubtedly best that she put as much distance between them as she could. As long as he was near, she would just keep embarrassing herself as she had twice already.

If she wasn't going to be near him, she might as well be in some tumbledown old cabin on the Illinois river outside of Tahlequah as anywhere else, not that she expected to stay there. The place was a mess, and her father would surely think to look there for them at some point. Until then, they'd be together, and eventually they'd find a safe place. And she would have kept her promise to her mom.

Maybe in a few years when Beau was older and no longer subject to the vicissitudes of Child Protective Services they could come home to Texas again. Maybe not. What would be the point anyway?

She wiped her eyes and looked forward resolutely. From

now on she would only look to the future. There was nothing to be gained by looking back.

"God has a plan," she said aloud, more desperate than ever to believe it, more determined than ever to yield to it.

No matter that it wasn't the plan she had thought it to be, her job as a child of God was to sublimate her desires to His will. Marcus had taught her that, and her mother before him. She wouldn't falter now just because her heart was breaking. She would see this through, and somehow she and her brother would come out on the other side, better than before, stronger than before, wiser than before.

And happier. She had to believe that, now when she had never felt so bleak.

"God has a plan," she whispered again, praying that losing her little brother as well as everyone else who had ever meant anything to her, including Marcus, was not part of it.

Chapter Fifteen

After many hours of prayer, Marcus had put himself to sleep on that Saturday night only to awaken in the black hours of Sunday morning with the rarest sort of pure and certain knowledge blanketing his mind. God had once again made wisdom from foolishness.

All this time that he'd been struggling against his own assumptions and calling it God's will, God had been preparing him. His own failures and faults had become the pathway to understanding, hopefully not only for him.

It was all so clear now. He'd begged God for a helpmate and then been quite sure that the only woman who truly delighted him could not possibly be the answer to his prayer. She hadn't fit his carefully constructed vision of what God intended, so he'd fought not to be affected, no matter how often or unmistakably God had thrust her into his path. There she'd been all along, the answer to his every desire, and he'd done his best to push her away. How stupid could a man be?

Just thinking of Nicole made him smile, and he never felt more firmly grounded, more sure of himself, more truly the man he wanted to be than when he was with her. It was afterward that he'd always started to question and assume and doubt.

He hadn't been just a fool; he'd been an ungrateful fool! In truth, the only difference between him and Dillard Archer was the saving grace and unbound wisdom of Christ Jesus, and because of that Marcus knew now what to say and how to say it.

Only Dillard could make the decisions that would set everything right, of course, for God so valued the personal choices of people that He would not violate their gift of free will. Now Marcus could only do his part and trust God to soften Dillard's heart. Hopefully, with weeks of sobriety behind him and time to think, rattling around in that empty house by himself, Dillard would be at his most receptive.

His mind full of the words he would say, Marcus had gone back to sleep, enjoying a truly untroubled rest, and risen early to meet his morning's obligations with a cheerful heart and calm assurance. Standing in the pulpit now, he looked out over the congregation and saw that Nicole wasn't there. He was disappointed but philosophical.

Perhaps it was for the best. This day's work must be done with finesse and dedicated concentration, and she could turn his mind to butter and his mouth to mush as no one else could. Besides which, he knew he'd have a difficult time keeping his intentions to himself, and he didn't want to disappoint her if he failed.

He greeted every congregant and shook every hand with smiling patience, knowing that Godly obligations must come first in any scheme. Once the building was empty, he left David to lock up and ran home to change into casual clothing before heading off to his sister's as expected, Connie's this time, this being Jo's monthly Sunday with the Cutlers. He no sooner walked through the door of Connie's magnificent home, though, than she thrust the telephone at him.

"Call Jolie's cell. She needs to talk to you. And it isn't the baby, I've already asked."

He never got to dinner. Connie had it on the table by the time he'd spoken with Jolie, Ovida and finally Larry, but Marcus couldn't have choked down a single bite by then. Not only was his stomach tied in knots, he knew that God had made other plans for this day.

"I'm sorry, sis. I have to go," he said, handing the cordless telephone to his bewildered brother-in-law and turning to hug the kids in their highchairs.

Larissa ignored him, busy as she was trying to feed Russell in his high chair, who in his laid-back fashion as usual, was perfectly content to allow her to do so. They were beautiful children, Larissa with her curls and Russ with his flame-red hair.

"Marcus, I couldn't help overhearing," Connie said, stripping off her apron. "Are you sure about this?"

"Going after Nicole? Absolutely. But I have something I have to do first."

Connie stared at him for a moment, standing there in her lovely home with her tall, quiet husband at her side, a worried expression on her face. "Jolie saw it first," she said, "but I'm not sure I really believed you were in love with her until now."

"Believe it," he said.

"It doesn't seem to fit," Connie murmured, "but God always knows best." She glanced meaningfully at her husband.

"How right you are," Marcus said.

She smiled and came to him with open arms. "Be happy."

He would if everything worked out the way he hoped. "Pray for me," he said, hugging her tight before he went out.

Half an hour later, he was standing on Dillard Archer's doorstep. Dillard didn't seem pleased to see him; neither did he appear particularly surprised. Without a word, he backed away, left the door standing open and turned to go into the living room. Marcus took that as an invitation and followed, closing the door behind him.

The first thing he noticed was that Dillard had left the furniture the way that Nicole had rearranged it. The second was an open book facedown on the seat of the recliner. Dillard picked it up and laid it aside, but not before Marcus had seen the title and recognized it as popular layman's work on the science of addiction.

"Might as well sit," Dillard rumbled, waving a hand desultorily as he dropped into his chair.

Marcus took a seat on the sofa and crossed his legs.

"I guess you're going to tell me what a jerk I've been and how this is all my fault," Dillard grumbled. Marcus inclined his head, spreading his hands, but before he could say anything, Dillard went on. "Well, don't bother." He looked away, snapping, "Don't you think I already know?"

Surprised, Marcus cleared his throat and leaned forward. "Okay," he said slowly, "now that we've established your responsibility in this whole fiasco, what are you going to do about it?"

Dillard turned sad, agonized eyes on him, muttering, "Everything I can, but you don't know how hard it is. My kids hate me, and I want to just drink that away!"

"They don't hate you," Marcus told him. "They're *afraid* of you, and *not* drinking is the only way to change that."

Dillard rubbed his chin, thoughtfully. It was cleanly

shaved, Marcus noted, and the hand that rubbed it was steady and strong.

"Even if Beau could forgive me," he said in a deep, thick voice, "Nicole never will."

"I think you might be surprised," Marcus told him.

Dillard snorted at that. "Why should she? I've done nothing but make her life harder." He looked away, adding softly, "And all she ever did was make mine easier. I never knew how much I depended on her."

"She's the dependable sort," Marcus said with a smile, "dependable, caring, smart, forgiving. She's forgiven me more than once, and I didn't even have to ask."

"You?" Dillard retorted, frowning. "What does she have to forgive you for?"

Marcus smiled wryly. "Believe it or not, sir, you and I have made some of the same mistakes where your daughter is concerned. We've both underestimated her, to our detriment, and she's the most loving, forgiving person I've ever known. Oh, and beautiful. Did I say beautiful? Not to mention unique, determined. Unforgettable, really."

Dillard's mouth twisted, but then he rubbed the hollow of his temple with a forefinger. "Figures it would be you," he said. "I always knew someone would look past that crazy wardrobe of hers someday. I just didn't expect it to happen this soon. Then again, she's mature for her age."

Marcus chuckled. "She sure is, which is why I intend very soon to ask her to marry me."

Archer flattened his mouth, but then he sighed morosely. "She really won't be coming home then."

"If she does," Marcus said, "I hope it won't be for long."

Dillard nodded, the motion heavy with resignation. After a moment, his gaze grew pensive. "She's just like her mom, you know. Suzanne was my rock, and after she was gone, Nicole became the only person in the world I could depend on, including myself. I don't know what I'd have done without her. Drank myself to death, I guess. Instead of taking care of her and her brother as I should have, I just tried to drink away my pain and let her deal with everything." He narrowed his eyes. "I don't know when it changed, when the drinking became the pain and not the remedy. Now I've lost them all," he said bitterly, "my whole family."

"I said I want to marry her, not take her away from you," Marcus pointed out dryly.

"Same thing," Dillard mumbled, "even if I have already blown it."

"No, it's not the same. And all Nicole needs is a reason to trust you and some time. I'm sure of it."

"What about the boy?" Archer asked in a gravelly voice.

"That may take a little longer," Marcus warned.

Dillard tucked his chin in disappointment, asking, "And what happens in the meantime?"

"If everything works out as I hope," Marcus told him forthrightly, "Nicole and I will marry, and Beau will live with us."

"I see."

"Until you can prove to everyone's satisfaction that you're capable of being a father again," Marcus added pointedly.

Archer sat up very straight, both feet firmly planted on the floor, his hands gripping the arms of his chair. "Do you really think I can?"

"Yes, Mr. Archer, I do."

Hope sparked in his eyes. "Might as well call me Dillard," he mumbled, obviously turning the possibility over in his mind, "if we're going to be related."

Before Marcus could point out that their hoped-for future

relationship was far from guaranteed, the other man suddenly drilled him with a very direct gaze. "How?" he demanded. "How can I get my family back?"

Marcus paused before saying, "Are you asking the man who wants to marry your daughter or the pastor?"

A muscle began to quiver along the lower ridge of Dillard's jaw. He looked down at his hands. "Maybe both," he said in a strained voice, his brow furrowed.

Marcus decided that it was time for a gentle prod. "Aren't you tired of being angry at God?" he asked softly.

For a moment, Dillard glared at him, but then a sort of weariness seemed to come over him, a tacit agreement with Marcus's assessment. "When my wife was sick," he said wearily, "I begged, I bargained, I raged. And Suze kept telling me, 'God will heal me, Dill. It just may not be in this world.' And I thought, what good is that? I just couldn't see any reason or hope in that." He shook his head. "But lately I've been thinking about something a fellow said to me in rehab. I was too mad to really think about it then, but—" he waved a hand "—I've had some time since, you know?"

Marcus nodded his understanding. "And what did this fellow say, Dillard?"

The other man leveled his gaze. "He said maybe I couldn't find any comfort in that because deep down I was afraid that I wouldn't be joining her in the other world where she's well."

"It doesn't have to be that way," Marcus said. "Because God's always willing to forgive."

"Even me?" Dillard rasped with acute hope.

Marcus clasped his hands together, momentarily bowing his head. *Thank You, God! Thank You!* When he lifted his gaze once again to the man whom he very much hoped would be his father-in-law, tears of joy stood in his eyes.

"Even you."

* * *

Marcus found her as the sun sank low against the horizon, trudging alongside the narrow road that wound through the craggy hills east of Tahlequah, dressed in a fluttery ankle-length skirt of orange organza and a white shirt that looked as if she'd slept in it. Since he'd passed her old car broken down on the side of road some miles back, he wasn't surprised, only relieved.

She stopped where she was, holding her long, dark hair up off her neck with one hand and looking so tired and bedraggled that he wanted to cry for her. Instead, Marcus put the car in park, got out and took her into his arms.

She leaned into him, asking wearily, "How did you find me?"

"Your father gave me a map." He felt her stiffen. "Come on," he said, moving her toward the car. "I'll explain as soon as we find Beau."

She let him help her into the passenger seat, then looked up at him with tears in her eyes. "What'll I do if he's not at the cabin?"

He brushed her hair back from her face and smiled. "Aren't you the girl too wise to cross bridges until she comes to them?"

"I'm not smart enough to stop and think," she scoffed in a trembling voice, "let alone wise."

"Oh, yes, you are," he told her, "wiser than you know. Now, how much farther?"

By her estimation, they were within ten miles of the cabin. According to the odometer on the dash, it was less than eight. Marcus turned where she told him and eased the car down the narrow, overgrown trail to the edge of the bluff, where the cabin perched, overlooking the Illinois River below.

It was a pretty pathetic sight. The roof had fallen in on one side, and the glass was broken out of the visible windows. The front door appeared to be missing. Its best feature was a familiar guitar stacked atop a familiar backpack on the ground-level porch right next to the space where the door should have been.

Nicole was out of the car and calling for her brother before Marcus had shifted the transmission into park. The boy appeared in the open doorway almost instantly, his dirty face streaked with tears. Even as Nicole gave a small cry and ran toward her brother, Marcus reached into the glove box for the papers he'd stored there before setting out, just as Beau fell into Nicole's arms, sobbing.

"It's all ruined. Rain got to the furniture. Even the floor's fallen through."

"I knew it couldn't be good," she said, surveying the damage over the top of his head.

"What're we gonna do?" he asked. "It was our last hope. There's nowhere else to go."

"Oh, Beau, this was never going to work anyway," she told him. "I thought for a minute that it might myself, but then I realized that as determined as Dad is, he'd just come looking for us."

"He never would," Beau insisted bitterly, wiping his face and adding more streaks in the process. "He'd have given up quick enough. He always has."

"I don't think that's likely to be the case anymore," Marcus said, coming to stand beside them. "I spoke to your father earlier today. He's a changed man in many ways."

Beau snorted. "I'll believe that when I see it."

"Maybe this will help," Marcus said, shaking open the folded papers and holding them out.

Beau squinted at them, frowning, but Nicole was quick to take them in hand. "What's this?"

He let her read until he got the first gasp, and then he began explaining the situation to Beau. "Your father's signed papers asking the court to grant your sister full custody of you."

"Where did you get these?" Nicole exclaimed, shuffling the documents.

"I had a lawyer draw them up," he answered before going back to his explanation to Beau. "Your therapist has endorsed the deal, too, and CPS will be making the same recommendation."

Nicole gave him another gasp just then, demanding, "Why are you pledging financial support?"

Marcus turned to face her, smiling as if his heart wasn't threatening to break out of his chest. "That's just a fail-safe plan," he said, "in case you won't agree to marry me."

Her eyes went wide. Beau whooped. And she dropped like a stone, sitting down hard in the dirt.

"Nic!" Beau cried, dropping beside her.

Marcus was already there, on his knees, gathering her up. "Nicole, are you all right? Sweetheart, say something!"

She clutched the papers to her chest and wailed, "Why?"

He cupped her face in his hands and laid his forehead against hers and said, "I love you, more than you can even imagine."

She threw her arms around him. "I love you, too!"

Marcus laughed, the sweetest relief imaginable washing through him. "I'm taking that as a yes."

"Yes! Oh, yes!" Suddenly she jerked back and shook a finger at her brother. "Let that be a lesson to you, Beau Archer! God does look out for us!"

Marcus couldn't have agreed more.

God was good. God was so good.

* * *

They married one month and three days later on the twenty-second of July. Marcus got a friend from seminary to perform the service at First Church Pantego, where each of his sisters had married before him. His sisters both cried. The baby, however, just three weeks old, slept peacefully through the whole thing in his mother's protective arms. Truth be told, Marcus himself shed a tear or two while repeating his vows, so overcome with joy was he. Nicole beamed through it all, from the very first moment she appeared in the doorway on her emotional father's arm.

She wore her mother's wedding dress. Marcus secretly found it a little too conventional for his tastes, but he knew how Nicole valued those things of her mom's and grandmother's, and since he valued her above all else in this world, whatever she wanted was fine with him. Marcus couldn't imagine a more beautiful bride anyway.

The wedding wasn't entirely conventional, of course. Beau, along with Nicole's friend Katrina, served as his sister's attendants while Marcus's two brothers-in-law stood up with him. And the reception took place in the vestibule, with Marcus standing at the back of the sanctuary shaking hands and smiling much as he did on Sunday following service. Except this time, his bride was at his side. He couldn't believe how right that felt.

The whole thing was done with a minimum of fuss and expense, frugality being Nicole's middle name. A fine trait for a minister's wife. Though, in truth, Marcus wouldn't have quibbled if she'd maxed out the credit cards and drained his bank account. A fine sentiment for a husband who knew his greatest blessings were not material.

During their month-long engagement, Marcus had moved from the old parsonage to the newer, larger house in the compound. Beau had kept him company, while Nicole had gone home to her father. Dillard had made great inroads during that time, and Marcus foresaw the day in the not-too-distant future when Beau would happily move back into his old bedroom.

Beau didn't know that Dillard was secretly making trips to and from Oklahoma to repair the cabin. The damage was significant, but not as bad as it had appeared. The building was still sound, and Dillard meant for the repairs to be a gift to his children, a material acknowledgment of the good times in the past and the grief he had finally laid to rest. Marcus had fronted him the money, but he was paying it back from the earnings of his new job.

While Dillard had rejoined the workforce, however, Nicole was taking some time off. She would finish her degree in the fall, work for a time in the church day care center, and then they would think about starting their own family. Marcus sensed that his ministry would deepen and broaden in ways he couldn't even grasp yet.

After it was all over, Beau happily went off with the Cutlers to give the new husband and wife some privacy. Nicole watched the last of their guests leave the building, then she followed along with Marcus as he shut up the place.

"Have you ever noticed," she asked suddenly, "that when you look back at something you can see the hand of God at work?"

He smiled warmly. "Oh, yes."

"It's a shame we can't see it at the time, isn't it?"

"Maybe we're not meant to," he said after a moment's thought, "at least not all the time, because He's teaching us what to look for."

"True," she agreed sagely. "God's plans are always perfect, after all."

"Perfect," he agreed, opening his arms.

Husband and wife were of one mind on the subject, as they would often be, for God's plans are indeed perfect and beautiful and imbued with a love so strong that it defies even the understanding of the most wise among us.

* * * * *

Dear Reader,

God wants only good things for us, and He's faithful to hear and answer our prayers. Sometimes the answer isn't what we want it to be, but we have the comfort of knowing that it's always for our best. What amazes me is that often our prayers are answered with such abundance that we can't believe God really means it! That premise is at the heart of Marcus and Nicole's story, *A Love So Strong,* but two others are also at work here.

Have you ever made a promise that you ultimately couldn't keep? I have. Eventually all worked out, and it was better for everyone than my original plan would have been, but not being able to live up to my word was an agonizing—and humbling—experience. I just had to accept that God's will ran counter to my promise. That experience is at the core of Nicole's personal story, but another bit of personal growth informed Marcus's.

Part of being a Christian is wanting to do God's will. Unfortunately we often assume we know what that is and have a hard time getting our preconceptions out of the way in order to understand what God is really saying. Thankfully, no matter how difficult we might make it for ourselves, God is patient, and He honors and blesses our desire to understand and do what is right.

My prayer for you is that you have that desire and are blessed with the greatest reward this life has to offer: love.

Arlene James

QUESTIONS FOR DISCUSSION

1. Nicole's father fell into destructive behaviors after the death of his wife. When confronted with loss and disappointment, what do you do to cope?

2. Marcus really wants to do the right thing at all times, such as when he calls the authorities about the abusive, alcoholic behavior of Nicole's father. Doing the right thing is often difficult and sometimes doesn't seem worth it. What might be some of the benefits of doing the right thing?

3. Though Marcus sincerely wants to do God's will, he missed or doubted God's answer to his prayers. Has this ever happened to you? Why do Christians sometimes miss or doubt God's answers to their prayers?

4. With a full decade between them, Marcus considers himself too old for Nicole. Does age difference truly matter in marriage? Do you know any couples with an age gap of ten years or more? How do they make their marriage work?

5. Nicole promised her dying mother that she would take care of her younger brother and father, but her father's destructive behavior eventually made that impossible. Have you or anyone you know ever been in a similar situation? What did you do?

6. Nicole reaches a point where she desperately wants to know why God allowed her mother to die when He could have healed her. Is it reasonable for Christians to want to know *why?* Have you asked similar questions of God? What about?

7. In many ways, Nicole and Marcus are opposites.
   Yet, they are also very alike. What is more important
   to focus on in marriage, the differences or the
   similarities?

REQUEST YOUR FREE BOOKS!

2 FREE INSPIRATIONAL NOVELS
PLUS A
FREE
MYSTERY GIFT

Love Inspired®

YES! Please send me 2 FREE Love Inspired® novels and my FREE mystery gift. After receiving them, if I don't wish to receive any more books, I can return the shipping statement marked "cancel." If I don't cancel, I will receive 4 brand-new novels every month and be billed just $3.99 per book in the U.S., or $4.74 per book in Canada, plus 25¢ shipping and handling per book and applicable taxes, if any*. That's a savings of over 20% off the cover price! I understand that accepting the 2 free books and gift places me under no obligation to buy anything. I can always return a shipment and cancel at any time. Even if I never buy another book from Steeple Hill, the two free books and gift are mine to keep forever.

113 IDN D74R 313 IDN D743

Name	(PLEASE PRINT)

Address	Apt.

City	State/Prov.	Zip/Postal Code

Signature (if under 18, a parent or guardian must sign)

Order online at www.LoveInspiredBooks.com

Or mail to Steeple Hill Reader Service™:

IN U.S.A.	IN CANADA
3010 Walden Ave.	P.O. Box 609
P.O. Box 1867	Fort Erie, Ontario
Buffalo, NY 14240-1867	L2A 5X3

Not valid to current Love Inspired subscribers.

Want to try two free books from another series?

Call 1-800-873-8635 or visit www.morefreebooks.com

* Terms and prices subject to change without notice. NY residents add applicable sales tax. Canadian residents will be charged applicable provincial taxes and GST. This offer is limited to one order per household. All orders subject to approval. Credit or debit balances in a customer's account(s) may be offset by any other outstanding balance owed by or to the customer.

LIREG05

TITLES AVAILABLE NEXT MONTH

Don't miss these four stories in October

A SOLDIER FOR CHRISTMAS by Jillian Hart
The McKaslin Clan

When Mitch Dalton entered her bookstore looking for help to find a present for his mother, Kelly Logan nearly fell over. This tall soldier was the classmate she'd once had a crush on. A friendship ignited, but with Mitch headed overseas could it ever blossom into more?

THE HAMILTON HEIR by Valerie Hansen
Davis Landing

Tim Hamilton accidentally damaged his assistant's car, but Dawn Leroux was more concerned with the people on her meal-delivery route than her vehicle. Stunned, Tim agreed to drive her on her route and found there was more to his assistant than he ever anticipated.

TIDINGS OF JOY by Margaret Daley
The Ladies of Sweetwater Lake

The opportunity to repay a debt he felt he owed to a woman he'd never met brought Chance Taylor to Sweetwater. Chance's arrival interrupted Tanya Bolton's routine...and brought her unexpected happiness. But the hidden obligation he struggled with meant Chance could lose Tanya—and his chance for a fresh start—forever.

A TIME OF HOPE by Terri Reed

Her church's new temporary pastor was everything Mara Zimmer was trying to avoid. Jacob Durand was young, good-looking and interested, but Mara had a devastating secret. Jacob didn't know what Mara was hiding, only that she made him long to make his position permanent.

LICNM0906